Novels by Kathleen O'Neal Gear
available from DAW Books:

Cries from the Lost Island

THE REWILDING REPORT

The Ice Lion
The Ice Ghost
The Ice Orphan*

*Coming soon from DAW Books

THE
ICE
GHOST

THE REWILDING REPORT #2

KATHLEEN O'NEAL GEAR

DAW BOOKS, INC.
DONALD A. WOLLHEIM FOUNDER
1745 Broadway, New York, NY 10019
ELIZABETH R. WOLLHEIM
SHEILA E. GILBERT
PUBLISHERS
www.dawbooks.com

ACKNOWLEDGMENTS

I appreciate my editor, Sheila Gilbert, more than she knows. She's the heartbeat of so many authors' books, including mine. Thanks, Sheila.

To all of the great people at DAW Books, I owe a special debt of gratitude. They work very hard to bring you the best science fiction and fantasy books in the world, and I sincerely appreciate their efforts.

My agent, Matt Bialer, is a cherished friend and the best literary agent in the business. It's been an interesting road, hasn't it, Matt?

1

❄

LYNX
923 SUMMERS AFTER THE ZYME

Mother Ocean is high again tonight, with an icy flush of wind.

I crouch in the doorway of our dome-shaped lodge and tie back the flap. Constructed of upright mammoth rib bones covered with bison hides, the lodge is around thirty hand-lengths across. A fire burns in the middle of the floor. On the other side of the fire, Elder Arakie lies beneath a mound of muskoxen hides with Xeno, the wolf, beside him. The wolf watches me with half-lidded eyes. Arakie hasn't moved since midday. He may still be alive. I don't know. Every morning I wake expecting to find that he has died and left to travel the Road of Light that paints a swath across the night sky. Arakie calls it the Milky Way galaxy. My people believe it is the road that all souls must travel to reach the afterlife in the sky.

Quietly, I sit down in the doorway to watch evening settle over the beach. It's one of those unearthly beautiful nights—mastodons trumpeting high up in the mountains, monstrous icebergs gliding ghostlike through the pale green zyme light—so beautiful it seems not to be of this world.

I have escaped to this barren seashore with a few books, a strange wolf, and a dying old man. Though Elder Arakie says

I'm a fool to think this is an escape. He says I'm lost and running from myself.

Very well, then, if you wish to put it that way, I have run here in the hopes of finding myself.

For a few blessed moments, I appreciate the endless, luminous hills of zyme that ride the waves as they roll toward shore. In places the hills of bioluminescent algae have grown so enormous they've toppled over one another and resemble hunched monsters five times the height of a man. Their green glow intensifies with the darkness, and the air fills with a pungent scent.

My people, the Sealion People, have many stories about the world before the zyme covered the oceans; it was a time of warmth when the world was filled with flowering trees and long-gone animals like coyotes and Cymric cats. Our elders repeat the stories over and over around winter campfires to teach the children about the Beginning Time before our creators, the Blessed Jemen, sailed to the campfires of the dead in ships made of meteorites. After the zyme, the Ice Giants were born. My people believe, as I once did, that they are alive and have voices that speak to our greatest shamans. Because of Arakie's lessons, I know they are monstrous glaciers that are still creeping across the world, gobbling up the land that living creatures need to survive. Today, the rumbling Giants rise so high they seem to touch fingertips with Sister Moon. Their jagged blue peaks are cracked and broken, veined with black crevasses that drop down to the center of the earth where rivers of fire flow. When I gaze to the north and east, all I see is mountains of ice. A few small pine groves dot the slopes, and here and there lines of black boulders slither up the mountainsides. Otherwise, it's just a vista of broken blue ice. To the west, the green blanket of zyme rises and falls upon the waves. It's only closest to the shore, where cliffs of ice meet the ocean, that a thin strip of freezing water remains free of zyme.

Xeno rises and flops down again in the firelit lodge behind me. He seems to be anxiously awaiting Arakie's departure from this life. The wolf is so human, I sometimes think he is one of our legends made flesh—one of the Jemen who learned to change into an animal and could never change back. In his sleep, Arakie often reaches out for the wolf and softly calls, "Jorg?" Then his voice trails away with the words, "I know it's been hard . . ."

I ponder whether that it is the wolf's ancient human name, or if Arakie calls out for a long-dead loved one?

An agonizing moan escapes his lips, and I turn to look at my dying teacher.

I shouldn't have brought Arakie here. He didn't want to leave his cave high in the Ice Giant Mountains. But the truth is, I was starting to feel as if I would be crushed by the sheer weight of words and numbers. Over the past nineteen moons, I have learned so much from this strange old man and from the last quantum computer in the world: Quancee. But I don't understand a lot of it. I'm an archaic human, one of the last surviving species created by the Jemen for the sole purpose of testing a hypothesis: could archaic forms of humanity survive the crushing cold encompassing the earth? Our ancestors had survived many Ice Ages before. The last hope of the Jemen was that archaic humans, and other re-created Ice Age species, would manage to find a way.

My friend, Dr. John Arakie, was the world's foremost geneticist. He believed in us.

Arakie has been rushing to teach me everything he can, but reading and mathematics are hard for me, and what little I have comprehended stuns me. Because of Arakie, the deep heavens now stand before me full of shapes I do not recognize. Wide circles of eternal motions. Brilliance impossible to see with my eyes. Darkness expanding forever in all directions. Things that are simply incomprehensible. Truly, I seem to understand nothing, not even who . . . or what . . . I am. *Denisovan.*

Arakie exhales, and his breath frosts in the cold air.

As I study him, the mournful howling of dire wolves carries upon the wind. Xeno's ears prick and a low growl rumbles in his throat. The big packs worry him. Arakie tells me Xeno is the last of his kind, an ancient wolf born long before dire wolves began to trot the glaciers like lords of the ice. I try to imagine how it must feel to be the last of his kind. There are times when Xeno points his nose at the sky and howls long and hard, then he listens for a response that never comes, hangs his head, and moves on. He never seems to lose hope that one day another of his kind will answer his call.

I reach for the ptarmigan I hunted this afternoon. When Arakie wakes, he'll be hungry.

Xeno lifts his head and gives me a feral accusatory stare, as though demanding to know what took me so long to start supper.

Quietly, I tiptoe across the lodge, skewer the bird on a spear of driftwood, and prop it over the flames to cook.

Arakie's voice is soft. "Everything all right?"

"Yes. We're safe. Go back to sleep."

He weakly pulls down the muskoxen hides to peer at me. His skeletal face is tight and pained, the paleness softened by the firelight. Thin white hair hangs over his sunken cheeks. "Worried . . . about your family?"

"We haven't heard any news in over two moons. Why have the runners stopped coming? My best friend, Quiller, used to come—"

"It's . . . cold, Lynx. No one . . . wants to travel."

"Or maybe the last Sealion People are running for their lives. The Rust People have hunted us down for generations. After the peace agreement fell apart, they must have started hunting my people down again."

His breath rattles when he says, "You're all warlike. . . . Thought it would help you."

"Sealion People are not warlike," I object.

Arakie just smiles, and it occurs to me that the last fight between Sealion People and Rust People was, in fact, started by Sealion People. In retaliation the Rust People slaughtered most of my village. I don't want to believe we are to blame for violence that has lasted centuries, but maybe he's right.

Arakie sighs. "You believe . . . in peace. So glad. If no one believes . . . peace . . . impossible."

Kneeling before the fire, I add more wood, building it up until flames leap and crackle beneath the ptarmigan.

"The last runner said there were only forty-five Sealion People left in the world. If the latest negotiations failed, over one thousand Rust warriors could have surrounded them in a heartbeat. There may be no Sealion People left. Except me." I pause to think about the Rust People, Neandertals, before adding, "You once told me that in the end one species would prevail. What if—"

"Just life, Lynx." He desperately sucks in a breath, struggling for enough air to say, "Species . . . go extinct. Others rise. At least . . . I . . . I hope they will."

His eyes fall closed.

Arakie tells me that he is probably the last modern human. Over the long centuries, I suspect that like Xeno he, too, has cried out again and again, praying another human voice from his long-lost people would answer, and, hearing none, hung his head and moved on.

"Sorry, didn't mean to sound sharp," I whisper. "I'm just worried."

"I know."

Reaching over, I quietly pull the hide up over his shoulder to keep him warm.

When he drifts back to sleep, I return to sit in the doorway and watch the beach trail while the ptarmigan cooks. As the darkness intensifies, the zyme fills the world with green light. Most of the campfires of the dead vanish in the onslaught, but I see two Jemen sailing through the sky in their ships of light. Arakie tells me they are empty, just satellites. He says a treasure trove exists in the sky if we could ever get to it.

Marvels of technology, they were placed in orbit during the great war to facilitate attacks . . .

My Sealion elders speak of that ancient war around the winter campfires. It occurred in the Beginning Time when the Jemen split in two. The leader of the Jemen—the Old Woman of the Mountain—ordered most of the Jemen to sail to the campfires of the dead. They became the Sky Jemen. But a handful of heroes willingly sacrificed themselves to remain in our world. We know them as the Earthbound Jemen. These heroes carved out a great hollow in the heart of the glaciers, a place where they hid cages of animals and plants, and vowed to continue their search to find a way to kill the Ice Giants. One day, when they've won the war with the Giants, they will release the animals and plants into a warm and beautiful world.

The precious books Arakie keeps in Quancee's cave, called the Rewilding Reports, are legendary among Sealion and Rust Peoples. The strange half-people, the Dog Soldiers, who travel with the Rust People, even claim to own one volume. I have read the few reports in Arakie's collection over and over. They document that there were many such caverns of animals around the world. I pray one survived.

The Rewilding Reports have taught me that Sealion legends are filled with fragments of the truth. Arakie has been trying to help me pull out the threads of fact and reassemble them, but his memory has been fading by the day. I fear that some of what he tells me these days is just as fanciful as our legends. Do I really believe that he created a genetic adaptation that allowed the Earthbound Jemen to change into animals so they could survive alongside the giant predators that fill the world? Arakie says that when he was stronger, he could change into a lion, or send his thoughts into the minds of animals. I have not seen him do it, though I have seen strange things that suggest he can: lion tracks that turn into human footprints and lead directly to a place where he sits. He also says I am one of the last people who carries a gene that allows me to bond with Quancee, and claims there are even a handful of people left who carry the Jemen's genetic ability to send their thoughts into the minds of people far away.

Despite my doubts, the Rewilding Reports do document the scientific efforts to achieve these miracles. For the most part, all I see in the books are diagrams of pentagons and hexagons. The building blocks of life, Arakie says. Incomprehensible to me.

I hang my head and wonder what I will do when he dies. When my teacher lies frozen and alone beneath the ancient stones of the mountains, how will I ever grasp anything without him?

A big wave rolls tufts of zyme across the shore. As the wave retreats, the tufts shine with an emerald fire.

I need time to sort through my melancholy.

2

❋

QUILLER

Utter blackness, so black it shimmers as though filled with silver dust. One more step, feel for the ice wall, brace my shaking legs, listen to the dark underworld groan.

I don't know how long I've been wandering in this honeycomb of caves, but I feel as if I'm floating, not really connected to anything solid. Just black air. That's what I'm becoming.

"Keep going. You're a warrior. The way out isn't far ahead."

Is it?

Hard to . . . to think. Has it been four days? Ten? The bundle of torches I carried ran out long ago, along with my food, and darkness has smoothed the edges of time, leaving me suspended in an emptiness broken only by the rumbling and quaking of the Ice Giants who smother the mountains above me.

With the toes of my mammoth leather boots, I feel for the undulations in the floor and carefully move forward.

The tunnel curves here. Warm air flows over me, coming from my left. Do I remember this adjacent tunnel? Must have a hot spring in it. The air smells of sulfur. Is this the hot spring close to the cave where my friends hide? Should I turn down this tunnel? No, no. It's just another passageway in the labyrinth. Don't get distracted. Walk straight. Don't explore any side tunnel, or you'll be lost forever in this womb of whispering Ice Giant voices.

With my hand against the freezing ice wall, I walk three more steps. Another three.

Just ahead of me, sparks pour into the gloom and crawl across the floor. What is that? A serpent of sparks, twining and coiling. Hissing. Everywhere that frightening hissing. Then I realize the sound is the rattling of the spears I carry in the quiver over my left shoulder.

When I blink, the sparks vanish, but I begin to see a rounded shape, a lighter darkness. My nostrils quiver at the mingled scents of blood and sweat, and I hear a low growl that I know as well as my own voice. *Crow. My big black dog.*

Relief surges through me so powerfully, I'm lightheaded.

I feel my way to the mouth of the tunnel and stop to look into the cave that opens up beyond. My eyes, so accustomed to the black underworld, can't seem to adjust to the dim light filtering into the cave from the world outside.

"We've got to surrender," a soft voice says. "They're coming in soon. You know they are."

"Of course, I know."

I see movement near the narrow crevice that forms the entry to the cave, but I can't make out the warriors, though the crevice is getting clearer—a gray slash about as wide as my shoulders and almost as tall as I am. Wisely, the guards must be standing off to the side, peering out at regular intervals, then drawing back out of enemy casting range.

When I softly call, "What's to see out there?" a black streak charges me from the left, barking and leaping. Happy to see me, Crow jumps up and places her big paws in the middle of my chest. "Hello, Crow," I say as I scratch the dog's ears. "I'm glad to see you."

"Quiller?" RabbitEar's deep voice sends a wave of relief through me. "Did you find a way out?"

My husband does not run to embrace me, and I know what

that means. The situation beyond the cave is so dire he dares not leave his guard post. Stepping away from Crow, I walk forward. She pads right at my heels with her tail swiping the air.

"No. There's a tunnel that continues on, but I ran out of torches and food. I was lost for a while."

"Quiller?" my eleven-summers-old son, Jawbone, calls sleepily from the darkness to my left, and I see a thin shadow rise and trot toward me to hug me around the waist. "We were so worried!"

I bend down to kiss the top of his blond head. "Are the girls all right?"

"Yes, they—"

"Quiller!" my daughter Little Fawn cries.

In moments, all four of my adopted children have encircled me and are hugging me and grabbing for my hands. Chickadee, four summers, is crying and clinging to my leg. I have only seen sixteen summers, but I found these orphans after their village was wiped out by a pride of giant lions and I adopted them into my clan.

"Shh," I say. "It's all right. I'm back. Everything's going to be all right."

"We've been fighting since you left," Jawbone says. "Rabbit-Ear says we must sleep when we can."

"He's right. You have to keep up your strength."

As I straighten, my gaze is drawn upward to the ceiling seventy hand-lengths above. The cave is about two hundred hand-lengths across. Dark shapes of people huddle against the walls. Or maybe they are dead bodies. I find it odd that no one else has called out. A few silver heads move to my right, so some of our elders are alive, and I see women hugging children. Are they all so exhausted and hopeless they can't even speak? Or are they under War Leader Mink's orders to be silent?

When RabbitEar peers out through the crevice again, his

burly shape is silhouetted against the green zyme light. His square face with its heavy brow ridge glows. He's seen two more summers than I have, eighteen.

I stroke my son's hair and say, "I want all of you to try to go back to sleep while I speak with your father."

"No, Quiller," Little Fawn says. "I want to be with you."

Her sister, Loon, is sobbing quietly against my bear-hide cape. I reach down to stroke her soft blond curls. "Quiet now. Others are sleeping. RabbitEar is right. We must all rest when we can. I'll come sleep with you soon."

Jawbone looks up at me with such love in his eyes they shine. Obediently, he releases his hold around my waist and says, "How soon?"

"Very soon."

"How soon is that?"

"As soon as I speak with your father, and understand what's happening."

"Come very soon, please? There are things I need to tell you," Jawbone whispers, and glances at his sisters as though he does not wish them to hear.

He is not a man yet, though he will be in two or three summers, but he so often seems much older. "I will. Now, all of you, go back to your hides."

My children drift away into the darkness and lie down together.

I carefully veer around the people sleeping on the floor, heading for RabbitEar; the sickly-sweet odor of death gets stronger. Two paces away, I see a glitter and my heart stops when I realize it's a baby. The bottoms of her boots are beaded and reflect the light streaming into the cave. We only bead the bottoms of boots for the dead to walk the Road of Light. My heart aches for her family.

RabbitEar risks stepping away from the crevice to wrap one

arm around me and crush my body against his. "I thank the gods that you're back. We need you."

While we embrace, another warrior immediately takes his place at the crevice, studying the hillside that slopes down to Mother Ocean. It's skinny young RedBoy, who's seen fourteen summers pass.

I don't want to wake anyone, so I keep my voice low. "How long have you been standing guard?"

"Long time," RabbitEar replies. "There are only twenty-two of us left, and just four warriors. Rest are dead. Runt can't stand guard and Mink had to sleep. He was stumbling weary. RedBoy just woke to take over for me, but he's only had three hands of sleep."

"How many are wounded?"

"One. Runt." He drops his voice to a whisper to add, "Belly wound. Bad. I thank the Blessed Jemen he's finally unconscious."

RedBoy adds, "Gods, yes. His weeping has kept us all awake for days."

I search the outline of the dead bodies stacked against the wall near the crevice. The source of the smell.

"I'll stand guard," I say and pull a spear from my quiver. "Both of you try to get some rest."

"No. You're as exhausted as we are. RedBoy can stand guard for a time. Come and sleep with me. I want to feel my arms around you. Besides, I heard you promise Jawbone you'd be there soon."

To RedBoy, I say, "Wake me in one hand of time, and I'll take over."

"Yes. Gladly, I will."

I shiver and flip up the thick collar of my bear-hide cape. As RabbitEar slips an arm over my shoulders and we start back for our children, RedBoy says, "Wait. Quiller, we talked it about it all day. I think we should surrender. Don't you think we should surrender?"

"I . . . Surrender?" My bleary mind can't seem to understand what he's saying. Crow sniffs the night air pouring through the crevice and utters a low growl, as though she knows something we do not. Her feral eyes have become wide zyme-lit moons.

"It's hopeless. We're beaten."

"What's happened? How long have I been gone? The darkness and cold have numbed my wits."

"Eight days. I couldn't believe it when I saw you step out of that tunnel. I figured you were lost in that maze and would never come out again."

RabbitEar tenderly hugs me. "I knew you'd be back. Wasn't a doubt in my mind." His red hair and beard suddenly flicker yellow, and I know campfires have been lit all over the slope outside that runs down to the sea.

"We have to give up, Quiller," RedBoy says.

"When War Leader Mink wakes, talk to him. It's not my decision."

"No, I—I know, but I thought if you and I agreed, it would carry more weight."

"Talk to Mink. You may feel differently."

RedBoy suddenly lurches forward to stare out the crevice. "What the . . . Come quick!"

RabbitEar and I rush back to stand beside him and peer out through the crevice. Hundreds of enemy torches are being ignited, reflecting from the faces of the warriors who carry them.

"What are they doing?" RedBoy asks.

My thoughts won't congeal, so it takes longer than it should for me to determine their strategy. The warriors are lining out in an arc. "Looks like they're preparing a sweep."

"A sweep? You mean they're going to sweep up the hill? Why? We're already trapped inside. There's no way we can escape!"

RabbitEar says, "Probably just a show of force."

"Maybe," I say. "Or maybe they're protecting elders who walk behind the arc."

"Their council?"

"Possibly."

Instead of watching the approaching army, I can't take my eyes from the magnificent vista. As the darkness deepens, the entire ocean shimmers and glitters with zyme. It could be a vast field of crushed emeralds. And high above, Sister Sky has begun her nightly dance, sending fluttering purple curtains and white lances of light across the heavens. The wondrous display becomes ethereal, changing from streamers to great towering arches and snapping ribbons that span the entire sky. The jagged peaks of the Ice Giants reflect the flashes and seem to move, swaying in time to Sister Sky's dance. For days, the only thing that kept me sane was the thought of getting outside into the light and fresh air. Gods, death is climbing the slope toward me, and all I want to do is stare at the stunning beauty of life.

Exhausted, I hang my head and long filthy strands of red hair fall around my freckled face. "Well. What do you want to do?" I whisper to my husband.

RabbitEar takes a new grip on his spear. "I'd better wake Mink."

"What's happening, Quiller?" a man calls from the depths of the cave, and I realize it's Runt. His voice is so hoarse, I almost didn't recognize it.

"Don't know yet. They're coming. That's all we know."

If I'd had more torches and food would I have found a way out? A way to climb to the surface and save the people I love?

"If we surrender, the Rust People might let us go back to being slaves," RedBoy says.

Runt growls, "You want salvation that bad?"

"You don't?"

"We're whipped, boy. They're going to kill us either way. May as well die fighting beside my friends."

Behind my eyes, I see the log cages where the Sealion People were imprisoned and hear the suffocating cries of the children begging for water. Hatred is a finely honed weapon inside me, one I plan to use on my enemies if I ever have the chance again.

After a pause, RedBoy says, "I could surrender."

"You have the courage of a worm." Runt finishes the sentence and suppresses a groan.

"It's been ten days since they trapped us in here! What's the harm in trying to survive?" RedBoy cries. "We just have to figure out how to do it."

"You figure it out. I'll never surrender." Runt curls onto his side. His pain must be unbearable, but he's not making a sound now.

"Quiller, what do you say?" RedBoy calls. "We're done for, aren't we?"

Crow rubs against my leg and when I unconsciously reach down to stroke her glossy head, she licks my hand.

War Leader Mink must be sound asleep or he'd say something to rally our spirits and keep us fighting until our last breaths. Or perhaps he's listening, taking stock of what his warriors think before he comments. The other Sealion People are mute, just listening. We all know we're staring extinction in the face.

Perhaps that's why the unthinkable possibility of surrender has filled me up. My soul is sliding out through the crevice into the phosphorescent darkness, running toward the tree-shrouded cove where RabbitEar and I have promised the children we will build a lodge. We'll hold each other in the firelight and watch the winter fade into summer. We'll grow old together, telling tales of the legendary Jemen, gods from before the zyme, to our children and grandchildren.

"Let's just get this over," RedBoy says. His skinny silhouette rocks from foot to foot, like a fledgling condor preparing to take flight. "Quiller, yell to the closest warrior. Tell him we're coming out."

From the darkness, Mink orders, "Get away from the crevice, RedBoy."

"But War Leader—"

"No one is surrendering."

Smoke blows into the cave and the strange clipped voices of Rust People ride the wind that blows up from the sea. They tend to drop letters, especially at the end of words.

I slide closer to the crevice. The slope resembles an overturned jewel box. In the blend of zyme glow and firelight, the bobbing torches seem suspended in a strange fog of pale green and gold. Shadows move in and block the torches, or dart before them as though running, probably warriors taking up new positions.

RabbitEar murmurs, "This has been such a farce. The Rust People could have rushed this cave and overwhelmed us at any time. They haven't even tried. Instead, they stand out there taunting us, casting a spear now and then to remind us they're there. Mocking our escape."

"Think their elders have been discussing what to do, and that's what this sweep is about?"

"More likely they're just tired of waiting us out."

As though laughing at us, the Ice Giants roar and shake the world. When the deep-throated rumbles fade, long grating shrieks echo through the cave. They so resemble human screams that everyone turns to look down the black throat of the tunnel in the rear, the dark tunnel I just escaped from. I hold my breath, fearing it is human. *Our enemies didn't find a way in through that tunnel, did they? Are they coming at us from both directions?*

Underneath the white-knuckle fear, another spear cracks the ice outside and makes me flinch and flatten against the cave wall. I watch the spear cartwheel down the slope like a string of emerald fire, the polished shaft reflecting the zyme glow.

RabbitEar softly asks, "How will they do it? Rush us? Just start crowding through the crevice, forcing their way in?"

"Probably." I expect my last sight of earth to be the leering face of a Rust warrior on top of me. They might try to keep me alive for a time. I plan to make sure they don't have the chance.

"Quiller?" War Leader Mink calls. "Come here, please."

I frown at his dark shape. "But Mink—"

"*Now.*"

Sighing, I walk back into the darkness and slump to the floor beside him. Crow stretches out and rests her chin over my knees. I say, "I'm not surrendering, if that's what you want to talk about."

"Didn't think you would."

Mink looks very much like his brother, Lynx, with a heavy-boned blocky face and shoulder-length black hair. His forehead slopes back severely and his heavy brow extends far beyond his dark sunken eyes. His bison cape is filthy and worn thin.

Something touches my arm, fumbles for my hand and takes it in a hard grip. Mink's fingers are thick-boned, rough with calluses, and warm with blood.

"Are you hurt?" I ask. "Where are you wounded?"

"My leg. It's not that bad." There's a small hesitation, before he says, "Listen. You have to take the women and children and run back into the honeycomb of tunnels. Somebody must survive."

"Without food or torches, we won't last long, Mink. Trust me. I've been back there."

"If you don't try, in a few heartbeats, the Sealion People will be no more." He tips his chin toward my children across the cave. "Wake them up and get going."

The idea of going back into that rumbling black maw wrenches my insides. "All right, Mink."

Faintly, he says, "Thank you." Mink has seen nineteen summers, but he seems much older. His dark eyes are invisible, just black holes in his face.

"Mink?" RabbitEar calls, and I can hear the panic in my husband's voice. "Could you come here?"

When Mink struggles to rise, I drag his arm over my shoulder and help him to stand up. "Let me support you to the crevice, then I'll go."

With his arm resting heavily over my shoulders, he limps to where RedBoy and RabbitEar stand. On the way, he says, "Did it occur to you that Lynx was smarter than the rest of us? After all, he's free."

"Been a long nineteen moons since he abandoned us, hasn't it?"

"It has."

Nineteen moons ago, we established a truce with the Rust People, and started peace negotiations. They had a new High Matron who argued that it was time to stop killing each other. It took five moons before peace was established, then we lived together in harmony until last moon. That's when their greatest holy man, Trogon, had a vision. He started raving that all Sealion People were sub-human beasts who had no right to walk as equals among the Rust People. We watched the ranks of his supporters swell until Trogon seduced them into madness. When the old man took the next step, murdered High

Matron Sunbird, and declared all Sealion People slaves, it was to thundering applause.

As we pass him, Runt fights to suppress sobs. All I see is an amorphous shape twisting, a man trapped between flight and fight, hovering at the edge of death like an eagle with clipped wings. His suffering will end soon, either by his own hand or one of ours. Probably Mink's—a final act of kindness from a loving friend.

RabbitEar leans back against the wall as we get closer, leaving space for Mink to peer at the slope outside. But Mink's eyes are surveying the fluttering light of enemy torches that reflect from the ice walls inside the cave. That's how close the army is. It's a macabre display, orange spirits bouncing behind crystalline panes. Some are so faint they seem buried deep in the ice, maybe struggling to crawl to the surface to slip into our cold tomb.

Mink says, "All right, Quiller. Let me go."

I step away from him, and he limps forward.

Outside, a war cry eddies across the slope, and a Rust warrior yells, "Are you pissin' yourselves, you cowards?"

When laughter erupts, quivers rattle with a thousand spears.

Mink turns to look into the firelit faces of the last Sealion People in the world. "I want all women and children who can walk to get back in the tunnels. Quiller is going to lead you. You'll find a way out. I know you will."

People rise like dark ghosts and move toward the tunnel. I see Mink's wife and two sons leading the procession, and I'm relieved to see them alive. My entire family, my parents, my sister and two brothers, were all killed in the last battle.

When I start walking back to join them, Mink grabs my sleeve. "Wait. Is that Trogon? I can't see him very well. You've been closer to him than the rest of us."

My adopted children are Rust People. Moons ago, I used to accompany them to visit their relatives in the Rust People camps. Trogon was always close by, watching.

I shoulder between RabbitEar and Mink to look outside. Over one hundred shiny, silver-clad warriors trudge up the slope with spears in their hands. All are blond and ugly with massive jaws. The shape of their faces has always fascinated me. Rust People have larger skulls and much heavier brow ridges than Sealion People do. Unlike Sealion People, who have many different colors of hair, Rust People all have blond hair, until they become gray-headed elders.

"The Dog Soldiers are marching right in front of him, blocking my view, but it might be Trogon. He's a big man."

Dog Soldiers stride up the slope side by side, their steps in tandem, clutching books against their chests. I'm surprised to see them here. Dog Soldiers are curious creatures, very different looking than the short muscular Sealion or Rust peoples. Because of my height, I've often been accused of having Dog Soldier blood. I don't think it's true, but it's possible. Legends say Dog Soldiers belong to an ancient and fierce military society, and my clan, the Blue Dolphin Clan, also comes from an ancient warrior society. As the Dog Soldiers get closer, I get a better view of the big man behind them. He has long graying blond hair and a beard that hangs to the middle of his chest.

"Yes," I announce to my crypt mates. "That's Trogon."

"Are you sure?" RedBoy gasps the last word.

"Absolutely. See that red lion painted on his silver cape? He's Red Lion clan."

Mink squints in confusion. "Why do they need the great witch just to slaughter a few Sealion people?"

"Don't know," RabbitEar says, "but I hope he doesn't plan to make another of his longwinded speeches. I'd rather die than have to listen to him."

"He wouldn't be here if he didn't need something from us," I say.

"What do we have that he could want?" RabbitEar asks.

Trogon's massive shoulders swing back and forth as he veers around the Dog Soldiers and climbs the slope toward us. Alone.

"Is he completely unafraid of us?" Mink asks.

"Maybe he's going to try and talk us into surrendering?" Hope fills RedBoy's voice. "Let's go outside and talk to him!"

"Get back," Mink orders.

Runt props himself up on one elbow. His voice is more a series of slow groans than words: "Maybe they're just . . . surrounding the cave . . . in case we try to escape in the night."

"Wouldn't need a hundred warriors to do that," I say.

"H—hundred?" Runt asks, stunned. "There are one hundred warriors with Trogon?"

RedBoy says, "They're coming in. This is our last chance to surrender before they club us to death like sealion pups!"

No one seems to be breathing.

Out over Mother Ocean, one of the Sky Jemen flies, just a white dot sailing across the Road of Light on his way to the campfires of the dead.

Runt says, "Let's pile chunks of ice in the crevice to block it."

"Ice?" RabbitEar responds. "I'll just spear the first one that forces his body through. Dead flesh will block it better than ice."

Pulling the long, mammoth-bone knife from my belt, I take a firm grip on it. The time for casting spears is over. What comes next will be hand to hand. Mink also draws his knife. Suddenly, I desperately want to see Lynx again. He's been my best friend since childhood. Not so long ago, we were to be married, but he decided to marry a woman from another clan. She's dead now. Seems like a lifetime ago.

RedBoy stalks forward. "You have no right to stop me. I'm beaten! I'm surrendering. You can come with me or not."

"Go on, then!" Runt growls. "Get yourself killed."

RedBoy shoves between Mink and RabbitEar, pushes me aside, and steps through the crevice with his hands up, shouting, "I surrender!"

A barrage of spears flickers in the torchlight.

"Get down!" Mink shouts and lunges to the side, while RabbitEar grabs me and flings me back against the wall.

Through the crevice, I see RedBoy. His body is alive with reflections, bristling with spears.

Runt calls, "Is he—"

"Yes."

Trogon has stopped twenty paces away.

"Quiller?" Mink calls as he struggles to rise on his wounded leg. "This is your last chance. Get in the tunnel with the women and children and run before—"

"Wait, Mink," RabbitEar interrupts. "Why are the Dog Soldiers walking forward? They never get close to battle. They always stand in the rear, reading from their sacred books to guide the carnage."

Supposedly there are only seven Dog Soldiers left, which means they'll be just as extinct as Sealion People soon. Oblivion is so close I can feel its footsteps in my heart.

The slope, the camps, the people standing around the fires, have all picked up the luminous zyme glow and appear to be shining green ghosts floating through the air.

"Tell me what's happening?" Runt begs.

Mink nervously licks his lips. "Two Dog Soldiers walked up to speak with Trogon."

"Why haven't they rushed the cave? Think they're going to try to take us alive?"

"Doubt it. Trogon knows we'll never—"

"*Let us talk!*" Trogon shouts.

Mink shouts back, "What's left to say?"

The old man climbs the slope carrying a torch. He's seen forty summers at least. Most people die in their early thirties, so he's considered ancient.

"He's coming up here by himself?" RabbitEar hisses.

Mink shakes his head. "Doesn't make any sense."

"Spear him now before he can get close enough to witch us!" Runt calls.

Mink's face has contorted, trying to figure out what the old man is up to. The Rust People consider him to be their greatest holy man. To us, he's a walking husk of evil, a legendary witch of enormous power.

Trogon stops less than five paces from the cave opening. He's completely vulnerable. We could kill him in an instant. His deeply wrinkled face has picked up the torch's gleam. "Send Quiller out. I 'ave to speak with her."

"Me?" I spin around to look at Mink. "Why would he want to speak with me? You're War Leader. I'm nobody."

Crow marches back and forth beside me, her back bristling because she understands the desperate tone of my voice. I bend down and say, "Crow, go and guard the children."

Her black ears lie flat, but she trots away into the darkness to stand with my children in the tunnel.

Mink and RabbitEar both look at me with questions in their eyes, and Mink yells, "Why do you want to speak with Quiller?"

Trogon props one hand on his hip, and his silver cape flares around him. "A wolf came to me, nosed right into my vision and transformed into one of the Jemen. And then there she was. Standing right in front of me in the dream. Quiller came to stand beside the Jemen."

"I did not!"

Mink yells back, "She's not coming out! If you want to talk to her, come in here."

"That'll be the day," I whisper.

Trogon moves his torch from one hand to the other. "I'll meet her halfway? Just in front of the cave."

"I'm staring at the body of the last warrior who went outside to meet you." Mink shouts. "Quiller's not coming out."

Trogon lifts his torch higher. His fixed stare is haunting. It's not just that the torchlight has turned his enormous eyes into amber moons, he never seems to blink, and the red lion painted on his shirt doesn't move. It's as though he's not breathing. Not really alive.

Two warriors down the hillside edge toward him, and Trogon holds out a hand to stop them. They obey, but fidget and take new grips on their spears. Voices begin to eddy through the semicircle of men and women that creates a big arc around the mouth of the cave.

Trogon calls, "Listen to me, Quiller! In the dream, I saw your friend Lynx camped on the shore two days north of here. A strange old man and the wolf Jemen were with him. I've heard this old man's name is Arakie. What do you know of him?"

My mouth opens to respond, but Mink calls, "That's why you're here? You want to know about an old man?"

"Send Quiller out. I must speak with her about it." Trogon uses the toe of one hide boot to draw an unfathomable design on the ground in front of him, and I wonder if he's witching us.

I whisper, "What's he up to, Mink?"

"I fear he's going to make you an offer you can't refuse."

"What could he possibly offer . . ." The bottom falls out of my stomach. My legs feel suddenly rubbery. "You think he captured Lynx?"

"No. He'd have already marched my brother up here and used him against us."

I glance back at Trogon, but he's not looking at the cave now. The old witch is gazing at the Road of Light that stretches across the heavens. Gusts of wind flap his silver clothing, sending out waves of reflected brilliance.

Trogon bravely walks closer to us. When he stands just outside, I can smell him. A bitter scent clings to his body. Something poisonous. A tang that claws at the back of my throat. Does he dry spirit plants and sprinkle them over his clothing? Or perhaps he makes a paste from the roots and rubs it into his temples to free his soul for otherworldly journeys? Our holy people do that as well. Is that why his empty eyes never blink? He's on a soul journey, flying through the night sky far away from his body?

"Very well," he announces. "I accept your offer."

We all exchange confused glances as the old man swaggers forward.

"What offer?" Mink says.

"I'm comin' inside to speak with Quiller." Trogon kicks Red-Boy's corpse aside, shoulders into the crevice, and orders, "Let me through."

When our gazes collide, my skin feels like it's on fire.

3

※

QUILLER

Mink, RabbitEar, and I fall back with our hands clutched around our weapons.

The old witch lifts his torch higher, and every fissure and crack in the cave flutters with shadows. He notes the dead piled against wall, then the women and children who huddle far back in the tunnel. Finally, his gaze focuses on my face. His examination seems to take forever, as though he's comparing what he sees now to the woman in his spirit dream, making sure we are the same person.

"Let us go and sit down," he says.

As he walks toward me, I back up to the center of the cave and adopt a fighting crouch.

Mink and RabbitEar silently close in behind Trogon.

As though completely unafraid, the elder sits down on the floor, leans his torch on a rock, and politely gestures for me to join him. "Please, sit down, Quiller."

"I'll stand."

His lips turn up, but no one would call it a smile. He's a caricature of a man, just the sort of monster you do not want to get too close to. I am much taller than he is, but his thick chest and shoulders leave no doubt about the outcome if he can get his hands on me. I'm not going to give him the chance. He may be old, but none of his life was spent lazing around campfires.

As he leans forward, the silver fabric of his clothing conforms to his bulging muscles.

"War Leader Mink," he says, "while we speak, I will not attack anyone in this cave. I give you my oath."

"What do you want?"

That unnatural smile again as he studies me. "You're pretty."

I have a freckled face with a broad flat nose, bushy red hair, and green eyes so large they seem bug-like. I'm anything but pretty. I'm in the process of formulating a response when RabbitEar sucks the air out of the cave: "Shut up, old man."

Trogon bows his head. I'm certain no one has ever spoken to him that way. Through the blond strands of hair that cover his face, his eyes are shiny fawn-colored beads, watching me. He gestures to the floor again. "Sit down, Quiller. *Please.*"

I hunt for any hint of witchery, but find none. What is it about Trogon that draws people to him on such an epic scale? I've spent my entire life struggling to understand men like this, but find them unfathomable. He's just an ugly old man with bizarre eyes.

I crouch down with my bone knife clutched in my fist. "Go on."

"After you appeared to me in the dream, I saw you climbin' the mountain, headin' to a cave. I've tried to soul-fly to find it, but it eludes me. The spirits must want you to take me there."

"There are a thousand caves in the Ice Giant Mountains. Which cave?"

"You mustn't play games with me. You see, there's no other reason for me to bargain with you for the lives of the last Sealion People."

My throat constricts with hope. "I'm not playing games. I don't know what cave you mean."

Trogon tilts his head. "Did you find the Old Woman of the Mountain there?"

"The Old Woman of the Mountain?"

Trogon's laced fingers clench until they go white. "You went into her cave. I saw you do it."

Confused, and frightened, I say, "I don't understand. What does this have to do with Arakie?"

"It's his cave. He lives there with her. The Jemen told me."

Mink silently steps forward. He's standing one pace behind Trogon. It's a simple lunge with his knife.

For the first time, Trogon blinks, looks over his shoulder at Mink, then his gaze moves to a tiny crack in the ice that slithers down from the roof; it resembles a thin black serpent. "I could escape anytime, you know."

Mink follows his gaze. "Going to change yourself into a spider and skitter through that crack?"

"No." He pauses. "Not a spider."

Trogon slowly unlaces his fingers, rests them on his knees, and stares unblinking at me. I feel like I'm caught in the gaze of a hungry lion.

"Forgive me for starin', but I can't see you. Are you gone?" he asks, and looks around the cave, as though searching for me.

"Move your torch. It's probably blinding you."

"No, it's not the torch. It's the blood." Trogon leans forward and squints hard. "Why 'aven't your sacred elders told you of this?"

"About the blood?"

"Yes, so much blood. I can barely see you through it. You're afraid and walkin' fast."

I ponder that. Sounds like a threat. "You mean I'm dead and walking through the skyworld? On my way to the campfires of the dead?"

"No. It's different. It's like you are an empty skin and blood fills you up inside, givin' you the shape of a woman. But you are not a woman. I don't know what you are."

Gods, he's strange.

He asks, "Don't your sacred elders care about this?"

"Maybe they don't see the empty skin."

Trogon squares his shoulders as though he finds that possibility disturbing. He leans very close to sniff me. "When you killed your first man . . . is that when the blood filled you up? The Jemen are strange that way. They don't want us to see the path too clearly."

"Lean back, elder, or you'll find my knife in your guts."

Trogon blinks curiously. "I could be wrong. Perhaps the livin' can't help you. Maybe the dead are your only hope. Perhaps your elders know this. I can't be sure, of course."

"You risked your life to come in here and tell me that the dead are my only hope?"

His eyes are endless amber reflections. Since he entered the cave, it has felt emptier than before, stripped of everything warm and light. "The Old Woman of the Mountain will send someone through the veil of blood, you know. You should prepare yourself for this arrival."

My voice is mocking, when I answer, "Oh, I will."

He doesn't comment, just rises to his feet and calmly walks between RabbitEar and Mink to leave.

Before he shoulders through the crevice into the luminous green night beyond, he looks back one last time. "Quiller? Would you bargain for your people, if I allow it?"

RabbitEar shakes his head so violently his blue medicine bag, which hangs from a braided cord around his throat, flops back and forth across his chest. "No, Quiller. You can't—"

"I would," I call over his voice.

"Then I 'ave one simple request. I must find your friend Lynx and the old man named Arakie. I wish you to accompany me. In exchange, I will allow your people to go free. I'll even order my healers to care for their wounds. That's a good bargain, isn't it?"

Mink scoffs. "Quiller, you can't believe a word he says. He's a liar. As soon as you step out of this cave, his warriors are going to rush us and kill everyone in here!"

I'm clutching my bone knife so hard my fingers ache. Glancing back at the women and children in the tunnel, I see Jawbone flickering in the torchlight. Crow stands beside him with her muzzle up, sniffing the air. The skirts of my daughters are visible just behind Crow.

"Mother?" Jawbone calls. It's the first time since I adopted him into my clan that he's called me that. He's clutching his boy's spear and shielding his sisters with his body. Like a slender arrow, he shoots out of the tunnel and runs to grab my hand. Looking up, he whispers. "A woman has been talking to me through the air. Elektra says she's coming back—"

"Come with me, Quiller! This is your last chance," Trogon shouts.

I have no idea what my son is talking about. I know of no one named Elektra. I squeeze his hand. "Jawbone, I love you with all my heart. Please, go and guard your sisters."

Tears stream down my son's face as he hugs me around the waist and says, "Mother, she wants to take you away from us. Don't let her take you!"

"I—I won't. I promise. Now, please, go guard your sisters."

"I love you," he says, then runs back to the tunnel to stand in front of my daughters.

In the gleam of the torch, I see Trogon's wide eyes narrow, listening. He extends a hand to me. "Come. The Old Woman of the Mountain waits for us."

I turn to my husband. More than anything in life I long to lie in his arms surrounded by our children, but I know I may never do that again.

"Keep our children safe," I tell RabbitEar. "Never leave them alone."

"Quiller, no. Everything he tells you is a lie! You know it! You've seen it over and over—"

"Don't come after me." I poke a finger hard into his chest. "Do you understand? Protect our children and our people. I can take care of myself."

"No, don't do this! Please . . ."

I unsling my quiver, hand it to RabbitEar, then shoulder through the crevice and walk to meet a man I have feared my entire life.

4

LYNX

Dawn's soft gray glow penetrates the smoke hole in the roof and falls across the lodge, waking me to the sounds of wind and surf, but I just lie beneath my warm hides listening to the uneasy rhythms of Arakie's breathing. He sleeps with his head pillowed on one arm and thin white hair veiling his face. One of his hands rests on Xeno's back.

The wolf never leaves him now, as though he's made a personal vow to guard the old man until his last breath. I'm sure he feels Arakie slipping away, just as I do.

I need to fetch water before Arakie wakes. He will need something hot to drink to keep him warm.

Quietly, I shove out of my hides and pull the tea bag from the tripod beside the low fire.

As I duck beneath the lodge flap, Father Sun crests the highest peaks of the Ice Giants, and a flood of yellow light rushes down the ice slopes. The zyme glow dies in the onslaught and slowly, inexorably, the sky shades from lime green to blue.

Out over the ocean, small dovekies flutter and soar, their eerie squeals fusing with the grinding of icebergs smashing through the floes.

Picking my way through the debris, I finally find a good place to kneel and sink my bag into the freezing water to fill it.

The earthy fragrance of glacial meltwater is powerful. Even

in the depths of winter, streams pour from the Ice Giants and flow into the ocean. Arakie says volcanoes live beneath the Ice Giants, constantly melting them and creating these streams. Filled with gravel and boulders, they are treacherous when sheathed with ice, like this morning.

My elders tell me such streams were once filled with so many fish a man could scarcely see the bottom, but that was before the ancient Jemen tried to destroy the Ice Giants by casting a necklace studded with gigantic mirrors into the sky. After that, warfare broke out and the zyme went wild, gobbling up the ocean.

To the east, the colossal bodies of the Giants resemble endless layers of blue-white mountain ranges receding until they blend with the sky. Black crevasses and verdant valleys studded with trees break up the vista, providing the only relief. The voices of the Giants are strangely soft today.

When the water bag is full, I draw it out and stand up. My fingers are so cold I can barely feel them. Beyond the bay to the south, where the freezing water has driven the zyme far out to sea, great cliffs of ice pack the shore, looking as if huge waves crashed there and froze in place, wave after wave spilling over the one before.

I'm surprised when I see Arakie duck beneath the lodge flap and stagger to the dead fire on the beach. The tripod that always stands there has toppled into the driftwood pile. "Elder?" I call. "What are you doing out here?"

He collapses to the ground and drops his white head into his hands.

Xeno noses through the flap and dutifully lopes to Arakie's side to stand guard over him.

"You should be inside where it's warm!" I call and break into a run.

"No man . . . sleeps in the cart . . . between Newgate and Tyburn."

Many of his phrases are nonsense to me, including this one, even though he has told me that Newgate was an ancient prison and Tyburn a gallows. "What are you doing out here in the icy wind?"

Arakie narrows his eyes at the zyme rising and falling with the waves. "Gazing . . . upon my sins. Helps me clarify . . . these last moments."

"I swear you're trying to kill yourself," I say as I run up and hand him the water bag. "Hold this while I get the tripod set up."

He takes the bag in knobby claw-like fingers. "If I wanted to kill myself . . . would have done it a long time ago."

"You should have at least carried a hide out with you to wrap around your shoulders."

He smiles weakly. "Too heavy. Couldn't."

"Let me get the fire going, and I'll fetch it for you."

Pulling the tripod from the driftwood pile, I spread its legs near the hearthstones, then take the bag from him and hang it in the middle. All the while, he squints at the zyme.

"What does that mean? Sins? I don't know that word."

"Oh, it's . . ." He seems to be considering what he'll tell me. When he speaks, he can only manage a few words at a time: "Not easy to explain . . . not without a lengthy discourse . . . on mercy and forgiveness. But . . . sins are the lies we tell our-selves."

I frown out at the zyme. "You were gazing upon your lies?"

"See? You did understand."

"I did not. How can a lie help clarify anything?"

"Foolish question. Once you know a man's lies . . . you know everything about him. In my case . . ."

He gasps and starts coughing as though he's being wrenched apart. The attack lasts so long, I panic, leap to my feet, and start pounding his back. His lungs are filling up with fluid. I've tried every spirit plant my Sealion elders have ever taught me about to cure it. Nothing has helped.

When the attack eases, I ask, "Are you all right?"

"Well, that's . . . relative. I'm dying."

I glance at the lodge. The door flap is whipping in the wind, revealing our sleeping hides inside. "I'm going to fetch the hide for you. If you like I can also bring out the leftover fish and make breakfast here on the beach."

Arakie has the bluest eyes I've ever seen—like the azure depths of the Ice Giants themselves. When he looks up at me, they are filled with love. His voice comes as a series of gasps: "Your . . . empathy . . . is such a surprise, Lynx. Many of my colleagues . . . said it was impossible."

"Does that mean yes?"

He manages a nod.

I hurry to our lodge to gather cups, the leftover fish, and a bison hide, all the while wondering who his colleagues were. Through the open flap, I see Arakie close his eyes and lean down close to Xeno. Is he sniffing noses in the way of wolves? Or perhaps he's whispering to Xeno? One of the Ice Giants lets out a sharp crack and a belly roar rumbles down over the beach, shaking the air, but neither Arakie nor Xeno pulls away. It's as though they are locked in some sort of feral communion. The wolf's tail thumps the sand. The sound is so soft it could be drumbeats echoing in the Land of the Dead. A sacred drumbeat . . . preparing the village of the dead for the great man's arrival.

My eyes blur as I duck out into the cold sea wind. Every moment I am with him now is precious.

When I crouch beside him, I set the cups and bowl on the sand, then drape the hide around his shoulders. "The Ice Giants sound angry this morning."

"Dwelling on my sins, too . . . I suppose."

"Why would the Ice Giants care about your lies?"

"Don't. Glaciers are . . . divinely indifferent. But they can't help but see them."

"What do you mean? The zyme?"

Gently, he says, "Knowledge . . . is a sharp knife, Lynx. You can use it to . . . to carve out your own conscience. Don't let that happen . . . to you."

"Is that what your people did?"

"There are those . . . who would say . . . I was the worst."

"You are not! You're the best man I know. The kindest man."

He closes his eyes a moment. "No. No. My arrogance. My belief in my own scientific . . . projections. Government wouldn't listen. When they took my family . . . I . . . I—"

"Doesn't matter. I'm sure you did what was right."

Lightly, he shakes his head.

Using one of the pieces of driftwood, I dig around in the fire pit until I find a few warm coals and rake them to the center, then place twigs on top and create a driftwood tent over them. Wind Mother will do the rest, but it may take some time, so I lean back on my elbows and frown out at the zyme, as he is doing. Sunlight glints from the tallest pillars that ride the waves like misshapen green humans. I gesture to them.

"Sealion People say that some of the last Jemen walked into the sea and turned themselves into zyme as punishment for creating it. Are there any parts of that story that are true?"

He frowns as though remembering things he'd rather not. "Oh, yes. It was . . . penance."

"I hope that's not what you plan to do."

"A pile of rocks . . . is all I need. A place beneath the pines . . . if you can."

He falls into a coughing fit that shudders his entire body. When he can't seem to get air, I start to rise, to go to him, but he holds up a hand to stop me. It takes several more agonizing moments before his coughing fit drops to wheezing.

My eyes do not leave him. It's as though I see him fading, turning invisible as I watch. "Elder, I wish you'd let me build you a burial scaffold when the time comes. That way your soul can look up, see the Road of Light, and find its way to the Land of the Dead. Being buried under a pile of stones . . . that's what Sealion People do to witches to keep a witch's soul locked in the earth forever."

Finally, he manages to get a full breath into his lungs, and asks, "Like the legendary Trogon?"

"He is the most evil man alive. I'd love to bury him beneath a big pile of rocks."

"He does have . . . quite a reputation."

"He earned his reputation by using a magical hook to draw out people's souls, twist them into knots, and put them back in their bodies."

Disdainfully, Arakie says, "Ever seen . . . one of these knotted-up victims?"

"Yes." As Wind Mother fans the coals, tiny threads of flame flicker through the driftwood. I bend down to rearrange the twigs. "A few of our people have been captured by the Rust People and escaped. When they returned to their families, they acted like animals. One young woman ate her own infant child. Another man murdered his son, who was a war chief Trogon didn't like. Their brains had become mush. They gnashed their teeth all the time. Their loved ones didn't allow them to live for long."

Arakie seems to be pondering that. As though speaking to himself, he softly asks, "Probably some . . . archaic technique of suggestion. Primitive psychiatry. Dangerous . . . psychotic . . . maybe."

As the flames rise higher, I add more wood, and roll a few of the hearthstones into the fire to heat. "I don't know what that means, Arakie. The man is evil. He's twisted the souls out of dozens of people."

"Psychotics can . . . convince people of . . . anything. History brims with examples. Hitler. Stalin. Lin Chang . . . of Euro-China."

As the wind picks up, surf batters the shore, and foam rolls almost up to our beach fire. When it retreats, lacy green filaments of zyme remain.

"Gods, it's c-cold this morning." He tugs the bison hide up to his chin and shivers.

My heart hurts. I rise and walk over to tuck the edges of the hide more closely around him. "Elder? I'm afraid. I don't want to lose you."

He glances at me, then seems genuinely affected by my words. He blinks away tears. "Don't be afraid. I . . . I will miss Quancee . . . and you. But it's good to finally see the path ahead."

5

QUILLER

We marched up the coast until well after midnight, then camped on the beach in a grove of pines to sleep. Throughout the night, I glanced at Trogon. I don't think he ever slept.

This morning, he's in exactly the same place, on the opposite side of the fire with his hands extended over the low flames and his silver cape flapping around him. Silhouetted against the green background of zyme-covered sea, he seems even larger and more threatening than he did yesterday. Long, pale wisps of his hair repeatedly tangle with his eyelashes and beard, but he doesn't seem to notice. I don't think he's really here. His wide eyes are filled with distance, as though he's soul-flying through unearthly skies.

I shift to readjust my bound hands, but it's a barely noticeable movement. I don't want to draw his attention. In exchange for setting my people free, I agreed to lead him to Lynx's camp, then he has agreed to set me free. I'm terrified of what will happen when he finds Lynx and Arakie, but even if all three of us die, it was a good bargain. Providing the Rust People did as Trogon ordered, by now the Sealion People are far away from the Rust villages.

Six warriors move to my right, rolling up their silver blankets and stuffing them in their packs. We'll be leaving soon. I don't know where the Dog Soldier went, probably up into the trees to empty his night water.

Trogon makes a strange sound and reaches down to touch the red bag tied around his waist. As he strokes it, his lips move, speaking to something I do not see, perhaps something in the bag. The conversation is apparently unpleasant. His nostrils flare with rapid breaths.

The lonely trumpeting of mammoths seems to bring him back to this world. He blinks and gazes around as though surprised to see the towering Ice Giants, the sea, and me.

"Oh, there you are," he says as though I'm the one who's been gone. "I'm always surprised to find your empty skin alive."

I shiver.

"Are you cold? Here, take my cape." He pulls the garment from his shoulders, walks around the fire, and tosses it over the shoulders of my bear-hide cape.

I know that it's called trayalon and supposedly lasts a thousand summers, but it's falling apart. Flakes of silver are missing, giving the cape a mottled appearance. It is warm, though. I can feel heat rising from it, as though Trogon is fevered and the trayalon holds his warmth.

"My daughter's ghost is whispering to me about you. May I ask you about these things?"

"Is that what's in the red bag? Your daughter's ghost?"

"Memories. She says I need to speak with you about your memories."

I realize I'm holding my breath, and let it out. "Memories of what?"

Trogon crouches in front of me. "Not what, but where."

I just stare at him, thinking he means the cave where the Old Woman of the Mountain lives.

But he says, "You 'ave memories that flew away to the Land

of the Dead and secreted themselves in crevices and holes in the ground. You must tell me about them."

He's a madman. Utterly insane. I twist my bound hands and wince when the cords cut deeper into my wrists. "What are you talking about?"

Trogon's blond brows pull together. "They are livin' things, little Quill. They breathe. They think. You must tell me about them. It's the only way I can help you," he says with genuine concern in his voice.

"I can't tell you about them, because I don't—"

"Oh," he says in a small polite voice, "I should 'ave known. You've forgotten them. The problem is . . . they remember you. Believe me, I've spoken with my own memories locked in the Land of the Dead. Like lost children cryin' in the darkness. They wait for me to pull them out of the crevices and turn them over in my hands."

His words spin bizarre images across my soul: memories weeping in dark crevices, waiting to be touched.

"Why would you do that? Why would you pull them out?"

As the morning warms, the green scent of the zyme overpowers the salty fragrance of the sea.

"You must do it, too. Or I can do it for you, if you wish."

"No, I don't wish."

Barely perceptible, he nods his head. "I understand. Memories 'ave fangs. They can rip you apart with little effort. But if you insist on keeping them locked in the darkness, I will never be able to help you."

"I don't need your help."

Trogon gracefully sits down beside me, but his gaze is focused on the billowing clouds sailing across the far horizon. "Very well. Then tell me about your friend Lynx."

The change in topics momentarily confuses me. "Why?"

"He's your age, yes?"

"One summer older. Seventeen."

"You were young lovers?"

"What makes you think that?"

"Your voice" —he touches his throat—"it gets soft when you speak of him. So tell me about him. What can it hurt? You loved him?"

With great caution, I say, "We were to be married, but in the end he married someone else."

He smiles. "You probably think that's one of the worst things that ever happened to you. It's not. But tell me, what's the worst thing that ever happened to Lynx?"

Shrugging my shoulders, I answer, "I don't know. You'd have to ask him."

"When I ask you a question, you'd better answer me. And don't lie to me. I'll know if you do." He shakes a fist at me. "Tell me why Lynx is livin' with an old man and not with his wife."

"She was killed by lions. A big pride attacked his wedding camp and slaughtered everyone except Lynx and one of the camp guards."

Trogon blinks. "So he ran away to live with an old man?"

"I don't know why he abandoned our people. I've never understood that."

He whispers in an insidious voice, "You hate men, don't you?"

The question is so outlandish, my mouth gapes. "No. Why would I?"

Trogon tilts his head first one way, then the other, studying me with each eye. "You may 'ave forgotten, but your hands remember. The fear lives in your muscles and sinew. I see it when you look at men. Unimaginable fear."

I know he is the great holy man of the Rust People, but my own people would wait until he wasn't looking, club him in the head, and bury him beneath a huge pile of stones. Then we'd move the entire village to make sure his ghost could not escape and find us.

Trogon wraps his arms around his drawn-up knees and hugs them to his chest. "You don't mind if I tell you what my daughter says about you, do you? They are not pleasant things. They may be hard for you to hear."

"I've heard hard things before."

His jaw falls wide open, revealing broken yellow teeth. I swear his soul has flown away again. He's staring at nothing.

"You were so small. Gods." Tears well in his eyes. "He used to come into your lodge at night."

"Who?"

Trogon squeezes his eyes closed. "He was so heavy. You couldn't get away."

I'm studying his facial expressions. They change so fast, I can't fathom what he's feeling. "I don't know what you're talking about."

The great witch sits quietly for a moment. "You begged him not to come. He—he was supposed to protect you. You never knew which night it would be. You were so frightened."

I am a seasoned warrior woman. I've fought in many battles against the Rust People and am considered by other Sealion warriors to be a brave person. But terror just grabbed me by the throat.

"Who did?"

"I—I don't know his name." As he wipes his eyes, he says, "Please don't be afraid. You're with me now. I will protect you. Do you know how to deal with the fear? Has anyone taught you?"

My answer is a light shake of the head.

"Takes practice," he says in a loving voice, as though I am one of his children. "When the body suffers you must leave it behind. Just put your soul in a rock or a clump of ice. It's all right for it to hide there for a little while. Don't feel guilty about that. You are still brave. Braver than you know."

He reaches out to stroke my hair, but seems to reconsider and draws his hand back to his lap. "I'm a healer. I will help you. You may speak with me about these things at any time."

My voice is so soft, I almost don't hear it. "Thank you."

I try to turn away from him, but he catches my chin with one big hand and wrenches it around to stare into my eyes again. His gaze travels down my throat and his mouth widens a little. When his gaze returns to mine, I glare at him with all the loathing I can manage.

"Your people, the Sealion People, believe that souls rise to the sky after death, isn't that right? You run to the Road of Light and follow it to the campfires of the dead?"

"Yes."

"Shall I tell you what really happens to the dead?"

"I don't care what Rust People believe."

He hisses, "Souls actually descend into the underworld, where they swim a great dark river to get to the villages of the ancestors."

"A river? Under the ground?" I'm frantically trying to understand the path to his Land of the Dead. I've seen rivers disappear into holes in the ice and never resurface. Is that what he means?

"It's in the Forgotten Country. You've been there. You've just drunk so much of its water, you don't remember."

"I've never been there."

"Oh," he says with a sigh, "yes, you 'ave. You've been there many times."

I'm afraid to argue with him. "Have you been there?"

"Yes. I . . . I . . ." He takes a moment to collect himself before he continues. "I'd seen four winters. My soul crossed into the

Forgotten Country and I traveled to the villages of the dead. I wanted to come back, but I couldn't recall the way. No one there knew the way back either."

Hesitantly, I say, "But you did make it back. You're here now."

That same strange half-smile. "No. I did not, little Quill. My soul is still there hidin' in a black hole in the bottom of the river. I can see the water flowin' over the top of me and the reflections of trees. Only my body is here."

His lips pull back too tightly across the teeth—like the rictus of a corpse. "Over the next moon, you must tell me every silly Sealion story. Especially your stories about the Jemen."

"The next moon?" My voice shakes.

"Yes. The Old Woman of the Mountain says she must speak with you in person, and the journey may take a long . . ."

The Dog Soldier emerges from the pines, and Trogon turns to watch him walk back toward the fire. Dog Soldiers all have very dark skin and strange flat skulls. Most have black hair, but a few, like this one, have red hair. I've never really seen one close up until the past few days. The Rust People protect them with their lives because only Dog Soldiers can read what's in their holy books. This one carries a shoulder pack. It must be heavy, for it swings from side to side with his steps.

Trogon cups a hand to his mouth, and calls, "Good mornin', Sticks."

The Dog Solider lifts a hand and picks up his pace. Around his neck he wears a powerful magical amulet, an ancient lump of rust suspended from a leather cord. I found one once. They're very heavy. My adopted children tell me they are ancient weapons. As he walks, the lump sways, leaving a reddish-brown arc across the trayalon fabric of his silver shirt. I have learned this is a mark of status. Other Rust People come up and reverently touch that arc to gain some of its power.

Trogon rises to his feet. "You must start searching for the

crevices where your memories cry, little Quill. We'll speak more later."

He walks out to meet Sticks. The Dog Soldier is two heads taller, which forces Trogon to look up into Sticks' black eyes.

I clench my fists and order my body to stop shaking. Can't seem to get enough air in my lungs. This must be how the old witch controls his victims. He plants memories like poisonous vines in the forest, knowing they're almost impossible to kill. I can feel them down there. The vines creep and slither, whispering in voices I almost recognize. And I have nowhere to run because they have twined so tightly with my muscles and sinew that I can't rip them out. I've never felt them there before. The only reason I do now is because he told me they hide there.

Stop it.

Those things did not happen. But . . . I half-remember them now. Long-ago eyes in the darkness. Something heavy on my chest.

Trogon and Sticks walk over to converse with the six warriors who are shouldering their packs and clutching their spears.

Sticks asks, "What did she tell you?"

Trogon says, "His wife was killed by lions."

I strain to hear more, trying to figure out how they plan to use that information against Lynx.

Finally, Trogon gestures to me and calls, "Quiller, come and walk beside me. We must know everythin' about your friend Lynx."

As I rise, dread makes me sick to my stomach.

6

※

QUILLER

When the shoreline curves inland, we head east into a large tree-whiskered bay. Beyond it, the Ice Giants loom like towering blue monsters. Their conversations seem subdued today. Distant lion-like roars rumble, but they're far away. Closer, I hear only whimpers and clip-clops that remind me of the magical running horses we hunted in the northern steppe lands. Old Hoodwink tells tales of ice horses that run with their tails flying through the deep caverns in the heart of the Ice Giants. He says they have icicle eyes and frozen blue manes.

"Elder Trogon?" the lead warrior calls and uses his spear to point to a haze of campfire smoke blowing across the bay.

"I see it."

Using the opportunity, my gaze locates each of my captors. Three warriors march in front of me, and Trogon and Sticks march behind me. Another three warriors bring up the rear. Eight against one. Nonetheless, I will escape. Every instant, I imagine myself fleeing up one of the mammoth trails that cut across the beach, or darting into an ice tunnel and crawling until my body becomes wedged in such awful blackness they can't find me.

"Is that what you saw in your vision, elder?" Sticks holds up a hand to shield his eyes against the blinding sunlit glare reflecting from the Ice Giants.

Trogon nods. "Yes." He's tied his graying blond hair back with a cord, but Wind Mother has torn strands loose, and they've tangled with his long beard.

"Then their camp is close."

Trogon scents the air like a wolf. "Yes, I smell them. The old man is dyin'. The odor of decay already fills him up and seeps from his mouth and ears."

Extending his arm, Trogon points to a crystal-clear stream of water pouring out of the glaciers. Enormous black boulders have rolled down the slope and cluster at the mouth of the stream where it empties into the ocean. "There. They are camped right there. We must use caution, for I fear the old man is more than he seems."

From behind us, one of the warriors bringing up the rear calls, "Elder?"

When I try to turn around to see him, Trogon orders, "Turn back around. Stare at that campfire smoke."

I obey, but listen hard to the conversation behind me.

Trogon says, "Predictable. Take care of it."

Footsteps pound away down the beach. Two men.

When I try to see what they're doing, Trogon grabs my arm and drags me forward. "Come, little Quill. Let me tell you a story about a great white bird who rolled a stone away from a tomb."

"How could a bird roll a stone—"

Trogon drags me closer and roughly whispers, "The bird was waitin'. Waitin' to see the dead fly away. Do you think she did?"

"I don't care."

Trogon shakes me hard to keep me from seeing the warriors trotting away down the beach and forces me to stare into his huge bottomless eyes. "Answer me."

"She must have seen the dead fly! You wouldn't have told me the story otherwise."

He grins at me with broken teeth. "Because there wouldn't be a story, little Quill. Think about that when we reach the Old Woman's tomb. The dead must take wing and flap away to the Road of Light. It's the only story that will save the world."

7

---❄---

LYNX

As evening approaches, the zyme glow is faint, just a hint in the sky.

I've been gone all day, hunting beneath a ceiling of low-hanging clouds. The goose tied to my belt flops with my steps. In the weave of pines to the east, giant lions silently creep along, paralleling my path. I clutch my spear more tightly, but I'm not too concerned. Since I've been with Arakie, the huge predators that roam the mountains and shore do not hunt me, they just watch as I pass. It's as though Arakie is the chief of the predators, and he's ordered them to leave me alone. Perhaps he can send his thoughts into the minds of animals, as he claims?

I wonder . . .

As I study the lions moving like smoke through the trees, I almost believe it. Why else wouldn't they run me down and eat me alive?

When I round the curve in the trail, I see the elder hunched before the struggling beach fire. Xeno stands guard nearby with one paw lifted. The wolf is staring southward. If it were a bear or dire wolf, Xeno would be barking wildly in warning.

Probably nothing. A skittering crab, perhaps.

Arakie lifts his head when he sees me, but does not raise a hand in greeting. He grows weaker by the day. If I followed the way of my people, I'd abandon him to the wilderness and move on. It would not be cruelty, but an act of compassion. His agony would be over much more quickly. By feeding and caring for him, I merely delay his journey to the afterworld.

Perhaps I should load him in a bull boat and paddle south to warmer country? But even if Arakie was strong enough to climb in a boat and head south with me for the summer, our slim window of opportunity is closing fast. Spring haunts the shoreline. The zyme is readying itself to rush in and swallow the last bits of open water. When that happens, traveling by boat will be impossible.

Arakie rasps, "People coming!"

I frown at the trail to the south, where tundra creates an open vista along the shore. "Where? I don't see anyone."

But there is something down there, for Xeno's attention is focused entirely on that trail.

"You shot a goose?" Arakie calls. "Good. Food to share."

Xeno suddenly growls, then barks and lopes back to the fire to lie down beside Arakie, guarding him.

It takes a while before I see the glypt that munches sea grasses at the edge of the surf. That must be what Arakie and Xeno see. Glypts are huge, round creatures, as tall as I am, and over twenty hand-lengths long. They are covered with hard gray scales that create an effective armor. Because they weigh forty or fifty times as much as a grown man, a single kill will feed an entire village for two moons. I'm surprised to see him alive. They're delicious, which means there aren't many left.

But as I get closer to our camp, the glypt utters a wheezy grunt and shakes his armored head at something to the south. As though he knows a threat when he sees it, the glypt breaks into a clumsy trot, heading toward the pines, where he crashes through the deadfall and vanishes.

Then I see them. Windblown capes blaze in the zyme light like greenish-silver flames.

"Rust People. Seven of them."

I'll never get over the fear in the pit of my stomach when I see silver clothing.

Trotting to the fire, I exchange a glance with Arakie. "Wonder what they want?"

Arakie's blue eyes narrow. As night falls, the firelight flows into his deep wrinkles, casting a tracery of shadows across his face. "To discuss news of peace?"

"Any fishing boat could have done that. Why send seven people?"

"Well . . . we will know soon."

"Hopefully, they're just passing through. In any case, it'll be dark soon. They'll want to stop for the night, and they will surely be hungry."

My stomach muscles are clenched tight, but I kneel, skewer the goose with a stick of driftwood, and prop it over the fire to cook.

8

---　❄　---

LYNX

It takes another hand of time before the Rust People have managed to walk around the bay, and by then it's dark and windy. The pines rock back and forth with their branches squealing.

As they come closer, my heart starts to slam against my chest. "Blessed gods, that's Trogon."

Arakie's white hair blows around his face when he swivels his head to frown at them. "Which one?"

"The big man with the long beard."

"And the others?"

Shaking my head, I say, "I don't know. Four warriors, one Dog Soldier, and one woman, I think." Something nags me about the woman. The way she moves is familiar.

"A delegation, then."

Rising to my feet, I pull my spear from where it rests near the fire, walk around, and place myself between Arakie and the oncoming warriors.

"Lynx . . . drop your spear. It's . . . seven against one."

"Yes, but I might be able to get Trogon, and that will rid the world of a great evil."

Arakie exhales the words: "Please, put it down."

"Do you really think this is an innocent delegation? Maybe the Rust People sent their greatest holy man to ask about fishing spots?"

My taut muscles seem to already be anticipating what horrors the next moments hold, but the more I think about it, the more I'm sure Arakie is right. My one spear is not going to be of much use in this situation. If things turn badly, it's best to try to talk our way through it. Reluctantly, I plant the butt of my spear in the ground . . . and walk away from it.

As the zyme pillars roll up and down on the crashing waves, the green gleam swells and fades, swells and fades. In its midst, the windblown tree shadows appear to be dancing across the beach, flailing fists at the light, striving to drive it back into the ocean from whence it came. It's an odd, unsettling effect.

They're twenty paces away when the wind blows back the woman's hood, and I see bushy red hair. "Quiller!" I break into a run.

Ten paces away, my happiness at seeing her dies, and I stumble to a stop. The expression on her face is grim, as though she's trying to warn me to run, and I see her straining against the bindings cutting into her wrists.

"Hello!" Trogon shouts with a wide smile. "Are you Lynx?"

Violently, Quiller shakes her head at me. She doesn't want me to tell him who I am. Why?

Trogon says something over his shoulder, and the Dog Soldier grabs Quiller's tied hands and drags her forward to speak with the old witch.

I cast a glance over my shoulder at Arakie, hoping he's noticed what's going on, but he just hunches before the fire like a skeleton wrapped in heavy hides. Xeno, however, has missed nothing. The big wolf stands in front of Arakie with his teeth bared.

Trogon wrenches Quiller's arm, and I hear him say, "I wish to enter their camp and speak with them. Tell them."

"Why can't you tell them?" Quiller fights against his iron grip.

"Your voice will ease their fears, that's why. Now, do it."

Quiller gives the witch a look of loathing, and calls out, "Elder Trogon requests permission to enter your camp and speak with you."

Before I can answer, Arakie calls, "Welcome!" and falls into a coughing fit.

"Kind of you!" Trogon shouts back and shoves Quiller ahead of him. The four warriors and the Dog Soldier surround them in a moving circle.

I back up all the way to the fire, where Arakie and I exchange a wary look.

As the Rust People approach, Xeno lifts his nose and scents the air. The hair on his back stands on end.

"It's all right," Arakie softly tells Xeno. "Lie down."

The wolf stretches out at his side, but his gaze never leaves Trogon as the old witch boldly strides right up to our fire and sits down cross-legged to Arakie's left. "Good evenin'."

I remain standing, watching the two elders exchange speculative glances. Trogon's eyes are tan, webbed with tiny red blood vessels. Sometimes the vessels seem to pulse and worm toward his dark shiny pupils.

Arakie keeps one hand on Xeno, making certain the animal doesn't rise into a threatening position, and says, "If you have cups . . . please help yourselves to the dried . . . berry tea," and gestures to the hide bag hanging from the tripod near the flames.

"Wait, elder," the Dog Soldier says as he kneels by the fire, removes his pack, and searches inside for two wooden cups. Then he dips one into the tea bag and draws it out dripping. He tastes the tea, rolls it around inside his mouth, and finally swallows. "It's safe." He hands the cup to Trogon.

"I thank you, Sticks."

Arakie gives the Dog Soldier a questioning look. "Sticks, like twigs? Or Styx . . . like the river?"

The Dog Soldier doesn't seem to understand. "Which river?"

"Never mind. Old story."

The Dog Soldier examines Arakie's small skull and jutting chin—not at all like the skulls of Rust People or Sealion People. Arakie is clearly something else, and Sticks knows it. "My People, Dog Soldiers, are story keepers. I would hear this story, if you will tell it, then I will decide if any of it should be kept."

"You only keep . . . parts you like, eh?"

"We keep the parts that are true. We discard the rest."

"I see." Arakie's eyes narrow. "Kind of hard to . . . tell the difference, isn't it?"

The Dog Soldier starts to respond, but Trogon says, "Leave us now, Sticks, and take the warriors with you. Arakie, Lynx, and I must speak in private."

The Dog Soldier bows slightly and pulls a book from his pack. I'm trying to read the title as he walks away with it, motions for the warriors to follow him, and together they trudge down to the edge of the surf thirty paces away.

"Quiller?" Trogon calls. "Sit down. Right here."

Trogon uses a fist to pound the sand, and she reluctantly sits down cross-legged at his side. He did not include her name in this "private" conversation, so I wonder why she's here.

"That's better. Now that I know you're not dead, I can concentrate. Please introduce me to your friends."

"Dead?" I say in confusion, and Arakie gives me a stern look, as though he wishes I'd stayed silent.

"Yes, she's not really a woman at all," Trogon says as he stares at me with huge empty eyes. "Just the shape of one. I'm not sure yet whether she's alive or dead."

When I start to comment, Arakie subtly shakes his head, and I close my mouth.

Arakie must have decided Quiller is not going to introduce us to Trogon, so he says, "I'm Arakie. That's Lynx."

"I suspect you already know who I am." Trogon's mouth curls in a superior manner.

"I do," Arakie says pleasantly. "Trogon the witch. Are you planning on sleeping . . . here for the night? Not sure I like that idea."

"Sleep? No. I'm always awake at night. That's when I feed."

There's a brief silence while Arakie evaluates Trogon, and seems to come to some conclusion. "That sounds scary."

Trogon smiles, then he gestures to the wolf. "That's an ugly animal. What's his name?"

"Wolf," I call from the other side of the fire.

Among the Sealion People, names have power. They shouldn't be given away without considering the ramifications of how they might be used. I don't want this evil old man to know Xeno's name.

"That's right," Arakie agrees with a pained smile. "Wolf."

"Wolf." Trogon growls the name and Xeno growls back, ready to meet that challenge with a lethal response.

Arakie's fingers twine in the scruff of Xeno's neck, but I doubt he can hold Xeno back if the wolf decides to attack Trogon.

"He's a strange creature," Trogon says. "Look at that narrow snout. And his gray hide shimmers in the firelight like the inside of a seashell. I've never seen one like him before."

"Don't imagine you have," I reply. "*Xenocyon texanus reecur.* He's a re-created Late Pliocene hypercarnivore. If you look closely, you will see that while he's as big as a dire wolf, his skull is longer and leaner, and he has four toes on his forepaws, whereas dire wolves have five. That's because Wolf's people are much, much older. They trotted the world over a million summers before dire wolves were born. Just like your friend Sticks. They're both well documented in the Rewilding Reports."

The Dog Soldier, who stands out by the surf, suddenly

stiffens and turns to give me a stunned look. Perhaps wondering how I know about the Rewilding Reports, which his people consider sacred. He has oversized ears, but it seems impossible that he could have heard us.

"I saw these strange wolves in a vision," Trogon says.

"Did you?" Arakie asks.

"Yes. A few days ago. One of the Earthbound Jemen came to my lodge in the form of a wolf and took my soul flying to a time before the zyme when vast deserts covered the earth. Strange wolves roamed the dunes. They looked like him." He jerks his chin at Xeno.

"Male or female?"

"What?"

"The Jemen." Arakie pronounces it Jee-man. "The one who came to you. Man or woman?"

Trogon's eyes narrow. "Why do you care?"

Arakie strokes Xeno's back until the bristly ridge of hair lies flat, but I can tell he's using Xeno as an excuse to mull over something. A strange, half-afraid expression comes over his face as he peers at Xeno. "What did he say?"

Trogon blinks. "Who?"

"The man who came to you."

As though frightened, Trogon snaps, "How did you know it was a man?"

"I'm praying it was. What'd he say?"

"Lynx knows what he said. Don't you, boy?" Trogon smiles at me with broken teeth. "The Earthbound Jemen speak to him, too."

With difficulty, Arakie says, "At least . . . you got that right."

Trogon's gaze slides back to Arakie. He looks truly worried now. "I came here to speak with you about the old woman. Order Lynx to sit down, so I can—"

"Sit down, Lynx," Arakie orders. "Man finally . . . wants . . . to get to the point."

I crouch near the driftwood pile on the other side of the fire, as far from Trogon as I can possibly get, and closer to my spear planted in the sand. "What old woman?"

Trogon places his tea cup on the ground and peers down into the liquid. He's so rapt by what he sees that I wonder if he's seeing the Earthbound Jemen there, or perhaps seeing visions of the future, as our shamans do. After what seems an eternity, Trogon lifts his eyes. "The Old Woman of the Mountain. Where is her cave? I need you to tell me how to find it."

Spreading my hands in a helpless gesture, I say, "Elder, every Sealion child hears the story of the Old Woman of the Mountain over and over around the winter fires, but I don't know how to find her cave."

"What are your stories? Tell me."

When I hesitate, Arakie nods to me. "All right," I say, "one of our stories says that the Old Woman of the Mountain was the greatest of the Jemen. She called the campfires of the dead down from sky and cast them at the enemies of the Jemen, who caught them in great nets and cast them back like a thousand flaming spears. The attack forced the Old Woman and her warriors into a deep cave in the mountains, where they locked themselves inside. Over hundreds of summers, the other Earthbound Jemen came to hate her. They drove her deeper into the earth and locked her and one lone guardian in the cave from which she could never again emerge. That's the story."

"Your story says it was the Earthbound Jemen who locked her in the cave? Interesting."

"Why?" Arakie asks.

"Because our stories say she was attacked by the enemies of the Jemen."

With a deep sigh, Arakie says, "Both are true."

"They can't both be true." Trogon sneers. "How could—"

"Doesn't matter," I interrupt. "I don't know where her cave is."

Trogon moves his unblinking gaze to me. In the gusting wind and wild firelight, his face is a shifting portrait of nothingness. There's no one there, no humanity to latch on to.

Trogon softly asks, "How close were you when the lions ate your wife?"

I suddenly feel as though my heart is about to shatter into a thousand pieces. Quiller must have told the old witch about what happened at my wedding camp. Why would she do that?

Arakie slowly leans back as though reevaluating Trogon, wondering something I cannot fathom. "Why do you want . . . to find . . . the old woman's cave?"

"She's called to me. She needs my help." Trogon shoves his cup across the sand with his hand.

"Help to do what?" I ask.

A small unpleasant smile turns Trogon's lips. Looking down at his cup, he asks, "Did you throw your wife to the lions to distract them so you could escape?"

I go rigid.

Arakie picks up a piece of driftwood and slams it into the fire, splashing sparks everywhere. "Leave. You are no longer . . . welcome here."

Trogon laughs as though he's truly amused by Arakie giving him orders. "You're a silly old man, aren't you? When I first learned of you, I thought you might be one of the last Earthbound Jemen. I was actually afraid to come here."

"Were you?" Arakie asks in deadly earnest.

"Yes, such foolishness. Now I know you are just a smelly old shrunken carcass—"

"Elder?" the Dog Soldier shouts and points upward. Sister

Sky has started her nightly auroral dance, sending fluttering purple curtains across the heavens.

As though it excites Trogon, he spins back around to me. "In my vision, Quiller leads me to her cave. You should come see the Old Woman as well. Your friend will be dead by morning."

"I'm not going anywhere. I—"

Arakie falls into a coughing fit. He seems to be suffocating. Watching him struggle for air wrenches my heart. Xeno frantically paces around him. When the attack lessens, Arakie wraps an arm around the wolf's throat and whispers something in his furry ear. I make out the words, " . . . don't do anything foolish . . . after I . . . gone."

Trogon laughs, "You're dead already. You're of no use to me."

Rising, he stalks around the fire. An emerald halo surrounds the old witch's body, spun by the zyme glow. As he passes Xeno, the wolf watches him with cold feral eyes.

Trogon stops less than one pace away from me. "Her voice is strange, isn't it? Words like icy tears shatterin' upon the ground. That's how it sounds to me. What does it sound like to you?"

"I don't hear voices, elder." My hand drops to rest on the mammoth-bone knife tucked into my belt.

Trogon watches my hand. "Do you believe the old stories that say the Jemen breathed upon ten-thousand-summers-old bones and they came to life?"

"No."

"Really?" He clutches the red bag tied to his belt as though there's something alive in there and he's reassuring it. Or perhaps being reassured by it. He's quiet for a long time. "You truly don't believe the Jemen can breathe upon the dead and bring them to life?"

I consider explaining the process of extracting and then cloning ancient DNA, but decide it would just make matters worse. Instead, I say, "I think the Jemen sailed away from this world a long time ago. If they ever existed at all."

"You're a very poor liar, Lynx. I can tell from your face that you are a deep believer. You must have—"

"Look!" the Dog Soldier shouts, "It begins!" and trots back to the fire with his sacred book clutched to his chest.

High over our heads, two satellites leisurely sail through the campfires of the dead.

"What begins?" Arakie asks.

"Elder Trogon's spirit journey. This is how it starts."

Trogon watches the points of light. After a time, his lips move in silent words, then he bows his head. "Yes, I understand. It will be done."

Arakie braces a hand upon the ground to steady himself. "You think the Jemen communicate through those balls of light?"

"Of course they do."

"It just communicated with you?" Arakie glances up at the satellites. "Just now?"

"Certainly."

"Fascinating," he says softly, as though to himself. "Probably drug-induced . . . hallucination, but. . . ." He turns to frown at Xeno as though asking the wolf a silent question.

Xeno stares hard at the satellite.

"Sticks?" Trogon calls. "Put the book in your pack and give it to me."

Sticks reverently kisses the book, kneels by his pack near the fire, and tucks it inside, then carries the pack to Trogon. The old witch shrugs it on over his shoulders.

When Trogon speaks again, his voice is soft and pleasant. "Make sure Lynx and the old man don't follow us. If I fail to return by the end of the moon, kill them, but not before then."

"Yes, elder." Sticks bows.

Trogon stalks around the fire, grasps Quiller's arm, and pulls her to her feet.

"What are you doing?" I cry. "Leave her alone."

Trogon drags Quiller stumbling out into the zyme-lit darkness.

"Let her go!" I charge after them. "Let her go!"

"Lynx, no!" Arakie shouts and takes a firm hold on Xeno. The wolf is snarling and yapping, trying to break free to follow me.

Two warriors pound across the sand behind me, chase me down, and throw me to the ground. When I roll to my back with my hands up, they aim their spears at my chest.

The Dog Soldier takes his time walking across the sand to look down into my eyes. "You're a fool." To the warriors, he says, "Bring him."

9

QUILLER

What's he doing?

Beneath the spreading limbs of a pine, Trogon sits, rubbing paste into his temples while he rocks back and forth. I can hear him gasping and see his breath condensing. Sounds like sobs. He has barely spoken to me since we left Lynx and Arakie, but throughout the night, he's been petting the red bag while he sings and weeps. Always low, barely audible.

We climbed the slope of the glacier until around midnight, then made camp. We're far enough away from the coast to have escaped the zyme glow, and the Road of Light is a brilliant slash of white across the indigo sky above me.

I watch Trogon for a while, then turn my eyes to the moonlight blazing from the Ice Giants, turning the mountains into a thousand deeply wrinkled ancient faces. Most have their eyes shut, but a few have shiny black boulder pupils. Their shrill whines drift across the slopes like the voice of the darkness itself, almost drowning out Trogon's weeping.

The old witch has repeatedly reached out to me in the darkness, but always closes his fist on air and pulls it back. My hands and feet are tied. I can't get away. What will I do when he finally does touch me?

When I exhale, my breath sparkles in the unearthly, reflected gleam cast by the Ice Giants. A warm front is moving up from the south. I can feel it on the wind that sways the pine boughs. The temperature is rising. This time of season, caught in the mountains, warm air is terrifying. By morning, freezing mist will engulf the entire world. We won't be able to see more than a few paces in front of us, but he expects me to lead him to the Old Woman of the Mountain, and I have no idea what he's talking about.

Craning my neck, I struggle to see through the weave of pines to the east. Maybe if I can identify a few high peaks or deep crevasses, I'll be able to get my bearings even in a shifting blanket of fog. I've only been this high once, and I did find an eerie cave, where strange symbols slithered across the stone walls. But I found no old woman there. Just broken cages stacked floor to ceiling. On the other hand, I didn't walk to the rear of the cave. Was there a woman back there that I did not see? I remember thinking that I heard whispers echoing from the stone walls, as though something was calling to me, beckoning me to walk deeper into the cavern.

The possibility that I might have discovered the cave of the legendary Old Woman of the Mountain worries me. What will he do to her if he finds her?

Trogon misses a breath, and I can't remember what I was thinking. My attention returns to the old witch beneath the pine and our gazes collide. There are no white streamers in front of his open mouth. He's not breathing. Just watching me.

His voice is a low rasp: "Have you remembered his name?"

"Whose name?"

"The man who used to sneak into your lodge at night."

"I haven't remembered because he doesn't exist. None of those things happened to me."

Trogon starts laughing and doesn't stop. It sounds like high-pitched yipping. In the distance, a dire wolf answers, then a whole pack breaks into mournful howling.

When Trogon finally runs out of air, his laughter dies, and he drops his face into his hands. "Gods, little Quill." He rubs his forehead hard. "You will remember. Soon. His name will shake you apart like an earthquake in your heart. But don't worry, I'll be here to help you. I'll be right here."

10

❄

LYNX

Soft footsteps from my left.

Firelight flickers on the backs of my closed eyelids. Warriors whisper to one another in the distance and someone throws another piece of driftwood on the fire, where it crackles. The flickers are brighter. Footsteps again, but now plodding through deep sand. The man stands about one pace behind me.

"I know you're awake," the Dog Soldier says.

"Not really."

Blinking my eyes open, I find myself lying on my side facing Arakie, who's sound asleep. Wind has pulled his hide down to the middle of his chest, and he's shivering. His face has gone a waxy yellow color. My people have been at war with the Rust People for one thousand summers. I have seen too many die not to know what that bloodless look inevitably presages. I long to go back to sleep until my world ends.

"I would speak with you." The Dog Soldier walks over to kneel near the driftwood pile, where the flickering firelight shimmers through the folds of his silver cape.

Gently, I pull Arakie's hide up to his chin, trying to keep him warm, then I search the camp for Xeno.

"Where's my wolf? Did you kill him while I slept?"

"No. He leaped to his feet and charged off into the trees. We tried to spear him, but he was too fast."

It's strange that after moons of clinging to Arakie like boiled pine pitch, Xeno would suddenly abandon him to run off. Did Arakie order him to?

Instinctively, I note the positions of the five warriors who stand out near the surf with their spears propped over their shoulders, talking, occasionally laughing. One more warrior trotted in out of the darkness around midnight, and a hushed conversation ensued. Apparently, there were supposed to be six warriors, but one didn't arrive. In the last glimmers of zyme glow, they look more like broken trees than men.

"The Rewilding Reports. You mentioned them earlier. Have you seen them?" Sticks wets his dark lips and stares at me as though his very existence hangs upon my answer.

For a while, I contemplate how he can misuse that bit of knowledge. Finally, I say, "Yes. Well, a few of them. There aren't many volumes left. I've heard that your people have one volume."

"Yes, though I've never seen it. Only elder Dog Soldiers are allowed to touch it."

"Of course."

Suspicion tightens his face. "How would you know the books you saw were the Rewilding Reports? They could have been other books. You wouldn't know the difference."

"I would know. I've read them."

Sticks' mouth curls into a snarl. "Your people are too primitive to learn to read. Dog Soldiers have been trying to teach the Rust People to read for generations, but they are incapable of it, and Sealion People are even less human than Rust People."

Tugging my bison cape closed over my throat, I say, "What was the book you gave Trogon? I only caught one word of the title. Desert."

Sticks fearfully jumps to his feet and runs ten paces away.

As though frightened, he keeps glancing back at me with his brow furrowed.

Arakie whispers, "Shouldn't have said that, Lynx. You just . . . gave away one of your advantages . . . and you don't have that many."

"Thought you were asleep. How much did you hear?"

"All of it," Arakie says through a long exhalation.

"He angered me. Can you believe he thinks Sealion People are so primitive we'd never be able to read?"

Arakie weakly lifts a hand and pushes hair away from his eyes. "Not so long ago . . . I would have said . . . the same thing. Still debating why you can."

"What conclusions have you come to?"

"Some left hemisphere skill . . . beyond Broca's area . . . something we missed." He lifts a feeble hand. "Help me sit up, will you?"

I move to help him, and he grunts in pain the entire time, before he manages to sit up and whispers, "Thank you."

"Dog Soldiers can read. Why would you think that Sealion People—"

"What makes you think . . . Dog Soldiers can read?" He gives me a knowing look.

Off to my right, Sticks turns and peers in our direction. We've been talking in low voices, but he's clearly listening to our conversation. Did the wind shift and carry our words to him? Or perhaps Dog Soldiers have more sensitive hearing than we do?

"I've seen them looking at books."

"Circumstantial evidence. At best."

"Are you saying they can't?"

Arakie shrugs. "Unlikely. Early on . . . we had special schools. Teachers worked hard to teach them. Huge failure. *Homo erectus* couldn't even . . . learn the most basic elements . . . of reading."

I'm sure he can't hear us, but the Dog Soldier tilts his head in our direction. His expression is rapt.

"If Sticks can't read, how would he know the word 'desert' is part of the book's title?"

"His species memorizes things . . . probably passed title down . . . over centuries."

Sliding over to sit closer to Arakie, I keep my voice to just above a whisper. "Before he comes over here, we must talk about Trogon's Old Woman of the Mountain. Is there someone up there that you haven't told me about? An old woman?"

For a time, he just stares into space with a thoughtful expression. "There's no old woman . . . living up there."

"So, Trogon's vision is false. He made it all up?"

Arakie squints at the mist creeping across the ground around us. The lower half of Sticks' body has vanished, leaving his upper torso to float in the air as if disconnected from his legs. "I wouldn't say that."

Confused, I frown at him. "Well, what would you say?"

"I wouldn't say anything. If I did, it would be dangerous for you."

"Why?"

"You'd try to find her."

I frown at him. "Then there is a woman living up there."

He shakes his head. "No."

"I don't under—"

"Listen." He points a finger at me. "I dare not answer . . . and I don't want to lie to you."

I'm so taken aback by his words that, for several moments, I just stare at him with my mouth open. "All right. Can you at least tell me why Trogon thinks Quiller knows—"

"Let's ask." Arakie gestures to the Dog Soldier. "Sticks, come. Let us speak . . . of the Rewilding Reports."

As the Dog Soldier hurries toward us, his magical amulet swings with his gait, leaving that distinctive rusty arc across his chest. He stops a cautious three paces away. "Yes?"

Arakie props one hand on the beach to stay upright, but I can tell he desperately wants to lie down. "I'll tell you . . . about the reports, if you tell me . . . why Trogon wants to find . . . the old woman."

"I will." The Dog Soldier nods. "If you will do something for me first."

"What?"

Sticks crouches down and his red hair flies around his face like windblown flames. "I wish to see your books. Your Rewilding Reports."

"I'd be happy . . . to loan you a volume."

Stunned, I stare at Arakie with my mouth open. This has to be a ruse that I don't understand. Arakie won't even allow me to carry one of the reports out of his cave to read it in the sunlight. Why would he . . .

Arakie's lungs rattle with his next words: "Will you allow Lynx . . . to run to my cave . . . and bring it back?"

What's he doing? Trying to help me escape?

Sticks shifts positions as though uneasy. "No. Of course not."

"Too bad," I say. "Your people had just been re-created when the collapse started. The Jemen were afraid the other two species were not going to make it, and they were frantic. I think you'd find that story very interesting."

"Then it . . . it's true?" He's almost breathless with excitement. "Our people tell stories about how the Jemen breathed upon the ancient bones of our ancestors and brought us back to life. But I can't find that story in a book. Have you—"

"Volume Delta."

"Volume Delta?"

Arakie coughs into his sleeve. "Yes. Delta chronicles the history . . . of the Rewilding Project . . . all the wrong moves . . . the petty jealousies and infighting . . . errors in calculations . . . mutations we didn't expect . . . the final disastrous actions we took to try and stop the government from exterminating—"

"You keep saying 'we.'"

Out near the crashing waves, one of the warriors laughs and another says something I can't hear. Their voices trail off in the rush of waves.

I say, "Sticks, your species were the longest surviving humans. They existed for a long time over a vast area. That's why there were so many variations, and that's what gave the Jemen hope. In the past, *Homo* . . . uh, Dog Soldiers had survived many different climate shifts." I lift my arm. "Notice that you have shorter arms and longer legs relative to your torso than either the Rust or Sealion peoples. You, however, are a very early example. Turkana Boy dates to around one-point-five million summers ago. Unfortunately, it was a foolish choice—"

"A catastrophic choice," Arakie wheezes. "Not mine . . . by the way. See how heavy Sticks' brow ridge is . . . how low the dome of his skull? I knew we . . . we should have opted for something around two hundred fifty thousand . . . but everything was falling apart. We were . . . grasping for straws, and the Turkana Boy sequence was the most complete—"

"What are you talking about?" Sticks' black eyes have gone huge.

"You," I say. "The species the Jemen used to make your people. *Homo erectus* recr. The Jemen called you Reecurs. Arakie wants to loan you the report that documents it."

Sticks eyes Arakie severely. "You are one of the Jemen?"

"Your turn," Arakie answers. "Trogon . . . wants the Old Woman of the Mountain? Why?"

The Dog Soldier nervously licks his lips. "He will flay me alive if he finds out—"

"Want Volume Delta . . . or not?"

Sticks swallows hard. "Trogon must kill her. If he does, his dead daughter will come back to life."

Arakie bows his head and frowns at the sand, and I can see the thoughts moving behind his eyes, evaluating possibilities. "The Jemen who came to him in the vision . . . the man . . . told him he had to kill the old woman?"

"Yes."

Fear lines his face. To himself, Arakie whispers, "He knows I'm dying . . . must figure . . . it's his only way out." Then he asks Sticks, "And why does he think Quiller knows the way to the old woman's cave?"

"In his vision, he saw Quiller inside the cave. She was walking through blue campfires of the dead."

Arakie stares at Sticks, but I can tell he's just understood something that frightens him. "Blue campfires of the dead?"

"Yes. She was walking on top of them, apparently on her way to the Land of the Dead to speak to the Old Woman of the Mountain."

Arakie starts to ask a question, but falls into a desperate coughing fit. I reach out and wrap an arm around his bony shoulders to comfort him and feel the death rattle that shakes his whole body.

The fit takes so long to stop that the Dog Soldier rises and walks around to the other side of the fire, giving Arakie time to catch his breath. Against the background of glowing green sea and wavering sky, Sticks seems larger than life. Almost ethereal. I'm noting the low dome of his skull when Arakie tugs on my sleeve to get my attention.

Through the wheezing, he softly says, "Start planning . . . your escape."

"You mean our escape."

"*We* can't escape. I'm too weak. Just have to find the right . . . moment for you."

It takes several heartbeats before I understand, then I shake my head. "No. No, I won't leave you. You need me."

"Quiller needs you more than I do."

"She's a strong warrior. You don't know her. You're sick—"

"Listen to me," he interrupts. "She *does* know the way . . . to the old woman's cave. You have to help her. If you don't . . . ."

I wait for him to gather to breath to continue. Finally, he says, "Trogon will murder her soul . . . long before he murders her body."

Streamers of mist creep across the ground and crawl up Arakie's back, then coil around his wrinkled face in a shimmering firelit halo.

"How could she know the way—"

"You know the way, too."

As the truth sinks in, my veins explode with tingling. "You think he means Quancee. She's the old woman?"

"Maybe," he says almost too low to hear. "Maybe not. We can't take any chances. Protect her, Lynx. She's completely helpless."

Fear warms my veins. Quancee is very, very old, born long before the Jemen sailed to the campfires of the dead, but is her crystal body alive? I think so, but I'm not sure the question has any meaning. If you can think and feel, you're alive, aren't you? "Arakie, they will kill you as punishment for my escape."

Arakie gives me an annoyed look. "Well, that would be ghastly . . . wouldn't it? It won't take me so long . . . to die."

"But—"

"You know I'm right."

Sticks tilts his left ear toward us and firelight flutters over his dark skin. Purposefully, he strides back and squats in front of Arakie. "If I tell you every detail of Elder Trogon's vision, will you tell me about Turkana Boy?"

"Of course." Arakie nods. "You go first."

11

"Chirp, chirp, little porcupine quill. Rise now," Trogon says and roughly shakes my shoulder.

When I drag myself up from a deep sleep, the thick coating of ice that formed over my warm bear-hide cape during the night shatters and falls upon the pine needles. It takes a while to blink awake enough to see that Father Sun has risen and freezing fog cloaks the Ice Giant Mountains. The pines resemble translucent spears of ice.

Trogon crouches at my side with a half-eaten rabbit leg in one hand. As he gnaws it, he smiles at me.

"Where's my breakfast?"

"No breakfast for you today, little Quill. We must be on our way to the see the old woman."

Finishing his rabbit, he tosses the bones aside and draws his iron knife from his belt. As he saws through the bindings on my ankles, I study his open pack, which rests a short distance away. Inside, I see a coil of green rope made from zyme, several small hide bags, and the sacred book Sticks gave him.

"Could I have water?" I struggle to sit up.

Trogon flicks a hand at the ground. "Pick up a chunk of ice and suck on it. You won't be thirsty anymore."

"I need food and water. I can't just keep climbing without—"

"Then perhaps I should blindfold you, wrap you tight in my

cape, and drag the bundle up the mountainside through the rocks."

"If you cover my eyes, I'll never be able to find the cave."

"Maybe I'll cut your eyes from your head and carry them in my hands. They know the way. They 'ave seen it."

When wind gusts, huge chunks of ice crack off the limbs and thump the ground. It gives me the excuse I need to break eye contact with Trogon. Gazing into his eyes is haunting. Gaze too long and you lose your soul in the emptiness.

I grab a chunk of ice with my bound hands and put it my mouth.

Trogon smiles as he walks over and pulls the rope from his pack. While he watches me, he methodically unwinds it. "Today, I will lead you like a camp dog."

Around the chunk of ice, I say, "You're going to tie a rope around my neck?"

"No." He returns, drags me to my feet, and ties one end of the rope around my waist. The other end, he forms into a loop for his hand to hold. "Now, walk."

"My feet are numb. You'll have to wait until I get some feeling back."

He tugs hard on the rope and, when I almost topple, he staggers back, off-balance.

In that instant, I lunge, slam my shoulder into his chest, and knock him backward to the ground. Struggling to get my bound hands around his throat, I roar, "I'm going to kill you! I'm going to kill you and your entire people! The Rust People will be just as extinct as the Mericans!"

Doesn't take long for him to grab me in muscular arms, flip me onto my back, then scramble on top of me and pin me to the frozen ground. He's a big man; his body is very heavy, pressing the air from my lungs until I can't breathe. I'm fighting with all my strength when I finally glare up into his face and find him smiling. "The Mericans killed themselves, little Quill. They were the enemies of the Jemen. They fought against the Old Woman and she wiped them out to the last child. They lived here, you know, right here, except it wasn't covered with ice back then."

Tenderly, he strokes my hair. "Did I mention that your husband is dead? What was his name? RabbitEar? Yes, he's dead."

Stunned, I almost can't find the breath to say, "You—that's a lie."

"The fool decided to follow our trail. Probably trying to rescue you. He gave me no choice."

The forest is so silent I can hear the tiny clicks my iced-over eyelashes make when I blink. "That's not true! He would have never left our children behind."

"He didn't leave them. And I do not lie. Ever. You will find that unpleasant, I suspect. No one wants to hear the truth all the time." A slight pause. "Your son. What was his name? Jawbone?"

My heart stops.

"You should know that even at his age, he was a warrior. He charged my warriors with a spear in his hand and cast it as hard as he could. He, at least, died quickly."

I see it unfold behind my eyes. That's exactly what Jawbone would have done.

"They told me your husband begged for mercy for the girls. For two hands of time, he begged, until the warriors got tired of his pleadin'. He cried for a while, I guess, then he stopped."

Cried for a while . . . after they killed our daughters in front of his eyes?

Trogon's voice is unearthly. "I'm so sorry, little Quill."

A strange vertigo fills me.

Trogon lowers his head and presses his mouth against my ear. "Do not attack me again. You're not good at this game."

12

※

LYNX

Dawn comes like the footsteps of the dead. Quiet. Not really there. Faintly perceptible in the mist that cloaks the seashore.

Throughout the night the warriors took turns sleeping. One scarred-face man currently lies on his back wrapped in his silver cape by the fire. Sticks stands near him with his feet spread, his hood up, sipping a cup of pine-needle tea. The sweet tangy fragrance of the tea rises from the old iron pot resting at an angle in the coals. Trogon took his pack, so the pot must have come from one of the warrior's packs. I can't see them, but I know they're out there in the mist.

Lions roar not too far away.

Rolling over, my gaze clings to the track pressed into the sand. Big lion track, and it's right beside Arakie's hand. Given the wind that constantly sweeps the beach, I wonder how the paw print could have survived. Not only that, people have walked all around this fire, which means it should have been obliterated long ago. Yet, there it is, staring me in the face, three times as big as my hand.

"Good morning," the Dog Soldier calls.

"Don't think so. You're still here." I sit up and yawn.

Sticks extends a hand to the wooden cups stacked beside the tea pot. "Drink some tea to warm yourself."

After slapping the ice from my bison cape, I reach for a cup and dip it into the pot. Steam billows as I set the first cup on the sand near Arakie. He will be able to reach it when he wakes. *Blessed Jemen, please let him wake.* His eyes are sunken in twin purple circles. Like water from a punctured hide bag, I feel my courage, what little I ever had, seeping away. When he is gone, there will be so little of me left I won't know who I am at all.

"He's not dead," the Dog Soldier says. "I checked him one hand of time ago, but his heartbeat is very weak. Fluttering like a bird's."

"Thanks for telling me." I dip a second cup of tea and hold it in both hands, while I wonder what Sticks wants. He's being extremely pleasant.

The Dog Soldier cocks his head to watch Arakie. "He's a strange old man, isn't he? Does he really believe he's one of the immortal Jemen?"

Over the rim of my cup, I blink at Arakie. His white hair shines in the firelight. Suddenly it's as if my father is lying there, leaving this world for a second time, and I'm desolate with the knowledge that I can't face life without his gentle strength.

"I'm pretty sure, at this point, he knows he's not immortal."

Sticks walks closer and crouches down. His dark skin reflects the firelight. "Do you believe it?"

I wonder what he would do if he thought it were true. Would he cut out Arakie's heart and keep it locked in a pot as a sacred relic? He might. "No, but I think he's a great storyteller."

"That's what I thought. If he truly was the last Earthbound Jemen, he'd use his magic to cast balls of fire from the heavens and burn us up, or turn into an animal and rip out our throats. He can't be the last Jemen." In Sticks' black eyes, I see one of the greatest dreams of earth wither and perish. "Our sacred books promise that the last Dog Soldier will meet the last Earthbound Jemen."

"That would be amazing, wouldn't it?" My throat constricts with emotion. Takes a while before I can speak again. "Wonder what they'd talk about."

"They'd tell stories of the beginning of the world. Stories that heal." He gestures to Arakie. "What are his stories? If you tell me, I give you my oath that I will keep the ones that are important."

Drawing up my knees, I prop my elbows atop them and frown at my cup. "Arakie rarely talks about his life, and when he does his stories are so astonishing I don't believe them. They are like the Wolf-and-Bear tales we tell children to teach them morality lessons."

Sticks lowers himself to sit cross-legged and his amulet thumps the front of his silver cape. "I still wish to hear them. Tell me, please."

"Well, for one thing, he says he was born on top of Sister Moon's head, and was so close to the campfires of the dead he went about cautiously lest they catch in his hair. He says he rode a streak of fire to get to our world."

Awe widens Sticks' eyes. "When was that? How long ago?"

"Before the Ice Giants were born."

Sticks scoffs, "That would mean he's seen over one thousand winters."

"Yes. Or he's a very good liar."

"Stories are not lies. They are truths hidden in words. Do you really think he's a liar?"

Bowing my head, I answer, "No, but I think . . . he gets confused."

One of the warriors out in the mist coughs, and I try to calculate how far away he's standing. Maybe twenty paces? With my cup, I gesture to Sticks' amulet. "What does that lump of rust mean? Only Dog Soldiers wear them."

When he glances down at the pendant, reverence softens his

expression. "This reminds us of the greatest story of all. It was just before the enemies of the Jemen cast crushed meteorites into the zyme and it started to cover the ocean that the Jemen breathed upon the ancient bones of my ancestors and brought us back to life." Thoughtfully, he corrects himself: "Re-created us."

"Yes, we are all Reecurs."

Petting the amulet, he says, "It is a story of death and rebirth. A story of redemption."

"Redemption?"

"Of course. My people believe that by bringing us to life, the Jemen saved the world."

The Ice Giants apparently heard us, for they roar with laughter and shake the ground so hard we both grab for the sand to keep from toppling—reminding us that they won the war, not the Jemen.

"You believe Dog Soldiers saved the world?"

"Not yet, but we will. When the last Dog Soldier meets the last Earthbound Jemen, he will give him our most sacred book. That was the covenant. We have protected the book for him. So long as a single Dog Soldier is alive, there is hope."

"But there are only seven of your kind left. What will happen if you never—"

"I will probably be the last," Sticks rushes to say, lest I finish that sentence. "I'm the youngest, twenty-two. The others of my kind have all seen at least thirty-five winters. When I give the book to the last Jemen, he will breathe upon it and the book will come to life and sail far away beyond the Road of Light until it finds the Sky Jemen and brings them home."

Fascinated by this story, I wonder what Arakie would make of it. The elder hasn't moved. The purple color that encircled his right eye has drained down and seems to have pooled in his cheek. His jaw has gone slack, leaving his mouth open. As I gaze at him, it's harder and harder to breathe.

"Must be hard knowing you will be the last Dog Soldier in the world."

"It is. Each day I see myself vanishing in the eyes of others. They look past me, not at me, and I know they want to move on, to start forgetting. I imagine elders feel this way. At the end."

All of me, everything I am, stares at Arakie. Not looking past him. Not moving on. I won't do that. And I dread the day that I must.

Sticks follows my gaze. "You love him?"

"I do."

My words hang suspended in the glittering fog.

"He was wrong, you know. I can read."

I take another drink of tea. "Then I guess I don't have to offer to teach you."

He seems taken aback. "You would teach me?"

"I would. If you'll let us go. But you'd have to do it now, while your warriors are blinded by fog. You can just tell them we escaped. In a few days, I'll meet you at Otter Point, and I'll bring Volume Delta with me. We'll start with that."

Sticks examines the eddying mist. "My people, Dog Soldiers, believe that letters are independent creatures made of light. Each is alive and superior even to the gods. Uncovering the radiance hidden in words is our life's work. I want to read the Rewilding Reports very much, but if you're gone when Trogon returns—"

"He's not coming back. My friend Quiller is going to kill him."

Sticks snorts in derision. "Trogon is the most powerful holy man in the world. His visions always come true. He will turn her into a mindless beetle. I have seen him do it many times. When he is finished with her, she will run in circles howling like a clubbed dog."

"You don't know her," I respond angrily.

"And you do not know Trogon's powers. I've seen him skin

his victims' arms and sew the skin into gloves while they were still alive and watching him. He . . ."

Abruptly, Sticks leaps to his feet and takes a step toward the tree line. I swing around to see what has caught his attention.

Close to the ground, the fog crawls. All I can make out are dark, wet tree trunks. Black stripes in a sea of shifting green mist. Then . . . gliding between them, yellow eyes flash. I glance back at Arakie. Did he send his thoughts into the pride? To call them here? Perhaps to give me a chance to escape?

Sticks yells, *"Lions! Lions!"*

"Arakie!" I shout and grab for his arm. "Get up!"

The warrior by the fire scrambles to his feet with his spear in his hand, just as the other four warriors blast out of the mist and charge toward us.

One man cries, "How big is the pride? How many do you count?"

"Too many!"

"We need to run into the ocean before they surround us!" Sticks shouts. "They won't follow us into the water!"

When I've managed to haul Arakie from his hides, I realize his body is cold in my arms, and the shock is like a blow to my belly. I clutch him hard against me. His head lolls over my shoulder. He's limp, but not stiff. Is there a chance that he's . . .

The pride lopes out of the trees and onto the beach. Six. No, seven. They're huge, taller than I am, and weigh five times as much as I do. Their golden coats have a green tint from the zyme.

The first warrior who breaks and runs starts the slaughter. Roaring, a lioness chases him down and sinks her teeth into his skull. As she flings him around like a child's toy, four other warriors scream and dash for the ocean, where Sticks is already swimming out into the surf as hard as he can. Two lions pursue them, diving into the ocean and paddling after them.

Gently, I lay Arakie down on the sand and tuck the edges of his hide around him. I've been fighting to keep him warm for so long, I can't seem to stop.

Three lions are now tugging on the first dead warrior, ripping different limbs from his body. When I look back out at the ocean, mist cloaks the surf. I can no longer see Sticks and the other warriors, but I hear them screaming . . .

Slowly, as though I have all the time in the world, I turn and walk toward the trees.

13

---------- ❄ ----------

QUILLER

I s that true?" Trogon calls.

The old witch climbs up the steep trail three paces behind me, his body swaying in and out of the fog that shrouds the mountainside while he chews a strip of jerky. He's been whispering all morning, carrying on conversations with invisible people, so I'm not sure he's talking to me.

"I asked you a question."

"Are you talking to me?"

"Yes, I'm talkin' to you."

"What do you want?" He cut my hands free so I could grab onto rocks as we climb, but they ache from where the cords cut into my wrists.

"Is it true?" Breathing hard, he stops and tugs on the rope around my waist to make me stop.

Sopping blond hair hangs around his bearded face. He shoves the last of his jerky into his mouth and chews it up. If I can just get my hands around his throat I will make him pay for what he did to my family.

Blessed Jemen, they can't be dead . . .

"Is what true?"

"Did you kill my grandson two summers ago?"

"I certainly hope so, but how would I know? What did he look like?"

We have left the trees far behind us, and now climb through a gigantic boulder field. At this spot, the boulders stand three or four times our heights and shine wetly with frozen mist. I have to grab hold of a rock to steady my feet. Freezing meltwater runs down the trail; it's very slick.

"He says you did. He plans to kill you in a few days."

"Is that who you've been talking to? Your dead grandson?"

"Yes, he's trotting around us like a hunting wolf. His pack is out in the fog."

"If he's a ghost, I'm not too worried about his threats."

"You should be. When my grandson attacks, all you'll see is a flicker of light at the edge of your vision, but it will distract you so you miss your step and fall over the edge of a cliff, or into a deep dark crevasse with no way out. He was very fast when alive, and even faster now that his body doesn't get in the way."

I turn and climb on through the cold shadows, sliding cautiously between boulders, where the mist and meltwater glisten. My boots are drenched. Each step I take squishes freezing mud around my feet. Despite my thick bear-hide cape, I'm shivering.

"How did he die? Remind me." My breath is a luminous haze that melts into the swirling mist.

"You crushed his skull with your club. He was bent over, dragging his best friend off the battlefield, when you ran up behind him and brained him. Then you killed his wounded friend. Good day for you, eh, little Quill?"

"Two Rust warriors in a matter of heartbeats? Very good day."

I remember that. It was the Moon of Velvet Antlers in the steppe lands. The Rust People attacked just before dawn. We were outnumbered twenty to one. While the women and children ran for our mammoth-hide bull boats, our warriors fought a retreating action. It's a miracle any Sealion People survived.

Carefully, I grab hold of a gray boulder and pull myself up the icy trail. It's getting steeper, and there's more meltwater babbling over the gravel.

Trogon must have seen me kill his grandson. That's how he knows.

"He's an evil spirit now, of course," Trogon says with a sigh. "He, and all of his friends, refused to travel to the Land of the Dead so they could remain in this world and kill more Sealion People."

"You believe that?"

"It's not a matter of belief. I know it's true."

"They are condemned to remain on earth forever? What a sad fate. Dead Sealion warriors travel to the campfires of the dead, where their ancestors greet them as heroes. They are loved and honored for eternity."

Trogon tugs on the rope, forcing me to stop walking. "If you look closely, you'll see my grandson and his war party."

I'm clinging to a rock with my wet boots slipping, frowning into the mist. All I see are birds. Fluffed out for warmth and almost hidden on the shimmering tops of the boulders, the snow buntings resemble frosty balls.

"See? He's right beside . . ."

Suddenly, I lose my footing and collapse to the trail.

In a heartbeat, Trogon is bending over me. "He tripped you. Watch yourself now." He blinks out at the rocky slope. "His war party is walking through the forest all around us."

I don't believe it, but . . . I swear I see a misshapen face reflecting in the ice that sheathes a black boulder. It flickers for an instant, then vanishes and appears again nearby. And more faces flash, darting about, as though flying from stone to stone. They seem to be all around me, but visible only as icy reflections.

Trogon whispers, "They are here to protect me, but I wish

they'd shut up. You cannot imagine what it's like to have dozens of evil spirits shouting at you to kill someone."

"They're ordering you to kill me?"

"Yes, my grandson tells me it was a mistake to let you or any of your people live."

Sitting up, I say, "I thought your grandson was going to kill me himself. Is he too cowardly to face me?"

Trogon's eyes are bright and anxious. "Not a coward. A dreadful beast. A monster." His voice trails off and he blinks. "I've always wondered why monsters are my only friends."

"Honestly? You can't be that dull-witted."

He chuckles at that. "You think I am monster." It's not a question.

Gasping a few deep breaths into my lungs, I surreptitiously note the way his iron knife hangs from his belt. Made from a cold-hammered meteorite and polished to a sheen, it's quite a prize. When I decide to make my move, I'll need to be standing to his left to cleanly pull it free. Constantly, every moment, I envision myself slitting his throat and pulling out his heart. That image is the only thing that keeps my soul from crumbling to dust and blowing away down the glaciers. I dare not start to mourn my family, for if I do, Trogon will use it to gut me like a freshly caught trout.

"Imagine," he says, "I started seeing evil spirits at the age of three winters, spirits that not even our most powerful holy people could see. Villagers were frightened by me. They began to shun me, to walk wide around me when they had to pass me. My mother left me alone with the monsters. I was an offering, you see."

"What do you mean? An offering?"

"A sacrifice. She gave me to the monsters, because while the evil ones were clinging to my clothes, they left everyone else in the village alone."

"Do you always prattle on about yourself like this?"

He doesn't comment, just stares into the mist as though he sees horrifying things out there.

Placing my boots with care, I shove to my feet and start walking. I haven't gone more than three paces when, at the base of the boulder, I see a wolf track. An odd track. I need to study it more carefully . . .

"No, no. I was my mother's pet," Trogon explains as though someone asked him a question. "She was a very powerful shaman. I saw her cut off my uncle's head with the wave of her little finger. Then she stuffed it in a trayalon bag and used it to play kickball." He's genuinely delighted by the memory, for he laughs out loud. "She taught me everything I know. Every spell and incantation. Every ancient story about the Jemen. Her soul lives inside me. I made sure of that. Caught it in a cup when it escaped with her last breath and drank it down."

The wolf track is large and covered with frost.

"Why did you stop?" Trogon shouts.

"I was listening to you, you old fool! I can't believe you prevented your mother's soul from traveling to the afterlife to be with her ancestors. That's cruel."

His massive shoulders swing as he shifts his weight, climbing the trail behind me.

When he halts two paces away, he uses his sleeve to wipe his runny nose. "She wanted to stay with me. She told me so many times. But I knew people would try to stop me, so I waited to kill her until we were alone one night."

The breeze suddenly feels immensely colder, cutting straight to my bones.

"You killed your own mother?"

In an exaggerated gesture, he forces his lower lip to tremble, apparently mocking my expression, and his words are as velvet soft as ermine fur. "Murder is not a crime, little Quill. Not when it's the only defense you have."

He's smiling now, his eyes so wide, it's bizarre and unnatural. "Your only defense against your mother was to kill her? What was she doing to you that was so—"

"I proved that offerings have teeth."

He blinks. It's an exaggerated gesture, as though he had to remind himself to do it, and I have the feeling I'm coming up on a precipice that drops into blackness.

"Like memories that hide in dark holes in the Forgotten Country?"

"Yes, just like that. Their souls have been lost in darkness for so long they aren't alive anymore. Just like empty skins filled with blood."

I stare at him. "Are you trying to say that I am an offering?"

"Oh, yes," his voice is languid and sensual, "yes, you are."

14

LYNX

As dusk overtakes the world, the fog shreds and small leaks of moonlight dart through the pines. They aren't much light, but I can make out Trogon's heavy boot prints in the frozen mud. Unfortunately, I have no idea where I am on the mountain. The fog has erased all landmarks. I can't see the Ice Giant peaks or the campfires of the dead to get my bearings. My only guide is the occasional track, or slide mark where a boot slipped. A little while ago, I found a place where Quiller stopped, and her wet boots repeatedly kneaded the earth. She's up there, maybe a day ahead of me. She's alive.

Exhaling through my nostrils, I watch the twin trails hang in the fog as though frozen in place, before they slither out into the darkness.

Water chatters to my left, flowing beneath a thick layer of ice. I've been trying not to think of Arakie. If he's gone, all I have to do is grieve, but I keep thinking that maybe he wasn't dead. Maybe he was just unconscious and I left him there alone and helpless on the beach, where he'd either be torn apart by lions, or tortured to death by Rust People. Why didn't I throw him over my shoulder and carry him with me into the trees? When I was far enough away, I could have laid him down and checked for breathing or a heartbeat.

But he was icy cold, and blood had pooled in the low spots in his body, as it does after the heart stops pumping.

"He was dead."

Keep walking.

Lingering doubt is eating my insides, sapping my strength, making it hard to focus on Quiller's trail. I think it's also the source of my building headache.

After I rub my throbbing forehead, I stare back at Trogon's tracks. The moonlight is a little brighter and I pray the fog is dissipating. If I could just see, I could move faster. But in this misty gloom, I dare not hurry. If I lose the trail, I may never find it again.

I go slowly, moving from track to track, but my gaze strays up the mountainside, trying to draw a line, wondering where Quiller is leading him. She's not headed to Arakie's cave. I'm sure of it. I've never been very good at tracking, but it seems to me that she's been weaving all over the face of the Ice Giants. Is she delaying in the hopes that I'm following her? Or maybe that RabbitEar or Mink is trying to find her? Could be. But knowing her, it's more likely that she thinks she's on her own, and is doing her best to find her opponent's weaknesses. She's the bravest person I know. She'll be looking for anything she can use against the old witch to kill him.

Here at the edge of the pines, I'm aware of new sounds. In the haze of moonlit fog, the deep-throated rumbles of bison carry across the glaciers, but it's the howls of the dire wolves that make blood pulse in my ears. They're getting louder as the pack trots down the mountainside toward me.

Quiller and Trogon's trail seems to lead straight into the oncoming pack, which means following it will be suicide.

Wind Mother suddenly stirs the fog, spinning it into a tiny tornado as if trying to get my attention. The tornado floats up the slope, bobs across a frozen pool of water, and gets bigger, pulling in more mist, turning dark as it disappears into the night, heading southeast.

I stopped walking and didn't realize it.

Arakie once told me that a man only finds his way once he's lost the trail and, ironically, the lost are the only true wise men.

I have a decision to make. Keep tracking Quiller in the hopes of rescuing her long before she reaches Arakie's cave, or abandon her trail and go straight there.

Arakie's voice whispers in my head, *"Protect her, Lynx. She's completely helpless . . ."*

He wasn't talking about Quiller. He meant Quancee.

My fingers curl into fists as a shudder moves through me that has nothing to do with the dire wolves. This is the same feeling I had at my wedding camp, just before giant lions attacked. There's something out there, and it's waiting for me to make a decision that will change the rest of my life.

That nameless presence was there nineteen moons ago, and it's here tonight.

I glance down at the tracks in the frozen mud.

Quiller's boot prints are perfectly clear, beckoning to me to follow them, even if they lead me into the middle of a pack of ferocious predators, follow them because she needs me. Everything that I am or ever hope to be depends upon her safety.

Walking off to the side, I take a few steps along her trail and slowly become aware that there's something wrong with the tracks. I'm following two people. But there are three sets of tracks here.

My eyes try to make sense of what I'm seeing. Quiller's boots and Trogon's boots sank into the soft mud and squished it up into foot-shaped rims, which are now frozen hard. The third set of tracks is on top, crossing at an angle, flattening out the mid-sections of a few of Trogon's boot prints. Kneeling, I brush away the windblown ice crystals that obscure the evidence. It's a large track from a careful tread.

A warrior's track.

Without moving, I examine the pines. One of the Rust warriors from the beach attack must have survived and is hunting me. I half expect to see him standing in the moonlit shadows watching, but all I see is eddying fog.

The dire wolves are getting closer, close enough that their barks make the hair on my arms stand on end.

I quickly brush at his tracks, trying to discern what kind of footwear could make these prints. They aren't smooth like a leather boot. A strange design is visible in places. Like tiny zig-zagging pebbles dimpling . . .

The bottoms of his boots were beaded with a pattern of chevrons.

Slowly, I straighten up. Why would a warrior be wearing the boots of the dead?

The dire wolves break into howls, and I charge away, trying to disappear into the fog before they can smell me.

15

QUILLER

By the time we've climbed high enough to get above the mist, the brightest campfires of the dead are winking out and the sky is shading from black to slate blue. For as far as I can see across the glaciers, rainbows shimmer. Born in the blowing ice crystals, their brilliant colors flare and vanish with the gusts. Rainbows before sunrise are uncommon and vaguely unreal. Legends say they are the youngest children of the Ice Giants playing chase before dawn.

When Trogon hikes up beside me, he's batting ice from his long beard. "Where's the cave? Can you see it now?"

I study the glaciers that go on forever to the east and north. Out there in the blue wasteland, I hear whisperings of life no part of my own. The magic here is strong and as old as the world. Often, the faint touch of icy fingers trails across the back of my neck and I know I must not turn to look at it.

Exhaling a white cloud, I say, "No. It's higher."

"You're not lost, are you? Or are you leading me in the wrong direction?"

Angry, I yell, "You're holding my best friend and an innocent old man hostage! I'm not going to risk their lives just to deceive you. Why would I? There's nothing in the cave but broken cages, anyway."

That startles Trogon. "Broken cages?"

"Yes, stacked floor to ceiling, dozens of them."

A look of sheer wonder comes over his face. "I did not see that in my vision. But if the Old Woman of the Mountain lives there, they must be the cages where the sacred animals were kept by the Earthbound Jemen. Why are they broken? Where are the animals?"

"How would I know?"

Trogon's brows lower and he gazes westward toward Mother Ocean, where a thick layer of fog cloaks the shore, but out beyond it, the zyme forms a solid green blanket all the way to horizon. It's luminous, the faint glow dying with the dawn.

I watch Trogon like a mouse does a crouched lion. All of my life, I've heard stories of the Sky Jemen and the Earthbound Jemen. As a child, I dreamed of finding that legendary cave and staring into the eyes of amazing, long-gone animals like spotted bobcats and peregrine falcons.

"How did you find this cave, little Quill? Your people are a sea people. Why would you come up here?"

"I was tracking a bison bull when a spark of light flashed above me, then a bright fiery trail blazed as one of the Sky Jemen tumbled through the sky over my head. He disappeared just over the curve of the hill, where a thunderous roar erupted and the resulting impact knocked me off my feet."

"One of the Sky Jemen fell to earth?" he says as though awestruck. "Was he dead or alive? Did you go look for him?"

"Of course I did. When he crashed, he dug a huge hole in the ice, and he was fiery hot, hissing and roaring, as he melted down into the underworlds."

Trogon gives me an incredulous look. "I don't believe it."

"I don't care what you believe. But that's when I saw the cave. Off to my left, there was a faint square of blue light."

"Blue?" he murmurs in a frightened voice. "Was it filled with the blue campfires of the dead? Did you walk on top of them?"

"I never saw any blue campfires of the dead, but I didn't go very deep, just to the broken cages."

I glance at his knife again. He's almost close enough that if I edge over . . .

Trogon is still staring off in the distance, seemingly lost in his vision, but he says, "Murder is never far from your thoughts, is it?"

"Not when you're standing this close."

Trogon grabs me by my collar and jerks me close to glare into my eyes. "Don't be foolish, little Quill. One of your daughters survived. She might wish you to come back to her."

The words are like a knife repeatedly plunged into my heart. He just told me my other two daughters are dead, and now I'm frantically trying to figure out which of my girls survived. Chickadee, maybe. Surely the warrior would not have wanted to murder a four-summers-old child? Then I have to remind myself that these are Rust People and they've been killing Sealion children for centuries. Or maybe it was Loon who survived, she was five . . .

Stop it. He's lying. He uses words to keep your heart bleeding. Don't let him.

"You old witch. I know my husband. If he came after me, he'd have never brought the children with him. They would have slowed him down, and he knows it. He'd have left them in the care of a woman of my clan, the Blue Dolphin clan. My children are safe."

He laughs. "Believe that if it makes you feel better."

His breath is so fetid, I turn aside. And freeze.

The big wolf stands in plain view, ten paces away, with his narrow snout lifted, smelling the wind. His gray coat flashes, and the tip of each hair shines like polished copper.

Arakie's wolf. His long lean body appears pale and ghostly in the pre-dawn gleam. What's he doing up here this high? Is Arakie here? Or Lynx? Hope almost suffocates me.

The animal takes a step and looks over his shoulder straight at me.

The hair at the back of my neck tingles. As though showing me the way, he trots up the hillside.

Trogon spins around, trying to see what I was looking at, but there's nothing there now. Just icy rainbows blowing across the slopes.

"What did you see? Your eyes went huge."

"A flicker. Probably nothing. Maybe your grandson."

"My grandson?" Trogon shoves me away while his gaze searches for ghostly war parties. "Where? Show me."

"Right there," I point in the opposite direction.

As though he sees his grandson charging straight at him, Trogon backpedals, trips over a rock, and tumbles to the ground. The force of the fall must have torn loose one of the ties on his silver pack, for the old book bounces out, along with curiously shaped rocks, lumps of rust, and other things I can't decipher. In less than two heartbeats, Trogon is back on his feet and standing in a warrior's crouch, as though waiting for me to attack him.

When I don't, he says, "Silly girl. You missed an opportunity. I'm surprised at you."

"I'm weak from hunger. Better to save my strength for the right moment."

"If you're waiting for me to feed you so you can build up your strength, you're going to be dead before you have another chance."

He slips his pack off his shoulders, kneels, and begins picking up the spilled contents, stuffing them back inside. He has to nerve himself to reach for the sacred book, but when he does, he tenderly kisses the old cracked leather binding, and gently tucks it into the pack.

"Why are you so afraid of your grandson?"

Trogon pauses with a lump of rust in one hand, then tucks it in the pack. "Monsters are monsters, even when they wear a beloved face. You should know that."

"I don't know any monsters . . . except you."

"Then you are deaf and blind."

Many of Sticks' belongings are still scattered across the ground, but Trogon rises and shrugs the pack over his shoulders, as if preparing to leave. Before he takes a step, his gaze darts over the mountains with an almost panicked look.

"Do you see your dead grandson out there? Is that why you're afraid?"

Trogon glances at me. "Monsters are everywhere. They've wriggled their ways deep into the hearts of all things, into the roots of grass and trees. Deep into human souls. Every time we breathe, we exhale monsters."

I watch my breath condense into white puffs and drift away across the slope. I see no monsters, just warm air going cold.

Trogon bows his head. "But I am *not* afraid."

Silence. For a long while.

"I am."

"Are you, little Quill?"

"Yes."

"Why?"

"You know why. Your mother's evil soul breathes inside you. I have no idea what she may make you do."

He smiles. "Nor do I."

"What does she feel like inside you?"

"A viper coiling in mud. She hisses. Her tail goes slap, slap. She watches me with strange unblinking eyes. Why do you ask?"

"Are you sure they're your mother's eyes?"

Trogon lifts his head and his wrinkles rearrange into unpleasant lines. "Who else's eyes could they be?"

"I wouldn't know."

Trogon seems to be searching his memories, trying to decide if they really are his mother's eyes or someone else's. "They're yellow eyes. Wolfish. Mother's eyes were blue."

"So they're not your mother's eyes. Do they belong to a man?"

"A man? Why would you think that?"

"Your eyes are tan, that's sort of yellow. Maybe your mother isn't the monster. Maybe it's your father or uncle—"

"Stop that!" he shouts in my face. "Say one more word and I will kill you!"

As the slate-blue sky shades pink above the peaks, the Ice Giants wake and stretch, shaking the mountains. Their grating whines shiver the air.

Breathing hard, Trogon looks away from me to blink at the southern horizon. It's a full ten heartbeats before he says, "You're getting better at this game, little Quill."

Softly, I respond, "I guess your memories do have teeth."

"Find the cave! Do it now."

"I'm trying. I've only been here once before, and it was autumn, not winter. Things look different."

"Climb."

When I turn to start up the trail, there's movement on the slope in the distance, a single wolf trotting along with his sunlit fur gleaming.

16

❄

LYNX

One moment the afternoon is sunny and bright, then the leading edge of the blizzard strikes and it's like an avalanche rolling over the top of me. The onslaught of wind claws through the curious ice sculptures that adorn the slope, shattering them and sending lumps of ice the size of lodges crashing down the trail.

Exhausted and half snow-blind, I can barely stay on my feet as I bull forward up the trail toward a cluster of giant boulders that appear and disappear in a wall of white. Those boulders may give me a little shelter from the storm, though if the cold continues to intensify, I'm not sure my heavy bison cape is enough to keep me alive until dawn.

By the time I reach the first boulder, tears are freezing on my cheeks, and the laughter of the Ice Giants rumbles through the storm, cold and as heartless as the towering stones that seem to lean over me in the fading light. Smoothed by the hands of the Ice Giants, they resemble misshapen eggs. I could be standing in a vast nest, waiting for alien creatures to peck through the black shells, spread huge wings, and flap away like the flame birds our legends say shot across the skies just after the zyme.

Every time I turn my head away from a gust, I stagger and almost collapse. It's only when I push into the middle of the nest and the wind is blocked that I allow myself to sit down and lean back against a boulder.

That's when I see the wolf huddled in a hollow at the base of the tallest boulder.

I'm so shocked, I gasp, "Xeno!"

My eyelashes, hair, and cheeks are crusted with so much ice, I can barely see him. He's sheathed with ice, as well, as though he's been huddling here for hands of time. Waiting for me.

"What are you doing here?"

The wolf doesn't move, and I have the strange feeling that he isn't real, just a trick of ice and exhaustion. In the surreal gusts of blowing snow, he looks ancient, his fur the aged yellow of mammoth ivory.

When I extend a hand to touch him, his eyes suddenly gleam—and I see glimpses of things I have never seen . . . shadows on the ground born of thunderous light . . . sprawled shapes of people, but not people . . . vast mountains falling down . . .

"What are you d-doing out here in the middle of a blizzard?"

Xeno lifts his big head and swings it around to search the snow blowing across my back trail. Sunlight pulses, here one instant, then gone, swallowed by the roaring white abyss.

It's as though he's entirely focused on something down there that he sees that I obviously do not, and it worries him.

"What's wrong? Do you see someone on my back trail?"

I turn my head around and strain to hear voices, or feet crunching snow, or breathing, but all I hear is Wind Mother wailing across the high country as though she's fleeing hunting Ice Giants.

"I don't hear anything except—"

Xeno stands up, shakes the ice from his coat, and trots up the trail.

Bewildered, I follow, calling, "Where are you going? We

should take shelter in the boulders until the storm passes! Xeno, come back. Don't you realize it's getting colder by the—"

The wolf breaks into a lope, ignoring me.

Flapping my arms against my sides, I call, "Where are you going?"

The climb up the slope through the blizzard feels endless. Arakie once told me time didn't exist, it was an illusion spawned by our inability to see beyond our own noses. He told me time would run backward if I was standing on the right hilltop. Circles within circles. Wide eternal motions that I seem incapable of grasping.

"Please, wait. I'm losing sight of you in the storm! Don't get too far ahead of me!"

When Xeno vanishes into the blizzard, I trot after him, trying to catch up. Where is he going?

Ahead of me, ghostly figures spin like smoky phantasms, dance across the slope, and melt into the storm. But I don't see Xeno, and I push on through the wild white veils. The snowflakes feel like gravel hurled into my face.

When I'm sure I've lost him, I turn around and start to head back for the meager shelter offered by the cluster of boulders.

The wolf's howl stops me.

"Xeno? Where are you?"

There's a yip.

I search the storm. Up the slope, a glow shines. Firelight . . .

With my feet slipping on icy rocks buried beneath the snow, I head away from it. Must be one of the Rust warriors.

"Hello!" a male voice calls.

Sounds familiar.

I stop. Up ahead, an ice overhang wavers in and out of the storm. It's darker blue, a shallow oval, hollowed out by wind and rain. How many people are in there? A low growl seeps through the air, coming from the direction of the overhang.

"Hello?" the man shouts again, and I see a burly figure crawl out of the hollow. Silhouetted against flickering firelight, he resembles a giant dire wolf standing on its hind legs. I see big ears pricked. It takes a few moments before I realize he's wearing a wolf-hide cape that drags on the ground. The hood still has the wolf's skinned face attached.

Fear makes me swallow hard. He takes a new grip on his spear and stands up. Xeno trots over to stand beside him.

Without realizing it, I've broken into a run, trying to reach him. "RabbitEar? Is that you?"

"Lynx?" RabbitEar charges down the hill. "What are you doing here?"

"I don't believe it!" I run toward RabbitEar and when we collide, we throw our arms around the other and laugh. "I'm so glad to see you!"

"How did you find me?" RabbitEar pounds me hard on the back. "I've been lost for days, wandering through this wasteland, trying to find Quiller."

"Long story, and I'm freezing. Let's go sit in front of your fire and talk. This is going to be a bad storm. We're going to have to wait it out."

"Yes, I can already feel frost growing on my bones."

17

LYNX

"This ice hollow isn't very big, but at least it's shelter." Rabbit-Ear's red hair and beard shimmer orange in the gleam as he ducks beneath the overhang and crawls back into the firelight.

Xeno trots in behind him and goes to curl up beside the tiny fire.

"I'm grateful for the warmth," I say, and drop to my hands and knees to crawl under the ice roof carrying my spear. The hollow is about twenty hands deep, just barely tall enough to allow us to sit upright inside. Chunks of bison dung are heaped near the fire, which is the best fuel up this high.

"Blessed Jemen, the fire feels good," I say in relief as I sit cross-legged before the flames. Firelight bounces around the ice, reflecting from each irregularity in the walls and low ceiling. "I'm shocked to see you, RabbitEar. I can't believe you're really here."

"I think I'm more surprised than you are. When I heard your voice, I thought I was dreaming." He gestures to the hide bag swinging from the tripod near the fire. "Dip a cup of packrat stew, Lynx. You must be starving. There's a wooden cup and bowl there. Grab one."

"Thanks, I haven't eaten since I ran away from the ocean."

"How long ago was that?"

When RabbitEar draws up his knees and wraps his arms

around them, the wolf's claws, still attached to the cape, scrape across the floor. He's one summer older than I am, eighteen. It's only been nineteen moons since I've seen him, but he looks older. Deep lines cut across his forehead and curve around his mouth.

"Three nights ago."

"Three?" RabbitEar rubs his forehead. "I've lost track of time, I guess. I feel like I've been up here tracking Quiller and Trogon since the beginning of the world."

As the storm roars across the landscape outside, a silent restlessness filters through the shelter, a low current of unease. We spent summers struggling for the attention of the same woman. I assume that's what it is. I cast Quiller aside. He married her, but I suspect he's still worried about me.

"How are your children?"

"Fine. I left them with the matron of the Blue Dolphin clan. She loves them. She'll take good care of them if anything happens to me or Quiller."

"I'm glad she married you, RabbitEar. You are the best husband and father she could have found."

He gives me a guarded look. "No regrets?"

"No. I'm aware of my many failings. So was she."

RabbitEar suppresses a smile and I reach for the wooden cup and dip it into the bag. The delicious aroma of boiled meat rises. It's too hot to eat, so I just clutch the warm cup in both hands. The sensation of warmth seeping into my fingers is such a relief, I don't want it to stop.

"How long has Xeno been here?"

"The wolf? Is that his name? He arrived the same time you did. I assumed he came with you. That's why I didn't kill him on sight."

I study Xeno, wondering where he's been since he left our camp.

"Where's everyone else? Where's Mink?" I ask, half afraid to hear the answer.

He turns to look to the southeast across the wavering, lead-colored vista of blowing snow. "Hiding somewhere in the ice caves high in the mountains. At least that was the plan. There are only twenty of us left in the entire world, Lynx. Gods, you can't imagine what it's been like the past few moons."

"The last I heard, the peace had been broken. What happened?"

He briefly squeezes his eyes closed as though to block the memory. "It all happened fast. Trogon murdered Matron Sunbird, and in retaliation, one of her relatives murdered Trogon's only daughter. After that, everything fell apart. There were riots and cries for revenge, then Trogon had one of his crazy visions. I swear it was eerie to watch all of the Rust People suddenly gather around him like dogs expecting a bone. He told them Sealion People were the cause of the problem, and once Rust People had cleansed the world of sub-human beasts— meaning us—all would be well again. They rounded us up and locked us in log cages. We broke out and ran, but they trapped us in a cave."

"How did you escape?"

The rumbling of the Ice Giants shudders the overhang. I wait for it to stop before attempting to sip the hot broth. It's rich and delicious.

"It's . . . complicated." He waves a hand through the firelight. "Trogon walked right up to our cave and forced his way inside to speak with Quiller. He said he'd seen you and an old man camped on the shore two days to the north. Quiller was in the dream, too. Supposedly she told Trogon the strange old man with you was named Arakie. He wanted to know what else Quiller knew about him."

At the sound of Arakie's name, Xeno whimpers. I reach out to stroke his back. "What did she say?"

"Nothing. Then Trogon said he'd seen Quiller climbing a mountain trail and going into a cave where the Old Woman of the Mountain lives. He demanded that she tell him where it was."

"Did she?"

"Of course not, Lynx. Quiller said she had no idea what he was talking about." RabbitEar's deep voice sounds strained. "That's when he offered her a bargain."

"What bargain?"

His green eyes flash in the firelight. "The old witch said that if she would lead him to your camp, he'd free all Sealion People. Mink and I both told her not to do it, but you know her, she has her own mind."

Quiller must have suspected that she would be sacrificing her own life, as well as mine and Arakie's. "Three lives in exchange for nineteen. It was a good bargain. Did he keep it?"

"Yes. As soon Trogon left with Quiller, the Rust People let us out of the cave, and we ran as hard as we could to get into the mountains. Once I knew our people were safely away, I ran back to the shore to pick up Quiller's trail."

"Mink agreed to let you go after her? Doesn't sound like my brother. He needed every warrior to protect our people, and losing you would—"

"I was going after Quiller no matter what, and Mink knew it. We have all seen the insane people who return to our village after Trogon is through with them."

"Trogon never suspected you were following his trail?"

"Of course he did. He sent two warriors to hunt me down. I ambushed one of them. The other finally gave up and trotted northward up the shore."

"Must be the warrior who came into our camp around midnight."

Using my fingers to dig a piece of packrat from the steaming cup, I blow on it before I dare put it in my mouth and chew. Down the slope I see the ghostly outline of a short-faced bear loping through the blizzard. "RabbitEar?"

He follows my gaze and clutches his spear, watching until the bear vanishes in the storm. "He was headed downhill, away from us."

"Think he smelled us or our fire?"

"Doubt it. Wind's wrong, but we'd better be alert. The wind could shift."

The roar of a bear thunders through the storm, but it seems to be fading as the animal gallops down the slope.

"There are two of us to find Quiller now. I pray she's all right."

In a deadly voice, he replies, "I'm going to kill that evil old witch. I give you my oath."

I can tell from his blazing eyes and the way he's clamped his jaw that nothing on earth will stop him from murdering the man he suspects is hurting Quiller.

Snow whips past outside. When the gusts sporadically slow and thin, flashes of sunset seep through and turn the largest flakes into whirling amber shards that fly away like autumn leaves. My breath now frosts where I sit before the fire.

"Did you see the warrior?"

RabbitEar stares at me like I've just dropped a boulder on him. "What warrior?"

"There was a . . . a man. I saw his tracks cross over Trogon's."

"I've seen no one else up here, Lynx. Are you sure you weren't just imagining tracks in the swirls of snow? I've seen snow and mist ghosts many times, especially over the past few days."

"His boot prints were awfully real for a snow ghost."

"Last night in the fog, I swore I saw my grandfather walking down from the campfires of the dead. He was calling my name. Looked just like I remember, before the Rust People bashed his brains out four summers ago."

"Well, the warrior's tracks were real."

The expression on his firelit face gives me a chill. For a moment, it's as though the world has gone lifeless, so dead and barren nothing could ever revive it.

"All right. I'll watch for him." RabbitEar tosses another chunk of buffalo dung onto the fire.

"I assume he's one of Trogon's warriors who's tracking me. Trogon ordered them not to let me go under penalty of death. But . . . did I tell you he was wearing boots beaded on the bottoms?"

His taut expression slackens. "No, you didn't."

"Yes. I saw the beaded pattern pressed into Trogon's track. What kind of a living man wears the boots of the dead?"

Tugging his wolf-hide cape more closely about him, he says, "I've never liked ghost stories, even as a child, and I like that one even less."

My thoughts flit around like moths in firelight as I try to pull puzzle pieces together . . . the storm coming out of nowhere . . . Xeno appearing sheathed in ice . . . RabbitEar in a firelit cave way up high in the Ice Giant Mountains . . .

RabbitEar tilts his head to stare at me. "One warrior would not risk his life to hunt you down by himself, not even if Trogon ordered it, not with all the giant predators up here, unless you have something he wants. Or . . ." RabbitEar stops to evaluate me. "Could be vengeance. Did you spear a member of his clan during the attack?"

I shake my head. "I didn't kill anyone. Which probably won't surprise you, given my reputation for cowardice."

RabbitEar's face is sober as he looks across the fire at me. "Tracking you through the blizzard wasn't easy. Means he's intent on catching you. Also means he's not going to give up easily."

"You mean the instant I think we've lost him, he's going to sneak up behind me and crush my skull with a war club?"

"Or spear you from a distance." When RabbitEar raises his eyebrows, the lines across his forehead deepen into dark furrows. "That's what I'd do."

My mouth goes dry. All I can think of is the Rust People's attack where my mother and father were murdered. I found their bodies. Mother was gone, but Father was alive. I carried him to Mink's bull boat, where he waited with his family, and we paddled out to sea. Father had suffered a belly wound. He was a strong man before the attack. We cared for him the best we could. He lived for a long time. Long enough to shred whatever courage I possessed in my soul.

I grip my cup and anxiously stare out at the blizzard. "RabbitEar, I don't think we need to pick up their trail tomorrow. I think I know where Quiller's going."

His head spins around. "Where?"

"Arakie's cave. Quiller's been there."

He pauses. "Are you sure?"

Gulping the last bites of stew, I set the cup on the floor, and wipe my mouth with the back of my hand. "Arakie told me that's where she was headed."

Reflections of firelight dance in his eyes. "How would he know?"

Uneasy, I shift positions, trying to decide what I should and should not tell him, wondering how much I can say before he thinks I'm as crazy as a foaming-mouth dog. "I don't know. Not for sure."

"But you believe him?"

"I do."

"Is Arakie still in your camp or—"

"No. He's on his way to the Road of Light. He was dying. Been dying since I met him. I stayed with him for as long as I could. Until it was over."

Gods, it was over, wasn't it?

RabbitEar's granite expression softens in sympathy. "I'm sorry, Lynx. When you abandoned us and went off to live with him, I was a little angry. We all were. You chose a stranger over your own people. But now, I understand. You were staying to help him. I'm sure you eased the burden of his last moons."

My voice shakes when I reply, "Someday, when we are all together again in the new Sky Ice Village, I'll tell you some of his tales. He's . . ." I can't continue.

RabbitEar frowns and glances away. After a short interval, he says, "I look forward to hearing his stories, Lynx. I'm sure he was an interesting man."

"He was."

As I reach for my cup on the floor, I see my reflection in the sheen of broth in the bottom. My brown eyes are shining tunnels that drop away into bottomless desolation, as though I'm waiting for the end of the world to arrive so this agony will finally end.

"Mind if I have a little more stew?"

RabbitEar gestures to the bag. "'Course. Help yourself. I made a lot, so I'd have plenty for breakfast tomorrow."

I dip up another steaming cup and blow on it to cool it, while I gaze at the storm hurling itself across the Ice Giants outside. Father Sun must have slipped below the horizon, for the snow has turned a bruised shade of purple.

As though he's been thinking about it, RabbitEar quietly says, "You know as well as I do that Trogon is the most powerful witch in the land. Killing him is going to be almost impossible."

"We'll find a way."

Xeno suddenly pricks his ears and stares out at the gusting snow, which makes RabbitEar whirl around with his spear up, prepared to kill whatever appears through the storm.

I search the growing twilight, expecting either a giant bear or ghostly warrior wearing beaded boots to emerge from the storm and crawl in here with us.

"See anything?" RabbitEar breathes the words.

"No."

While I pet Xeno, the big wolf braces his chin on his paws and continues watching something out in the snow that neither I nor RabbitEar see.

18

QUILLER

The sound of Trogon's footfalls changes as he steps from crusted snow to frozen wolf tracks, crust to tracks.

He's following me very closely this morning, probably because he removed the rope from around my waist, coiled it up, and tucked it into his pack. I can't run in this knee-deep snow, and he knows it.

Here and there, Wind Mother whispers across the slope, stirring flakes into languid streamers that creep near the surface like spectral serpents. I glance at them to make sure they are not alive, then continue up the mountain, following the wolf's trail. Not a single cloud floats across the intensely blue sky, which means I have to keep one hand lifted to shield my eyes from the blinding glare of reflected sunlight or I can't see the rut in the snow left by Wolf, and it's the only break across this great expanse of white.

All around me, where drifts and cornices disturb the breeze, a masterpiece of long drawn-out notes, the purest I have ever heard, drifts upon the wind. It's a flutelike accompaniment to the constant deep-throated rumbling of the Ice Giants. I long to stop and listen, but I dare not. The last time I stopped to catch my breath, Trogon slammed his fist into my back, knocked me face-first into the snow, and ordered me to keep going.

Besides, the cave is up there. I can see the distinctive shape of the mountainside. We should reach it by sunset.

"This is an odd wolf, eh, little Quill?"

I keep slogging up the hillside. "All wolves are odd."

"Not like this one."

"What do you mean?"

"I mean I've never seen a wolf that moves in a straight line. Usually, they trot around sniffing out lemming trails, rolling in the snow, digging dens, pissing on drifts. This wolf seems to know exactly where he's going and he's heading there like a cast spear." Trogon pauses. "Is there something you'd like to tell me about him?"

I cast a glance at him over my shoulder. "I don't know anything about him."

"He's the same wolf that was at Lynx's beach camp."

"What makes you think that?"

"I saw his tracks yesterday before the storm. He has only four toes."

Shrugging, I reply, "Well, the rut is half-filled with snow now. Maybe it isn't a wolf's trail. The oldest people in my village say there are ice ogres that flit across the snow wearing the faces of dead warriors who fell from the sky in a long-ago war. They only have four toes."

"How do they know they only have four toes?"

"They've tracked the ogres."

Trogon chuckles. "Your people tell foolish stories."

The freezing air up here hurts my lungs, but I keep inhaling just to learn it. Along the sea, the scents of salt, damp sand, and zyme are always sharp and powerful, but up here in the heart of the Ice Giant Mountains the fragrances are more subtle. When I draw air into my lungs, I smell the earthiness of glacial meltwater and the faint tang of frozen mammoth beds that hide beneath the snow—a mixture of wet fur, urine, and dung.

I rub my arms. "Blessed Jemen, it's colder than I ever thought possible."

"I've seen it colder, so cold it left muskoxen standing frozen in their tracks in meadows, dead as stones."

As I walk through the frozen puffs of my own breath, they frost my face and hair, turning my head into a mass of clattering icicles. But the sunlight is stunning. The higher I climb, the more brilliant it becomes. The vast glittering snowfields stretch away in every direction, and towering above them are gigantic blue peaks speckled with pines.

"Tell me more foolish Sealion stories."

"I don't think I will."

"Why not? Are you afraid I'll laugh?"

"No. I'm saving my breath for more important things."

"Still thinking of running away?"

My boots crunch as I labor up the rut made by Wolf. The rut is almost completely filled with snow here, which means he must have made it in the middle of the night. I swear, it's as though the animal is leading me straight to the strange cave I found last autumn.

"You were heartbroken when I told you about your husband and son, but you haven't asked me any questions about your dead daughters."

He's trying to pummel my heart to raw meat. When I am finally so overcome with paralyzing grief that my will to resist him ceases, he will have me exactly where he wants me. I must not fall into that trap. If my family is truly dead, they would want me to survive. RabbitEar's ghost would be here close by, protecting me, trying to help me defeat this old witch. I feel him out there, just beyond my fingertips.

Soft laughter drifts on the wind. "I like you."

"Do you?"

"Does it please you that I like you?"

"No, it doesn't."

"I think you like it. I think you like it when any man takes an interest in you. It was pleasurable, wasn't it? The first few times he slipped under the hides when you were a child? You felt special. And I make you feel special, too. That must be confusing for you."

His voice has dropped to that soft threatening coo. That's part of how he does it. There's a scared little girl hiding inside every woman, and if he can just force me to see through her eyes, I'll be scared, too. The problem is that I am scared. Every time he returns to these unremembered moments, my heart suddenly thunders. I hear breathing not my own, and soft whispers that sound very much like Trogon's voice.

Steeling myself, I say, "Did that happen to you? Did a man slip under your hides when you were a boy? The man with the yellow eyes? You must have been terrified."

"Ummm, dangerous, little Quill. You must be desperate for me to stop talking."

"I'm interested. I want to know—"

"No, you don't."

Unconsciously, I reach up to grasp the medicine bag hanging from a braided leather cord around my throat. I can feel the silver glow encased in the bison fur that rests inside and know my spirit helpers, Bull Bison and Sister Moon, are alive over my heart. They give me strength.

"But I'm certain you want to know how your girls died. You've thought about it, haven't you? Wondered what our warriors did to those poor innocent little girls before they slit their throats? How long they kept them alive?"

"The only thing I wonder is how I'm going to kill you."

He laughs again.

When I stop and turn around to glare at him, his eyes narrow, waiting for the scared little girl to show her face.

"I know how badly you want to know. So, I'll tell you. Your little girls died sobbing for their mother. Quiller, Quiller, where are you? I want my mother."

For a few heartbeats, I can hear my girls. Little Fawn was the oldest. Nine. Her voice is the clearest, screaming my name. Chickadee was the youngest, but she would not have been calling to me. She'd have been crying and reaching out for Loon, her five-summers-old sister who was her best friend.

Despite his smile, his eyes are glassy and stone cold. "Don't you want to know which one survived?"

As Father Sun rises higher in the sky, reflections dance around the snow and throw a strange funereal light into my eyes. I thank the gods for sunlight that blinds.

"It wasn't the toddler," he says.

When I turn away and start hiking up the trail again, shadows fall across my path, indistinct, hazy, little more than gray smudges.

"Soon," I call over my shoulder.

"Soon, what?"

I bow my head and laugh. "I'm going to plunge a stiletto through your guts."

19

✻

RABBITEAR

Just before dawn, Wind Mother scoured the Ice Giants, hurling snow and ice crystals high up into the dark blue sky. They're drifting back to earth now, filtering down through the morning gleam, raining sparkles of light across the entire vista. The Ice Giants seem to be watching, too, for they have gone quiet and still, as if enjoying the beauty.

Propping my spear across my knees, I swivel around on the rock where I sit just outside the ice overhang to gaze at the white slopes below. In the distance, a herd of helmeted muskoxen wind down one of the many game trails that crisscross the faces of the Giants. Their gray fur is laden with ice crystals, making them resemble moving snowdrifts.

For most of the night, while I kept watch, I thought about where Mink had finally settled the Sealion People, and my children. We talked about the caves high in the mountains, far from the clutches of the Rust People and their evil Dog Soldiers. That labyrinth of caves—mostly lava tubes—is unpleasant, but it might be safe. Many of the tubes slither around and surface again in hidden places, providing routes of escape. The other possibility is the caverns to the north of here that dive through solid rock and head into the deep underworld, reputedly the caverns where the last Earthbound Jemen hauled crates filled with magical animals to save them. Often, our people hear haunting choruses rising from those caverns, yips and high-pitched squeals. Our shamans tell us they are the voices of long-vanished creatures like Osprey and Red-Tailed Hawk, animals still guarded by the Jemen and awaiting the moment when the Ice Giants disappear and the world turns warm again.

When the wolf walks out from beneath the overhang, his nose up, sniffing for danger, I whisper, "Morning, Xeno," and scratch his ears. "Where did you go in the middle of the night? Off to hunt for snowshoe hares? You were gone a long time."

Xeno drops to his haunches at my side, and scans the vista as though he smelled something worrisome on the wind.

"You must have been hungry. I'm hungry, too."

Taking a deep breath of freezing air, I exhale it slowly, and watch the frosty cloud drift away in a glittering stream. Since dawn, blood has been charging through my veins with such force that I feel I'll burst wide open. The almost supernatural urgency is more animal than human, as though a starving dire wolf has been born in my body, and I'm on the hunt of my life. Imagination is the worst gift of our Jemen creators. Every muscle in my body is shouting at me to rise and get on the trail, to find my wife before Trogon hurts her even more than he already has. I know what ordinary Rust warriors do to captive Sealion women, and I fear those torments are pale in comparison to what the legendary witch may be inflicting upon the woman I love with all my heart.

Close to the ground, a giant owl sails through the sparkles with his gray wings shimmering. For such a big bird, he's unnaturally sleek and silent.

Xeno turns to look back behind us where Lynx sleeps curled on his side before the low fire. My friend has been making soft agonized sounds, as though dreaming of frightening moments, either in the past or waiting for him in the next few days.

Reaching out, I pet the wolf's warm fur. "You're a beautiful animal."

Xeno vigilantly continues to scan the Ice Giants, his gaze lingering for brief moments on each boulder and curling tendril of snow, possibly searching for Quiller with the same desperate ferocity that I am.

I wrap an arm around his side and hug him against me. "We'll find her. I promise you we will. We'll free her, and we'll kill Trogon."

The wolf's front paws knead the snow, as though he's afraid and doesn't know how to ease it, except to stop dallying and trot off to continue our quest.

"We'll leave soon. Lynx says he knows where she's going. We're going to have to trust him. Can you do that?"

Lynx must have heard his name. I hear him roll over.

Turning, I study him. With his heavy brow ridge and skull that slopes back severely, he looks very much like his brother Mink. Except for his eyes. War Leader Mink has the hard un-yielding eyes of a man who has faced death countless times and knows its wiles. Lynx, on the other hand, has doe-like brown eyes. When he jilted Quiller to marry Siskin, he was still a boy. Before he could marry, he had to become a man by killing a great frost bear. He couldn't do it. He got to the den, saw the bear and her cubs, and fell to his knees in tears. In the ultimate irony, Quiller killed the bear for him so that he could become a man and marry another. That's how much she loved Lynx.

That fact is never far from my thoughts. Though I know she loves me, I often fear she loves Lynx more. She's certainly loved him the longest.

Lynx expels a troubled breath and rolls to his back. I doubt he slept at all after leaving his beach camp. I haven't slept in days either, but I don't feel tired. I feel unnaturally buoyant and focused on the task ahead.

Looking into Xeno's shining eyes, I say, "I wish I had your skills. You're strong and you can run forever. If only I could do that."

At some point, I will have to sleep, and I dread it.

"You didn't wake me at midnight," Lynx calls.

"You were completely exhausted, Lynx. You needed the rest more than I did."

I watch him rise, rub his eyes, and crawl out to sit just beneath the overhang with his gaze roaming the Ice Giant Mountains. His heavy cape is sprinkled with ice crystals that glitter in the sunlight.

"Looking for the ghost warrior in the beaded boots?" I ask, only half-teasing. "Haven't seen him."

"He's out there. Believe me. But, no, I wasn't looking for him, I . . ." His voice trails off as he shakes his head. "I was looking for an old man."

"An old man? You mean Arakie?"

"Yes." Lynx flips up his hood and shivers. "He came to me in my dreams. He was so real, I expect to see him climbing the trail behind us."

Shifting on the rock, I carefully aim the point of my spear away from him. "What did he say in the dream?"

"He told me he's searching for me, and I can feel him out there, trying to find me, to help me."

The pain in his voice makes me hurt deep down. He must have loved the man very much.

"That makes sense," I gently say. "The dead remain here for ten days to make sure the living are all right, before they trot off for the campfires of the dead. I imagine he is out there searching for you. He's probably worried about you."

Lynx fumbles with his hands in his lap. "RabbitEar, can I ask you a hard question?"

"'Course."

"You have been forced to leave the bodies of many friends on the battlefield while you retreated. Did you ever . . . feel . . . they might . . ."

"Still be alive? Many times."

I can see the dread on his face, and I understand that smothering guilt with perfect clarity. I add, "But even if they were, if I'd tried to help them, to tend their wounds, or drag them from the field of battle, I'd be dead, along with many of the people whose retreat I was supposed to be covering."

"Do you still feel guilty?"

"I will always feel guilt for leaving them behind. But, in the end, everything is about numbers. Warriors are always asking themselves, 'If I do this, how many can I save, how many will I lose.'"

Lynx rubs Xeno's neck, but doesn't comment.

"Arakie is dead, Lynx."

He stares down the steep white slope at the cluster of black boulders. "Is he?"

The dread on his face is so great, I nod and look away. "How many Rust warriors were there? In your camp?"

"Five warriors and one Dog Soldier, plus seven lions, but I know at least two of the warriors were killed by lions. The rest, along with the Dog Soldier, had been chased into the ocean and were swimming for their lives."

"So, if Arakie was alive, he would have almost immediately been killed by the lions, or any surviving Rust People. I think you can stop worrying about him. He doesn't need you any longer."

Lynx drops his face into his hands. "I know, I just . . ."

When he doesn't finish, I say, "Let it go. There's nothing more you could have done."

As the sunlight changes, the jagged peaks of the Ice Giants resemble colossal smoky-quartz crystals that have been broken with a hammerstone and cast across the crests of the glaciers. Some of the largest chunks lean at such precarious angles, I'm sure they will crack off and tumble down the face of the Giants with the next ice quake.

"I wish Quiller was here. I've relied on her my whole life to tell me what's true and what isn't."

"She is good at that." I smile. "Even when I know she's wrong, I still believe her. It's the forceful way she says things. Her confidence leaves no other possibility."

Lynx laughs.

Xeno pads over to Lynx and noses his hands, as though trying to shove them away so the wolf can look at him. When Lynx lowers his fingers, Xeno growls in his face.

"Lynx? With six Rust People and seven lions all prepared to kill you, how did you escape?"

"I just walked out of the camp."

I stare at him from the corner of my eye. "I wager there's more to that story than that. The lions were slaughtering everyone else and they simply let you trot away?"

"I can't explain it, but that's how it happened. I hugged Arakie, laid him on the sand, and ran away into the trees."

That seems so unlikely, I tilt my head. Then I remember his wedding camp . . .

"I would say I find that hard to believe, but I was at your wedding camp. I remember finding your body being guarded by two lionesses."

Frowning, he blinks at the blowing snow. "I'm sure they were just saving me to eat later."

"That's not what it looked like. They were curled up around you like protective lovers."

Lynx and one badly mauled warrior survived. Everyone else had been killed and eaten, including his beautiful new wife, Siskin. Only Lynx walked away without a scratch. Like icy fingers drumming down my spine, a haunted shiver moves through me.

"When you ran from the beach camp, did any lions chase you?"

"No."

After a long pause where I try to imagine how that's possible, I say, "You're a strange one, do you know that?"

"I guess I am."

"Do you remember when you were at the council meeting after your wedding camp was attacked?"

"How could ever forget it? Half the young warriors were calling me a filthy coward and saying I'd thrown my wife to the lions so I could escape. I thought the council was going to order me thrown into the zyme or make me an outcast and order me hauled off into the Ice Giant Mountains and abandoned, while the rest of the village moved on down the coast. I was terrified."

I lift a finger to make my point. "But our shaman, Old Hoodwink, said he thought you'd spent the night of your wedding journeying from this world to the other side of the campfires of the dead. He said that explained the old man who came to you on the trail, and the fact that the giant lion, Nightbreaker, told his pride to protect you from the other animals. Hoodwink said the old man was Nightbreaker in human disguise. A spirit helper sent to guide you. He said you were alive because an old spirit-filled lion saw something inside you that none of us did. Something powerful. Something important. Maybe something critical to the survival of the Sealion People." Lowering my finger, I solemnly add, "I believe that. You're a born holy man."

Lynx lowers his eyes to frown at the snow blowing around his boots. "I'm no holy man, RabbitEar. Holy men have the courage that comes from an understanding of the spirit world. I've been scared my whole life."

"Who hasn't?" I ask with a touch of scorn. "I've been afraid my whole life, too, and never more afraid than when Quiller shouldered through the crevice and walked out to meet Trogon. For a few heartbeats, my muscles went so rigid, I couldn't move."

"The difference between you and me is that you did move. I know you helped Mink get our people out of that cave and to safety before you left to search for her. That's who you are, RabbitEar. You're a warrior. You protect our people, no matter what."

I wonder at that statement. There have been so many people in my life who died because I could not protect them. I still see their faces. Just before the spear lanced through them or the war club crashed down, every one of them was begging me for help. I just couldn't get to them in time.

"You have other skills, Lynx. I truly believe you walk with one foot in this world and one foot in the spirit world. You see and feel things that others do not."

He swallows hard, before he says, "Arakie told me that some of us, me included, were given an extra gene by the creators that would allow us to speak with them even across great distances."

"What's a gene?"

His brows pull together. "Something they added to our bodies, like extra ears."

I stare at him, trying to visualize that, thinking how ridiculous it sounds. "Well . . ." I lift a shoulder. "If you hear one of the Jemen calling, and he or she wants to help us, say yes. We need all the help we can get."

When Lynx smiles, I reach over and pound him hard on the back. "Now, stop dwelling on the past. We need to eat the last of the packrat stew and get moving. Quiller may not know we're out here trying to find her, but she's hoping we are, and we're not going to let her down."

Lynx nods. "I'll build up the fire, then drop a hot rock into the stew bag. Bring you a cup when it's warm."

"I'd appreciate that. Xeno needs a bowl, too. He was gone hunting most of the night, but I'm sure he's hungry. There isn't much to catch up this high."

Lynx nods and crawls back beneath the overhang, where I hear him tossing more chunks of bison dung on the fire. Hidden in the dung are the remnants of the bison's last meal. When they catch, the sweet scents of burning grass and willow twigs rise with the smoke.

"You all right?" I ask as Xeno lies down at my side and a barely audible growl climbs his throat. His gaze is fixed unblinking on something down near the boulders.

I see nothing. Nothing threatening, anyway. What worries me is that there is something down there, some colorful shimmer left by a ghostly warrior wearing the boots of the dead, or the shining tracks of an old man climbing up toward the Road of Light, but only Xeno and Lynx can see it.

Absently, my gaze leaps from cloud to cloud, until my head is tilted far back, seeking some sign from the Blessed Jemen that we are not alone in our quest to save Quiller. I was serious about needing the help of the gods or the dead. Trogon's reputation is horrifying. I have no idea how we're going to kill him and rescue Quiller. If only the Jemen were watching over us . . .

"Almost ready," Lynx calls.

Reflexively, I suck in a breath and blink. Ice crystals glitter as they leisurely drift across the slope below.

"Thanks," I call back. "We need to get going."

20

❄

QUILLER

Five paces ahead of Trogon, I kick my way through a drift and wade up the mountainside toward the grove of pines. When I reach the first tree, I grab hold of a branch and look around. The grove is a pitiful sight, for winter has conquered and beaten down the towering trees, cracking off huge limbs and leaving them lying in the snow, forlorn and dying. Everything seems dead. There is no birdsong. No howling of wolves or trumpeting of mammoths. There's no sound of water trickling beneath the ice. The cold has frozen it solid, and driven the last warmth from the sunlight that falls like diamonds through the weave of branches.

"Why did you stop? You said we're very close to the cave. Keep movin'."

Trogon's eyelashes, cheeks, and hair are coated with ice crystals from his freezing breath, leaving his ugly face barely recognizable: a disembodied frost mask bobbing along my back trail.

Lifting an arm, I point. "The cave is right up there. Just around the curve of the hillside."

"You're sure?" He almost can't contain his excitement. "This is it?"

"Do you see that crater in the snow? That's where I saw the Sky Jemen crash into the ice and melt his way down into the underworlds."

"Go on, then. Hurry!"

Reaching from branch to low-hanging branch, I break trail through the pines. In places, the snowdrifts rise to the middle of my thighs. It's hard going.

His boots crunch no more than a pace behind me.

"The Sky Jemen revealed the entry to you. Do you realize that? You found the cave because you were meant to bring me here."

A clump of snow falls out of the pines and thumps on the ground. Trogon stops, pants, "In fact, I'm sure you were born to bring me here."

"You think my entire life has had one purpose? To be your tool?"

"Of course."

I am filled with such loathing for this man that I can barely endure it. "If the Jemen really wanted you to come here, why didn't the Earthbound Jemen who came to you in your lodge simply lead you here?"

"Because you had to do it."

"Why?"

He's breathing heavily, struggling through the drift where I just broke trail. "The Old Woman of the Mountain said she must speak with you. She ordered me to bring you with me, and she is the chief of the gods."

"Was. Was the chief."

"What do you mean?"

"Don't you know the Sealion People's story of how the Old Woman of the Mountain was trapped in her cave? Have you never heard it?"

"Not the whole story, no. Just bits and pieces from Sealion slaves we've tortured."

A potent gust of wind almost topples me before I manage to

turn my shoulder into the storm. Small snow tornadoes careen through the trees before melting into the next gust.

I trudge forward again, placing my boots with care. "It's been one of my favorite stories since I was a little girl. Old Woman of the Mountain was heartily disliked among the Jemen. After she ordered all of the other Jemen to sail to the campfires of the dead in ships made of meteorites, she and the rest of the Earthbound Jemen knew they had to learn to turn into animals or they'd never survive the awful cold after the Ice Giants were born. Most of the Earthbound Jemen chose lions, wolves, saber-toothed cats, or bears. Some became mammoths or bison. A few selected the bodies of eagles and condors. But the Old Woman of the Mountain longed to live forever, which meant she had to become more like the Ice Giants than any of the other Jemen."

"Then she became an ice creature?"

"Yes. She changed into a woman with ice fangs and skin made of snow crystals. Once she changed, however, she discovered that she could only eat tears. So she visited the other Earthbound Jemen at night, crept into the dens where they slept, meadows where they grazed, or trees where they perched, and drank their tears. She lived entirely on the tears of the other Jemen."

Trogon laughs. "Silly story."

"Then I won't tell you how it ends."

At the curve, the snow has blown the hillside clean and I can see mammoth tracks pressed into the frozen mud of the trail. The crater where the Jemen fell to earth is a huge glittering bowl of snowdrifts. I can't see the cave yet, but the view is stunning. Curtains of snow blow across the vista of smoking volcanoes.

He asks, "How does the story end? I want to know."

"You want to hear the ending of a silly story?"

"I should know every story about her before I must face her."

Boulders as tall as I am create a sheltered pathway two paces ahead. The snow isn't as deep there, so I head for it. "The Old Woman of the Mountain drank so many tears she almost killed off the Earthbound Jemen who fed her. Their hearts dried up and almost blew away in the storms that raged at the Beginning Time."

"The other Jemen must have hated her for what she'd done to them."

"They did. They hated her so much that they chased her and her lone guardian into a deep cavern and locked them inside forever. She couldn't kill her lone guardian, so she didn't live on his tears, and without tears to sustain her, she froze solid. But she was still alive, trapped forever inside a body made of frozen tears. Supposedly only warm blood can thaw and awaken her."

"Curious. When I hear her voice riding the air around me, it sounds like frozen tears falling upon the ground, ice shattering, the shards clicking and pinging as they bounce away."

A branch creaks when Trogon grabs it and leans upon it to steady his sliding feet. "I've been wondering about something the old man on the beach said."

"Something Arakie said?"

"Yes. He said both of our stories about the Old Woman were true. How can that be? We say it was the enemies of the Jemen who locked the Old Woman in the cave, but you say it was the other Earthbound Jemen who did it. How could both stories be true?"

"The Earthbound Jemen who came to your lodge didn't explain it?"

"No."

Propping one hand on a rock to steady myself, I catch my breath before I turn around and look at him. "You never mention seeing people."

"What?"

"In your vision. When the Earthbound Jemen came to you in your lodge and took your soul flying across the vast deserts that covered the world in the Beginning Time, did you see any people? You never mention seeing anyone."

Trogon abruptly goes still. Behind his eyes is endless night. He must be reliving that vision. I don't know what he hears or sees, but it's so terrible I dare not ask.

In a dreadful voice, he finally says, "Wind Mother had gone mad. She'd killed the voices of the Thunderbirds, of singing rivers and whispering trees, and raged across the deserts, whipping up sandstorms that covered the entire the world. In the ocean of sand, I saw half-buried stone villages that went on forever. The strange lodges were empty, like abandoned cocoons." I can hear him swallow. "That's when the Jemen created the zyme and turned it loose in Mother Ocean. That's when the Ice Giants were born."

I wait for him to tell me more, but when he doesn't, I slog through the last drift and hit the mammoth trail, placing my feet in the animals' enormous frozen tracks. The mud was wet when they walked here, squishing up around their heavy feet. Maybe walking in their trail wasn't such a good idea. It may be clean of snow, but the irregular icy surface is very slippery.

"Then there were no people?"

"I saw a handful of strange-looking bison running. Spots of trees. Mother Ocean was huge. She'd swallowed most of the land. I think the last people lived in the sky world, for I saw thousands of Sky Jemen crisscrossing the campfires of the dead in their ships of light."

"Thousands?"

"Yes, flashes and streaks of white blazed everywhere I looked."

The cave comes into view when I round the curve of the

hill, and it appears even more unnatural now in the daylight than when I first saw it at night. Dangling icicles, twice my height, drape the entry like a curtain of great frozen stalactites.

Trogon hikes up behind me and sucks in a breath when he spies the cave entry. "Blessed gods, it . . . it's square. Just as you said. I've never seen a square cave before."

"Nor had I. When I first saw it I couldn't believe it. It's so perfect, I thought it might have been hewn from the stone by the hands of the Ice Giants."

He frowns. "More likely the Jemen. I thought you said it was filled with blue light?"

"It was, but maybe you can only see that glow at night."

Trogon has been pushing me up the icy trails at a killing pace, but now, for the first time, he hesitates.

"Do you think she's in there, little Quill?"

"I told you, I never saw an old woman in this cave. Are you suddenly doubting your vision?"

He licks his lips. "I did not see a square cave."

"You also said Lynx and I led you here. But it's just you and me today."

"Yes, but . . . I never saw the cave entry. When I saw you and Lynx, we were all inside the cave, and it was a big cavern sparkling with the blue campfires of the dead. You walked upon them, little Quill, as though they were a sacred hide spread at your feet, a cushion for your steps as you journeyed out of this world and into the glittering world of the Old Woman of the Mountain."

"Did you actually see the Old Woman? What did she look like?"

Smiling grimly, he answers, "Like an ice creature made of tears. Come along now. She's waiting for us, and we're going to have to knock some of those huge icicles down to get inside."

21

❄

LYNX

By midday Wind Mother is kicking up her heels and howling across the glaciers as though waging war on the groaning Ice Giants.

"Where's the cave?" RabbitEar asks. "Show me."

Xeno has been leaping through the deep drifts and now stands twenty paces ahead of us, looking startlingly copper-colored against the snow as he scents the air.

Shielding my eyes, I squint into the blowing ice crystals, get the lay of the land, and extend my arm. "It's around the curve of the mountain. Maybe another one or two hands of time away, depending upon how much snow blocks the path."

"All right. Let me take the lead. I'll break trail for us. I'm not as exhausted as you are."

"I don't know why not. I haven't even seen you nap."

He doesn't bother to comment, just walks past me, wades through a drift, and leads the way around the shore of a frozen glacial lake that is as crystalline and blue as the sky above us. I follow behind the huge dire-wolf hide that he wears; it rocks back and forth across the snowdrifts with its ears pricked and the hind legs scratching wavy claw marks in the white.

Xeno scrambles through the drifts on the slope above us, jumping up from a deep hole, then diving down into the next drift, only to leap into the air again.

It's hard to keep up with the pace RabbitEar is setting. He's moving out like a great frost bear loping across the white wastes, desperate to find his wife. Though he was supposed to wake me at midnight to keep watch, he never did. RabbitEar must be so weary he can barely see straight, but he shows no signs of it, and I'm certain he will run until he finds Quiller or literally falls down dead.

When my boot slips off an icy rock buried beneath the snow and I almost topple face-first into a drift, I call, "Please, slow down, RabbitEar. I can't keep up."

He hangs back a moment, waiting for me while he surveys the horizon. "Is the cave near those pines?"

The grove of pines that whiskers the side of the mountain like a dark green line is visible in between the veils of gusting snow.

"Yes, we need to go through the pines and around the curve of the hill and you'll see it."

When I hike up to stand beside him, RabbitEar stamps his feet to get the blood moving, or maybe to dislodge the snow caked to his pant legs. "This is a foreboding place, Lynx. After we left you on the shore and paddled away, did you find Arakie and he brought you here? Can't imagine why anyone would come to this awful place by accident."

I smile, remembering the wonder-filled days I spent with Arakie learning numbers and words from many ancient human languages. Despite the difficulties and feelings of grotesque inadequacy, I would give anything to live through those days again.

"He brought me here. He lived in the cave, off and on, for most of his life, I think."

RabbitEar bats the snow off his hood and the wolf's ears turn from white to gray. "Alone?"

Nodding, I reply, "He was an Outcast among his people. He'd been alone for a long, long time."

"Why did they outcast him?"

The trumpeting of mammoths echoes across mountains, rising and falling, as though the entire herd is on the move, thundering down the winding trails that lead to the sea.

"I wish I knew the answer to that question, but he never really told me. I think it had something to do with the zyme."

RabbitEar pauses, and watches Xeno trotting straight for the pines. "The zyme?"

Shrugging, I don't know how to answer that question without discussing things from the Rewilding Reports, things I'm sure RabbitEar will not understand. Still, I try to choose my words carefully. "You know how our creation story says that in the Beginning Time, the world was hot and covered with vast deserts, and people were starving by the thousands, so the Jemen created the zyme to feed people?"

"'Course."

"I think Arakie may have created the zyme, or had a hand in creating it."

RabbitEar looks down at me as if to discern when my soul flew out of my body, leaving an empty-headed idiot behind. With a smile, he says, "You're telling me he was one of the Jemen and had seen over a thousand summers pass?"

"Yes, and I know it sounds impossible."

"Well . . ." He hesitates. "No. But you said Arakie was dead, and our stories say the Earthbound Jemen are immortal."

"You believe that?"

His head waffles back and forth and it's as if the empty wolf eyes are scanning the vista. "You don't?"

"I think they learned how to live very long lives, but they faced death just like we do."

A sadness comes over RabbitEar. "Hope you're wrong. I want the Earthbound Jemen to be alive and caring for the precious animals they hid in cages in the underworlds until they win the war with the Ice Giants. Once the war is over, they will release magical falcons into a warm new world. I long to see them sailing through the skies above me."

As though trying to ease that epic loss, a woolly rhinoceros lumbers through the snow near the frozen lake. They are solitary creatures, about one-third the size of a wooly mammoth. What's she doing up this high? They are grazers and there's very little dead grass up here. As though trying to keep my attention, the animal shakes the snow from her reddish-blond coat and sniffs the wind, which must be laden with our scents.

RabbitEar flips aside the big wolf paw and rubs ice from his red beard while his gaze moves from the rhinoceros and on down the slope. After a time, he points. "Lynx?" A long pause. "Is that Arakie?"

I whirl around with a sickening mixture of fear and hope swelling around my heart.

Climbing the mountainside far below us is a man. He's too far away to tell much more than that, but it can't be Arakie. He moves like a strong young man, bent on reaching us where we stand on the ridge trail.

"Can't be Arakie. He was old and sick. Must be the warrior who's hunting me."

"The warrior with the beaded boots?"

"Probably."

Worried, I swing around to search for Xeno. He's far ahead of us, trotting across a stretch of gravel, headed for the pines.

RabbitEar studies the distant figure. "See the way he moves?"

The man uses a spear as a walking stick to help him navigate the drifts, but despite that he has a distinctive swagger. Sealion People move differently than Rust People, less . . . authoritatively. "I do."

"He's of the Rust People. No question about it. Must be one of the warriors who survived the lion attack on the beach."

"What should we do?"

RabbitEar pushes his hood back to get a better look and the wolf's ears poke out of the back of his head. "A few moons ago, I would have waited, ambushed him, and left him for dead. But we can't afford the time. We have to find Quiller before Trogon kills her. Once she's served her usefulness, there's no reason for him to keep her alive."

"I know," I say softly. My gaze has not left the warrior, and as I watch him move up the slope, a nagging certainty fills me. "RabbitEar, I think I know who that is."

"You can see that far?"

"No, but there's only one person it could be."

"Who?"

"The Dog Soldier. His name is Sticks."

Rolling his shoulders, RabbitEar shrugs his heavy cape higher. "A Dog Soldier wouldn't be this brave. They're never alone, and they never engage in any dangerous activity. They always let others fight for them while they stand in the rear shouting orders or reading from their books to guide the course of battle. Besides, why would a Dog Soldier be chasing you?"

I breathe deeply and mull that over. "He knows there are books in Arakie's cave."

"Books? He would risk death a hundred times over to get to books?"

"I think he would do anything to get his hands on the Rewilding Reports."

RabbitEar pulls his hood lower over his face to block the wind, and the snout at his fingertips appears to be sniffing the air, scenting for the Dog Soldier. "What are Rewilding Reports?"

"They're . . ." How should I explain? "They're Beginning Time stories. One of the stories is about the creation of his people, Dog Soldiers."

The wind batters RabbitEar's cape, sending the wolf paws flopping around him as though the long-dead animal is clawing the air for enough purchase to leap into the sky world and run to the Land of the Dead. "What's in the book that he wants to know? What does it say about his people?"

How do I explain to my friend things I do not understand myself? Inside his wolf's-face hood, there's a brief shimmer as his pupils reflect a passing gust of icy wind.

"There's one story . . . At the end, just before the Jemen sailed to the campfires of the dead, they believed the Dog Soldiers were a catastrophic mistake. They wished they'd never created them."

RabbitEar releases my sleeve. "The gods hated his kind? That's the last thing I'd want to know if I were him."

"I think he just wants to understand why."

"There are only seven Dog Soldiers left. What does it matter now?"

"Dog Soldiers spend their lives searching for the light that hides in words. Maybe it's just about finding light."

"Light hides in words?"

"In the letters that make the words. He believes that each letter is a living creature made of light."

RabbitEar makes a deep-throated sound of disgust. "So when Dog Soldiers read they are actually speaking with creatures made of light? That's what reading is about?"

None of what I'm saying makes sense to him, I can see it on his face, but why would it? Sealion People have no written language. Words are spoken. The concept of letters is completely alien to him.

"Yes, well, sort of. The letters tell stories, just as our elders tell stories."

He gives me an odd evaluative look. "How do you know that, Lynx?"

"Sticks told me."

"No . . . I mean . . . that these strange creatures of light are like our elders? You sounded like you believed it."

I hesitate because I am already considered to be a strange person by my people, and I'm afraid that if I become even more alien they may well outcast me in the same way that Arakie's people outcast him. With Arakie dead, all I have is my people. Nonetheless, RabbitEar has been my friend my entire life.

"Arakie taught me to read."

He stares at me. "Like a Dog Soldier?"

"Don't say it like that. You make it sound evil."

RabbitEar twists his spear in his hand. "Well, I don't know how to feel about that, Lynx. Dog Soldiers use these creatures of light to kill Sealion people."

"I know, but I have read books that will help Sealion people to live better lives."

"How?"

Down the slope, thankfully far away, a pack of dire wolves trots along a game trail with their tails up and their coats glistening in the sunlight.

"I read stories about how to melt iron for tools and turn clay into pots."

"What's wrong with mammoth-bone tools and hide bags?" RabbitEar asks a little hostilely.

"Well, you use a bow drill to make fires. Your drill is made from a sharpened stick of wood. Imagine if it were made from iron?"

He gives me a skeptical sideways glance. "I can use my bone knife to sharpen the tip of my wooden drill. How would I sharpen iron? Not only that, a few too many iron tools in one of our bull boats and we're going to sink to the bottom of Mother Ocean the next time we're paddling south along the coastline."

Defensively, I say, "Before the zyme, the Jemen melted iron to build enormous lodges thousands of hand-lengths tall, and they used—"

"Who would want to live in such a thing? I'll take a bison-hide lodge on the beach any day."

Ice crystals have accumulated and formed ledges on my cheekbones that burn like fire. I knock them off and return my gaze to Sticks where he resolutely climbs the slope. As he gets closer, I can just make out the low dome of his skull, which is so different from mine or the skulls of Rust People. Why did Arakie mention that? He thought it was important. I don't recall anything from Volume Delta that explains why that's important, but perhaps I read it and didn't understand what the words meant. There are so many words in the reports that are simply nonsense syllables to me. I can sound them out, but they have no meaning. Arakie promised that when I knew more, he would explain . . .

Like a hard fist to my belly, grief momentarily bludgeons me. I have to close my eyes until it passes. When I open them again, I find RabbitEar staring at me.

He rubs his frozen face, then extends a hand, silently querying which of us is going to take the lead. "You want to break trail or should I?"

22

LYNX

The sweet tang of pines carries on the wind.

The storm was so powerful it scoured the snow completely off long strips of the mountainside. Rather than slog through snowdrifts, I'm using the open patches of gravel and dirty ice, leaping from one to another like a giant lion, then trotting where we can, heading for the pine grove that whiskers the curve of the mountain.

I've lost sight of Xeno. His trail across the slope above us was visible for a while, but it vanished in a rim of eyebrow-like cornices.

Panting behind me, RabbitEar says, "Took us longer to get here than you thought. You said two hands of time."

"Sorry. I found the fastest path I could."

When we enter the mosaic of shadows cast by the flailing branches, I hear the long drawn-out howl of a wolf. It's almost ghostly, rising and falling with the gusts like a hawk struggling to ride the fierce air currents that rip the upper reaches of the sky. The kind that twist the clouds into fantastic creatures.

When the howl comes again, closer this time, I turn to RabbitEar. "That's Xeno."

RabbitEar holds a hand over his eyes to scan the grove of trees. "I don't see him. You sure that isn't just another wolf?"

"I know his howl."

Ice crystals coat the pointed ears of RabbitEar's hood, and

glitter when he lowers his hand and turns to face me. "He's an odd pet, Lynx,"

"Xeno is not a pet. He belongs to himself. He's as wild and ferocious as they come."

"Tear out your throat on a whim?"

"If he doesn't like you, yes. He followed Arakie's orders, but not mine."

RabbitEar smiles as he wraps one of the wolf legs around his throat with the kind of flourish worthy of a high clan matron. "Where did you find him?"

"He found me. Or rather, he found me and Arakie."

"And he's stayed with you ever since?"

"He comes and goes as it pleases him. He's often gone for weeks at a time."

Picking my way through the trees, it doesn't take long to realize there's a solid sheet of ice beneath the snow. "Careful here, RabbitEar," I call over my shoulder. "This gully must have been running water a few days ago. This is more like skating than walking."

"Already know that," he says, and I hear twigs snap and crackle as he grabs for the nearest branch.

Two small ponds decorate the forest floor ahead. They're flat and frozen smooth, easier for walking, but I have no idea how deep they are, or if there's still water beneath the layer of ice.

"You're not planning on walking across those frozen ponds, are you? The last thing either of us needs is to get wet. That could be deadly."

I shake my head. "I'm not walking across the ponds. I know there's no time to build a fire to dry out."

"Good. I was worried."

When we manage to slip and slide our ways to an opening in the trees, I turn and gaze down the mountain looking for the Dog Soldier, but I don't see him. As the sunlight shifts toward afternoon, however, every undulation casts a shadow, and think I see his trail, like a dark line, cutting across the slope Our trail is more serpentine, weaving from one gravel patch to another. Like the venerated warrior he is, RabbitEar has taken great pains to hide our numbers, placing his feet exactly in my tracks, so that it looks like the trail of one man.

"Are you all right?" RabbitEar asks. The wolf claws, hanging from the skinned leg that wraps his throat, have acquired a layer of ice and appear to be sculpted from perfectly clear quartz crystals. "Something wrong?"

"No, it's just . . . I don't see the Dog Soldier."

Where is he? Surely, he can't be moving any faster than we are? So why can't I find him? He should be visible on that open slope for hands of time, unless he's taken shelter behind one of the boulders. The line of trail that I think belongs to him doesn't seem to lead to the boulders, however. It climbs in an almost straight line, as though, no matter how difficult the climb, he's taking the fastest route to reach me.

"Lynx? Come on, we have to go." RabbitEar's boots crunch the snow, closing the distance between us, until he stands right next to me. "We can't stop."

"Do you see the Dog Soldier?"

"No, but forget about him. He's the least of our worries right now."

Nodding, I turn back to the forest trail. It isn't more than thirty paces to the cave.

When I take the first step, my foot hits ice and skids out from under me. Crashing backward, I ricochet off RabbitEar's shoulder and tumble face-first to the ground. Pain slashes through me as my forehead bounces off a rock hidden beneath the snow.

Dazed, I struggle to get up, but my arms won't hold me. The last thing I hear before blackness swallows the light is Rabbit-Ear crying, "Lynx!"

23

❄

QUILLER

When we enter the cave, Trogon pulls his knife and takes my arm in a hard grip to keep me from going any farther. His gaze traces the dark cave's square shape, then lifts to the ceiling one hundred hand-lengths over our heads and drifts across the walls. There's only enough light for him to see the peculiar drawings near the entry. He glances at the wood pile and stash of torches leaning against the wall, but makes no move toward them. He seems awestruck by the black curls scrawled across every flat rock face. They are so fine and beautiful, they look like there were painted with tiny twigs or bison-hair brushes.

"What are the pictures?" he murmurs, but the cave magnifies his voice so that it resonates from the walls.

"How would I know? I didn't draw them."

"Some of them remind me of the letters in the Dog Soldiers' books. Do they tell stories?"

"The last time I was here, I thought they might be stories."

Trogon drags me another seven paces deeper into the cave. "The last time you were here there was a blue glow. Could you see more? How far back do the images go?"

"They cover every wall for another one hundred paces, but that's as far back as I went."

As Trogon examines the higher images, his pale hair trails down the back of his cape. "I see no pictures of people or animals. Just wavy lines. Are they supposed to represent Mother Ocean?"

"Maybe, but there are handprints back there." I gesture with my chin.

"Clan symbols?"

I shrug.

Ahead of us, the rattle of the Ice Giants' retreating steps fades along the stone walls, dying away into the deepest recesses.

Trogon cocks his head, listening for more, then he squints down the black throat of the cave. "Where are the broken cages?"

"Far back. You'll never be able to see them until the blue glow returns at nightfall. If it returns."

"Yes, I will."

He gestures to the torches leaning against the wall near the entry. "We'll carry several of those with us."

"Aren't you afraid? Afraid she's back there watching you? Coming for you with her ice fangs bared?"

A faint smile from the old witch. "Do you know what true fear is, little Quill? It's the moment when you are most alive. The whisper of a spear before it strikes. The whir of the ax falling. You must never run from things that frighten you. They are doors that lead the way home."

"Empty gibberish."

"Fear reveals who you truly are, little Quill. It bares your soul for all to see, which can be devastating if you are a coward."

"I'm not a coward, so I—"

"Let me tell you about bravery. I have sat with my victim before the fire, in my lodge, or upon a rock—and pressed my lips against her throat to feel her blood rushing through her skin, enjoying it for as long as I could . . . then walked away, killed another, and returned the next morning to sit down beside her again, to that smell of terror, to that personal intimate death. That is bravery, little Quill."

My breathing has gone shallow. He's looking straight at me, but he's far away, lost in pleasant reverie. When he blinks and sees me again, he notes my breathing and appears lazily amused, as though I've failed some test of nerve.

"The courage of the battlefield is one thing," he says, "but when you know what's happening, when you know your murderer is seducing you, that is quite another."

He pulls the rope that hangs off his belt and grabs my wrists. While he ties my hands, I struggle, but he's much stronger than I am, and I need to save my strength. I've had very little food or rest, and my opportunity is coming, somewhere back there in the darkness. I've been planning my attack for days. If only my muscles weren't so weak . . .

"Besides," he goes on softly, his eyes never leaving mine, "the Old Woman doesn't come for us. You take me to her. I have seen it. We must gather a bundle of torches and continue our search."

Trogon drags me over and shoves me to the floor along the wall, then he points a stern finger at me. "Stay there while I get a fire going."

He walks to the torches, pulls four from the stack, and ties them together to create a bundle to carry with us.

I was here on an autumn night, but it still smells stale and ancient, like moss that's been growing in darkness for a thousand summers. There's also a hint of something else today. I can't quite place it. The trailing odor of wet fur, maybe.

Trogon kneels, unslings his pack, and opens the top to pull out a strange device. It glints in the sunlight pouring through the cave entry, polished iron, made from meteorites. After he arranges a small pile of twigs, he thrusts the device into the center and clicks it. I see sparks fly. Doesn't take long for the twigs to catch fire.

"What is that thing?" I call.

As though momentarily confused, he looks down at the

device and replies, "It's a strikes-a-light. It's been passed down through my family for many generations. I forget how primitive your people are. You smack two chert cobbles together to create sparks, don't you?"

"On occasion, but a bow drill is more useful, not that you actually care."

The constant cries of the Ice Giants rumble through the rock, occasionally shaking the cave. When I entered this cave last autumn, I heard strange sounds, like the clicking of claws on stone and indistinct purring. Which made me wonder if a lion den hid back there in the darkness. Hopefully, the lions are still there. Trogon is a bigger target than I am.

He reaches for a torch and holds it in the flames until it blazes to life, then he ties the bundle of torches to his pack, stands, and stalks back to me with his cape flaring about his legs.

"Get up, little Quill. Take me to her."

"I have no idea where to go. What if she's not here? What if this is the wrong cave? I told you, I never saw—"

"Then I guess you are useless to me. Do you wish to be useless?"

He reaches down and the tiny touch of his fingertip pressed against my throat sends a disturbing shiver through my body. I lurch to my feet and back away from him.

"All right, but I'm telling you I have no idea what we're going to find!"

"Just walk."

Trogon stays close behind me, and I have the feeling he's using my body as a shield while he repeatedly lifts his torch to examine the curious drawings. When we reach the place with the handprints, he halts and holds his torch closer to them. "Small handprints, like a woman's or a boy's."

"A boy would have had to be standing on a ladder to paint so high on the wall."

His gaze drifts up, following the handprints. The highest are twice his height. "Unless he was flying in a ship of light."

My eyes narrow, trying to imagine a ball of light floating in front of the handprints while they were being painted.

Trogon leans forward to sniff them. "This isn't black paint. It's old blood that was absorbed by the stone. There's so much of it, the artist must have been bleeding to death when she smeared it across the images."

"Maybe the Old Woman of the Mountain wasn't using her own blood."

"You think she tore out a man's throat with her ice fangs and used his blood to obliterate the images?" He's mocking me, making fun of our story.

I pause, wondering. The images all run together in long curling strings, thousands of them. "I think she was a story killer."

"If these images tell a story, you're right. She didn't like the tale."

His gaze roams over the wild stripes and circles that continue down the wall for as far as he can see, blotting out line after line of drawings. In the fluttering torchlight the old blood seems to tremble, as if not even a thousand summers can diminish her rage.

He gestures with the torch. "Let's move on."

We walk for another one hundred heartbeats before entering the gigantic chamber filled with ancient cages.

Trogon's breathing hisses through his nostrils. Broken rectangular boxes are stacked atop one another all the way to the ceiling two hundred hand-lengths above us. The bars are made from a material I have never seen, so black it's almost luminous.

"Blessed gods," Trogon says. "You were telling the truth. Some of the cages look as though they were chopped apart with an ax."

He waves his torch around, watching the light catch in the glittering splinters of broken bars and slide over the black material like liquid gold. When he lowers it again, the torch-light congeals into an unholy halo around him.

"This must be where the Jemen took the cages of animals to protect them. Why would they have released the animals before they'd won the war with the Ice Giants?"

"Maybe the Old Woman of the Mountain and her lone guardian got hungry."

Trogon cautiously edges closer to the cages and squints. "Teeth marks. Some of the animals tried to gnaw through their bars. That makes me think there was no one left to care for them and they were desperate to escape."

"Or they got scared when they saw the other cages being hacked apart."

The Giants let out a low grating shriek and the cave quakes so hard I stumble. Trogon braces his feet and leans against the ancient cages to steady himself.

"Lead me deeper."

I blink at the darkness ahead. The flickering torch illuminates the square shape of this cave, but I can tell that it narrows back there.

I walk on.

The cavern starts to shrink, growing smaller and smaller until I see a round hole in the stone—perfectly round, as though the ancient Jemen fashioned huge drills to cut it from the rock—a tunnel just tall enough for us to walk through standing upright.

"It's pitch black in that tunnel. I'm not going in there without light. If you want me to lead, you have to give me the torch."

Trogon hesitates, eyes me suspiciously, then hands me the torch. "Go on. If there's something hideous in there, I want you to get eaten first."

For an instant, I consider shoving the torch in his face and diving for his knife on his belt . . .

As though he can read the tracks of my thoughts, he says, "Don't be foolish. If you force me to kill you now, you'll never see if my vision is true."

"I don't care if it's true."

He smiles. "Don't you want to see her, little Quill? By now, you know most of the things I've seen are real. You know she's there. Just ahead of us. I think you want to look into the eyes of a legend as much as I do."

He's right, of course, I do want to see if the Old Woman of the Mountain is in this cave. Extending the torch in front of me, I can see far enough ahead to know this tunnel leads to another cave. The cave must be big, for it swallows the torch-light as though it does not exist.

"There's another cave up there, a big one."

He punches me hard in the back. "Go on, then. Proceed into the tunnel."

I haven't taken more than four steps into the round hole when Trogon whirls around and looks back toward the cave with the demolished cages.

"Did you hear that?"

I listen. "What?"

"Quiet!" He pulls his knife from his belt.

I don't hear anything. Except . . . water. I hear water washing over rock.

Trogon rips the torch from my hand and snuffs it out on the floor. "There's someone coming."

When the torchlight vanishes, the tunnel fills with a faint blue gleam. Trogon spins around to stare at me, then past me, to the cavern beyond, from which the blue gleam originates. His face is a mass of contradictions, as though he's too stunned to speak.

Then I hear it. Footsteps.

Quietly moving through the last cavern.

24

❄

QUILLER

H urry," Trogon hisses and uses the sharp point of his knife to prod me forward toward the huge blue cavern. "And don't forget that your last little girl needs her mother. If you shout for help I'll plunge my knife into your throat and leave you to bleed out on the floor."

"There's a ledge up here. I'll have to jump down."

"Do it."

With my bound hands, it's difficult to negotiate the drop. I have to sit down and slide over the edge, where I land hard and stumble across the rock below. Above me, Trogon's massive body glows in the blue gleam as he stands and stares wide-eyed at the huge dark sea that spreads before us. It's a stunning sight, motionless, too calm to be real. The source of the blue gleam comes from tiny pinpricks of light, like glittering turquoise flakes, that sprinkle the shore.

"Blessed Jemen." Reverence fills his voice. "The blue camp-fires of the dead."

Trogon jumps down from the ledge and grabs my arm in a rough grip. "You did not see this last time?"

"No. I didn't come this far."

Trogon pulls me back against the wall and tilts his head up, watching the precipice as though waiting for someone or something to peer over the ledge.

But I can't take my eyes from the underworld sea. The water is pure black, so black that the faint blue glow skims from the surface, giving it a luminous sheen that extends as far back into the cavern as I can see. Just above the waterline, all around the walls, other square tunnels jut off. One hundred or more.

Trogon hisses, "I told you. If we just keep walking, we will find the Old Woman."

That possibility terrifies me. Because if he really was visited by one of the Jemen, then the Old Woman of the Mountain is here, hiding in her cave, waiting for me to lead the powerful witch to her tomb. And she ordered Trogon to bring me along so she could speak with me . . .

My blood goes cold.

When no one leans over the ledge, Trogon's grip upon my arm relaxes slightly, and he turns back to me.

"You must walk across blue campfires, just as I saw you do."

"They're not the campfires of the dead, they're speckles of some kind of blue zyme."

Jerking me away from the wall, he flings me forward into a shambling trot. "Her cave is close now. Very close."

"But how do I get there? Look around! One hundred square tunnels lead off from this cavern."

Certainty slackens his expression. "You'll lead me there. Just keep walking."

Sighing, I walk across the glints of blue zyme and follow the curving shoreline. The deeper I go into the bowels of the Ice Giants, the more zyme there is, covering the shore and floating upon the vast sea like small glowing islands. As the gleam intensifies, swelling to fill the cavern, I feel increasingly off-balance. Must be the reflections. All around me, blue light wavers, coming in surges that mimic the slight waves washing upon the shore.

"I did not see that," Trogon softly says from behind me.

When I look back at him, he's gesturing to my boot prints in the wet sand. As each fills with water, the disturbed zyme shimmers and turns it blue.

My breathing sounds loud. "You didn't see the square entry to the cave. You didn't see the dark sea or my blue footprints. What else did the Jemen hide from you?"

"Many things, I suspect. The gods are under no obligation to tell us everything."

I walk deeper.

The blue glow silhouettes what look like gigantic arms thrusting up from the black water, reaching for a ceiling hidden in darkness high above.

My heart actually aches from the majesty. A strange lattice weaves patterns through the air, huge toppled beams overlapping, others hanging down as though about to cut loose and spear into the dark water. At the far edges of the cavern, phosphorescent sea fog crawls along the walls as though alive and moving to encircle us.

"What were they doing in here?" Trogon asks in a voice filled with wonder.

"Who?"

"Look up. Can't you see through the lattice to the rock above? This enormous cavern is square. It was hollowed out by the Jemen. And see the beams still attached to the walls? They are layered, as though the ancient lodges were built one atop the other all the way to the ceiling." He tilts his head back to look up and his mouth falls open. There is no ceiling. The layers vanish into darkness high above us. "When I was a child, our greatest holy people told stories about ancient villages that stretched forever beneath the Ice Giants."

I don't respond, for I'm trying to judge how high the ceiling might be. The faint glow isn't strong enough to reveal it, but if I concentrate, I can see vague shapes up there, blocks and triangles. Something that appears to be circular. All I can say is that the roof of the cavern must be thousands of hand-lengths above me.

While Trogon gapes in silence, I listen for footsteps, but whoever, or whatever, was coming through cavern of broken cages has gone silent. The only sound now is the slight hiss of waves.

"She's back there somewhere, little Quill. We must continue on until we find her."

I shake my bound hands at him. "Are you listening to me? Which tunnel should I take? Which direction should I go? Tell me, and I'll start walking."

He exhales into the darkness that is not quite dark. And not quite empty, for I feel eyes out there, examining us.

"Your feet know the way. Just walk. You will find her."

25

❄

LYNX

Blackness gradually shades to gray and I flex my fingers, fighting against the nausea to open my eyes. I can't convince myself to sit up, but I can roll to my back and look at the snow-laden pine boughs above me, shimmering in the afternoon sunlight. Not too far away, I hear cracking and snapping, as though boots crush the ice secreted beneath the snow.

"RabbitEar?" I call in a weak voice. "I'm awake."

My voice spooks the birds and a flurry of wings erupts in the trees as they take wing and fly away into the cloud-strewn sky.

"Hello?"

I keep expecting him to lean over me with a concerned look on his face, or grab my arm and help me sit up. When he doesn't, I manage to roll to my hands and knees and choke down the sickness rising in my throat. Gods, my head feels like it's being pounded with a granite hammerstone. Did I crack my skull? Is that why my vision is fuzzy? Shaking my head to clear it just makes me feel worse.

Frosted deadfall and rocks surround me. The wind has stopped, leaving the forest quiet, the drifts piled beneath the boughs sculpted into odd unearthly shapes that resemble hunching beasts. I don't see RabbitEar.

If I'm correctly calculating the slant of sunlight, I've been unconscious for at least one hand of time. I have to get up. Hoping to ease my belly, I scoop handfuls of snow and put them in my mouth. Each time I swallow, my belly seems a little better.

I jerk my head up when a low threatening growl reverberates from the boulders scattered between the trees, and look for my spear. Where's my spear? While I pat the snow searching for it, I watch the wolf.

Mostly hidden in the weave of tree trunks, a wolf stands less than five paces away with one front paw lifted and his shining eyes fixed on me as though he's not sure I'm real. I can't find my spear.

"Xeno?"

When a breeze sways the branches, sunlight falls across his body and he appears and disappears with the wavering shadows.

"Xeno? Come."

The big wolf lopes over.

"Where have you been? Where's RabbitEar?"

Xeno drops to his haunches at my side and vigilantly begins to examine the forest, as though expecting an alien creature to claw its way up through the snow and leap for our throats at any moment.

"Hold still." I grab hold of Xeno's thick neck fur and drag myself to a sitting position.

While I stroke the wolf's back, I call, "RabbitEar? Where are you?"

Wind-blown flakes have filled our tracks completely, leaving a smooth white surface where our trail once rutted the snow. The only fresh tracks belong to Xeno. I don't see my spear anywhere. Either RabbitEar took it, which seems unlikely, or it's completely covered with snow.

Did he try to wake me and when he failed decided go on without me? He was desperate to find his wife. Would I have done that? Left an unconscious friend behind in the snow if I thought the person I loved most in the world was about to be killed? I try to put myself in his place, but I don't think I could have left RabbitEar lying alone and unconscious, food for any predator that trotted by, and gone on to find Quiller. Nonetheless, it's a choice I'm glad I didn't have to make.

Xeno paws at my leg again and growls, telling me it's vitally important that I stand up.

"Give me just a little . . ."

Bracing my hand on Xeno's shoulder, I stagger to my feet, and almost fall before I catch myself and lock my shaking knees. Blessed Jemen, it's like I'm seeing the forest through a thin pane of ice. Everything is distorted.

Xeno slides out from under my hand and trots off in the direction of the cave. When I don't immediately follow, he charges back and viciously snarls at me.

Stumbling around in a circle, I try to find any hint of which direction RabbitEar might have gone. Though I pointed in the general direction, he's never been to Arakie's cave before. How will he find it without me? When it occurs to me that all he has to do is hike up through the trees and around the curve of the mountainside and he'll see it, I realize I'm not thinking very well. When my forehead slammed into the rock, I must have knocked my soul loose. My thoughts are a jumble of nonsense.

"Have to get to the cave."

I start forward, but my lurching gait makes it almost impossible to continue without falling. The first time I trip and pound forward with my arms circling, I realize my vision is even more blurry and I can't figure out why, then it occurs to me that warm blood is trickling into my eyes.

I have to lean my shoulder against a pine trunk before I can balance well enough to lift a hand and swipe it across my forehead. My fingers come back red.

Wiping blood from my eyes, I call, "RabbitEar?"

Two more tottering steps. Look around. Listen to the distant whinnying of horses, before I take another step. The pain in my head is almost unbearable.

Xeno has stopped in the trail with his tail straight out behind him and his nose pointed toward the cave, telling me there's something up there. The wolf tiptoes forward in utter silence, then, like a wisp of smoke, fades into the dense weave of trees and disappears.

Gripping a limb with both hands, I take a few moments to eat the snow that frosts the bark. I'm so thirsty. I eat more. If I just had time to lay my head in a snowdrift for a while, this headache . . . Then it occurs to me that my head has been lying in a snowdrift for at least one hand of time, which means this is as good as it's going to get.

A faint breeze stirs the forest, lifting snowflakes into the air and wafting them around me in a glittering dreamlike haze.

I stagger forward, shouting, "RabbitEar? RabbitEar? Xeno . . ."

The weight of the snow has snapped off branches and strewn them across the slope. I have to step over or around each obstacle, which means it takes forever to climb through the trees and reach the mammoth trail that leads past the mouth of Arakie's cave. By that time, my heart is thundering, but my headache is slightly better. I'm no longer choking down vomit each time I gasp a deep breath.

"RabbitEar?"

No answer.

"Xeno?"

The wolf must have trotted this way, but Wind Mother has been busy blowing snow across the slope, erasing all signs of life. If I can't find Xeno's or RabbitEar's trail, I have no way of knowing if Trogon and Quiller beat me here.

My spine stiffens when I see an icy man-shaped depression

in the snow. The arms and legs are sprawled, as though the person was thrown facedown onto the trail.

When I stagger over to it, the hair at the nape of my neck prickles. If a man had lain here and melted down the snow, which later froze, it would look like this depression. Did Rabbit-Ear fall down here?

"Hello?"

My voice barely carries in the cold air.

I continue up the slope, climbing, stopping to breathe, climbing, searching the mountainside. Amid the drifts that fill the huge crater where Arakie said a "bit of flotsam" had fallen to earth, there's a slip of light moving through the crater, dodging behind drifts, and I swear I hear a woman sobbing very softly.

Lifting my arm, I shield my eyes from the brilliant glare of sunlight off snow.

A cloud of frost crystals floats around inside the crater. Maybe that's what I heard, wind whispering around drifts. Might have also been tree branches snapping in the freezing air behind me . . . but it sounded like it came from ahead of me. From the crater.

I lower my arm and think about it. If I'm hearing things, maybe I should sit down in the trail and wait until my soul returns to my body.

But I can't. If Quiller and Trogon are ahead of me, they are already in the cave.

Taking my time, I place my wobbling feet with care, and continue on up the trail.

The flat expanse of frosty tundra to the south is luminous, dotted by a line of smoking volcanoes that disappear in thick clouds. Arakie once told me that the massive weight of the Ice Giants had split the earth all the way down to its core where boiling rivers of fire flow, and given birth to the volcanoes.

Faint sobs ride the breeze.

The sound is arresting, haunting even.

For several moments, I can't move.

"Are you out there?" I call. "Where are you?"

I glimpse movement to my left and whirl around panting, expecting the unknown woman to rise up from behind one of the drifts, but I see only tendrils of snow creeping across the slope like icy fingers.

It isn't until I reach the mouth of the cave that tracks appear, or rather distinctive long rakes in the snow, left by the trailing wolf claws on RabbitEar's cape. And Xeno's distinctive paw prints. He was running when he entered the cave, stretching out, flying across the floor, as though in a hurry to get somewhere. Enormous icicles as wide as I am lay battered and broken on the ground. Xeno leaped over several to get into the cave.

"RabbitEar?" I call.

Stepping into the cave between two remaining icicles that stretch from the roof to the ground, I feel a sudden relief. I'm home. Everything is as we left it. The ancient inscriptions scrawled across the walls run all the way back into the far darkness. The torches by the entry . . .

Then I notice the small fire near the torches and my breathing dies in my chest. It's burned down to gray ash, but it can't be more than two or three hands of time old. Several torches are missing from our stash.

Shuffling forward, I head for Arakie's cave, where I know he kept bags of medicinal plants. A cup of his special willow-bark tea will ease my headache, and perhaps Quancee will be able to tell me . . .

When a shadow leaps from the darkness, grabs me and slams a hand over my mouth, I don't even struggle. I see wolf ears silhouetted in the gloom over my left shoulder.

"Be quiet, Lynx. They're back there in that big blue cavern."

26

LYNX

When RabbitEar lowers his hand from my mouth, I whisper, "If you know where they are, why haven't you followed them?"

"I was worried about you. I was going back to see if you were awake, and make sure you hadn't been trampled by a mammoth."

My jaw aches from where he wrenched it. I lift my hand to rock it back and forth to ease the pain. "Did you build the fire by the entry?"

RabbitEar shakes his head. "No. I assumed Trogon or Quiller did. When I first got here, I could see a torch flickering in that tunnel back there and I heard voices. Then someone snuffed out the torch. I was afraid Trogon had heard me and snuffed it so it wouldn't blind him while he hunted me down. I flattened back against the cave wall with my spear up, ready to kill him when he emerged from the tunnel. But he never came out."

"Where's Xeno? Have you seen him?"

"Yes, he raced past me a little while ago. When I called to him, he didn't even slow down, just ran harder."

RabbitEar walks away and grasps his spear, which leans against the wall. In the deserted darkness ahead, the black lines scrawled across the stone appear to hover in the air, disconnected from the rock. "What are these?"

My gaze drifts over the inscriptions, remembering the sadness in Arakie's voice when he spoke of them. "Passages from books no one has read in a thousand summers. Some are love letters. A few are prayers to gods that died long ago. Most are mathematical formulas the ancient Jemen believed important to preserve." I start to walk across the cave, but a surge of dizziness stops me.

RabbitEar catches my arm and holds me up. "Feeling sick?"

"Yes, I . . . I cracked my skull, I think."

"Then you're going to have a hard time keeping up with me. You should probably stay here, while I run ahead."

"No, I'll keep up." Blinking my eyes clears them somewhat. "There's a cave in the back where Arakie kept medicine plants that will ease my headache. Help me get back there, and I'll be ready to help you."

RabbitEar turns to look at the torches. "How far is it? If we light a torch, Trogon will know we're following him."

"The next three hundred paces require a torch. Let me get my feet under me and I'll gather up a few. Can you use your cup to scoop up warm coals from the dead fire? We'll grind out the torch when we've made it to the ledge that's up ahead. After that we'll only light torches when we have to."

"You look weak enough to topple at any moment. I'll do it," he says and walks over to kneel before the small fire.

As he unslings his pack, he glances back toward the tunnel where he heard Quiller's voice, and his jaw clamps tight. I know he's desperate to find her. Any delay is too long for him.

Drawing out his cup, he scoops it full of coals and tucks it back in his pack, then wrenches it around so that it's wedged between other objects and sits upright. If the coals spill, there's a small chance they could light his pack on fire.

RabbitEar removes the coil of rope from his belt and strides to the torches. "I'll bundle several torches together and tie them to the top of my pack."

"I can carry them."

"You're dizzy already, Lynx, let alone with a swaying bundle of torches on your back. I'll carry them. By the way, where's your spear?"

"Lost it. I have another one near the cave with the medicinal plants."

"We could use a few extra spears. How many do you have?"

"Just the one. Sorry."

As he ties the torches to the top of his pack, his hood tugs sideways until the wolf's snout points at my face, staring at me through empty eyeholes.

"If you light one torch, I'm sure I can carry it," I say.

"I'm skeptical, but all right."

RabbitEar pulls another torch from the stack and stuffs it down into the coals, then he blows on them, fanning the coals until they glow red. He continues blowing. When tiny flames lick up around the head of the torch, he blows harder, and fire crackles through the shredded bark, illuminating the cave.

RabbitEar's gaze roams the walls. "I don't like this place, Lynx. I feel despair oozing from the walls."

"I'm not surprised. They were hopeless at the end. All they could think of was leaving one last message for loved ones who'd been dead for hundreds of summers."

"They left messages for ghosts?"

"I don't think they were thinking well at the end. And they may have been praying that, through some miracle, their loved ones were still alive somewhere in the world or among the Sky Jemen."

I stagger ahead, occasionally weaving before I get my legs under me, but managing to walk past the inscriptions and to the mouth of the tunnel, where I stop to brace a hand against the rock.

"You all right?" RabbitEar calls.

"It's going to be narrow for a few paces, but then the tunnel opens to another cave."

"I know, Lynx. I told you. I've been back there. Are you sure you don't want me to lead? What if Trogon is waiting in the next cave?"

It stuns me that I forgot he told me he'd been all the way back to the big blue cavern. My memory is jumbled up, filled with gaps.

"Then it's best that he kills me instead of you. Quiller has a much better chance of surviving with you fighting for her than with me fighting for her."

I carefully lead the way to the cave of the broken cages. They are only faintly visible this far back, just black bars against a lighter gray background.

"Lynx, is this . . . ."

"It's one of the caves where the Earthbound Jemen took the cages of animals. Arakie said there were many more around the world."

"Thank the gods," he whispers. "When I first saw these, it was like watching my greatest dream die before my eyes. I actually wept."

In the dirt at my feet, I see Xeno's tracks. He stopped before the cages for a time, as though paying his respects before trotting on for the next cavern. I wonder if he sat here, pointed his nose at the ceiling, and howled long and hard, as he does in the world outside, hoping to hear another of his kind answer his call?

27

RABBITEAR

I don't see Quiller or Trogon." I step around Lynx to get a good look at the ledge where he stands.

As I lift the torch higher, orange light flutters over the smooth black surface of a vast sea, creating perfect reflections that are impossible outside.

"Let me jump down first, so I can make sure the old witch isn't waiting down there to brain us with his club."

Lynx takes the torch from my hand and sags against the wall of the tunnel, while I slide over the edge, landing almost silently on the stone floor. My gaze slowly travels around the cavern, searching the darkest corners, then focusing on the flickers of what appear to be blue zyme that sprinkle the shore.

"All right, Lynx." I lean my spear against the wall. "Slide over the edge and I'll catch you before you hit bottom."

Above me, I see Lynx sit down on the ledge, holding the torch tightly as he eases over the lip. I grab his torch arm on the way down and hold him upright while his legs wobble for purchase. I'm not sure, even with a cup of willow-bark tea, that he will be able to help me find Quiller, and that leaves me in a frightening position. Can I take the old witch by myself? I have to, so I guess it doesn't really matter.

"I'm all right now, RabbitEar. You can let go."

"You sure?"

"Yes, really."

I release his arm and reach for my spear again. Lynx lifts the torch, then points. "It's just up ahead."

As we walk, I can't help but stare across this strange underworld. The sea is so black and shiny it could be a colossal pool of oil. We saw black oil ponds oozing from the ground in the far northern steppe lands. We used it like melted bear fat to oil our spear shafts and waterproof our hide boots.

"Is this a sea or a lake?"

Lynx halts on the shore, his feet surrounded by blue glitters, and says, "Arakie called it a paleo-ocean, which means it's very old. He said it surfaces in many places beneath the Ice Giants. It's been cut off from our ocean for so long that the zyme never had a chance to spread through these underground caverns."

"But aren't the blue sparkles zyme?"

"Bioluminescent algae. Similar, but different. This is natural algae. The zyme was created by the Jemen."

"Are there fish in the sea?"

"Once, a long, long time ago, fish thrived in these waters. I still find their skeletons."

As I look across the cavern, I'm speechless. Heavy black beams crisscross the air above us. It's a jumble, broken, and ancient. Long ago, many of the beams fell and now spike up from the water, towering over us, and half or more of their length is beneath the water.

"How far back do these caverns go?"

"They go on forever beneath the ice, but there's no food down here, so a man can't never carry enough with him to truly explore all the tunnels."

"It's . . . beautiful. Astounding. What are the beams?"

"They used these beams in the same way that we use mammoth ribs to support our lodge covers."

"So these are toppled Jemen lodges?"

Lynx nods as he walks forward and ducks into a square tunnel.

I'm not as tall as he is, so I don't have to bend down to enter the tunnel, but I do have to step over the fallen rocks and rubble that block the floor. I can see that this cave was once rocked up, sealing it, as though to hide whatever is inside. The rock wall must have collapsed over time. Why didn't Arakie ever clean it out? But perhaps, at his age, he wasn't strong enough to carry the heavy debris.

Many smaller round tunnels branch off in all directions, but Lynx bypasses all of them. Finally, he ducks into a square tunnel and continues back into the darkness for another twenty paces until he reaches an ancient door, falling off its hinges. When I follow Lynx and step through the door, fear constricts my throat.

"Where are we?"

"Don't be afraid."

Strange rectangular panes of ice—or maybe they're flat sheets of mica crystals—cover the roof, floor, and walls. The upper panes shattered and fell long ago, leaving shards upon the floor and gaping holes in the walls. The blue gleam from outside shines through them and reflects from the long shelf in the rear lined with things I do not understand . . . metal objects with no rust, blocks with crumbling leather bindings, which must be books, for they resemble the books the Dog Soldiers carry, and clear tubes like reeds made of ice. Colored powders fill several of the tubes.

When one of the panes winks, I leap back. "Blessed Jemen! What's that?"

Lynx stares at the pane while it winks three long red flashes. Three short green flashes. Three long red flashes. It repeats over and over.

"She's calling for help. But I can't help her. Not even Arakie could. When the rest of the Jemen stopped coming, Arakie no longer had the tools he needed to repair her."

"She?"

"Yes, and I know you don't understand how that's possible. I don't either, really."

"You said the rest of the Jemen stopped coming. I thought the Sky Jemen sailed away forever, leaving the Earthbound Jemen behind alone to continue the war against the Ice Giants?"

"No, they returned for a time, bringing supplies. Then, one day, they stopped."

"Why?"

"Arakie didn't know. He suspected they were all dead. But he hoped they had sailed far away, following the Road of Light deeper into the campfires of the dead."

"If they were going to sail away forever, wouldn't they have told him first?"

"There was a war. I think they were forced to abandon the Earthbound Jemen, but I don't know for certain."

Lynx lifts a hand and places it against one of the panes. When he closes his eyes, he asks, "Quancee, do you know he's dead?"

A liquid shimmer passes through the panes, like tears glazing an eye, and Lynx's shoulders heave with silent sobs.

My gaze darts over the crystalline chamber. "Her name is Quancee? Is she alive?"

"I'm not sure how to explain her. Does she think and love and feel sadness? Yes, but her body is made of these clear panes." Lynx strokes the panes, as though petting a lover. "She has the gentlest soul I have ever known."

When my pulse pounds, I take a step backward. "A soul?"

He seems to be listening to a voice I cannot hear. Finally, he nods, whispers, "Yes," and lets his hand fall.

I'm not sure if he was answering me, or a silent question from Quancee.

"Will she let me touch her?"

"I think she'd like that."

Lynx backs away and, swallowing hard, I walk forward and place my hand against the blinking pane. My chest suddenly expands with air and emotion fills me, as though a birdlike spirit has slipped inside me and is fluttering around, testing the edges of my body. I'm frightened, but I don't pull away. The sensation is not unpleasant, just intense. Strange images flash behind my eyes, explosions of light spinning through darkness that goes on forever, and despair so deep I can't . . .

When I jerk my hand away, tears are streaming down my face. It's as though, for a few instants, I looked out through her eyes, knew the campfires of the dead were winking out, and felt alone for the first time in my life.

"I feel . . . h—hollow," I say in a halting voice.

"After a while, you get past her loneliness and touch her joy. The more I am with her, the more I ache for her companionship when I must leave. Arakie said she was my true spirit helper and had been since long before the Ice Giants were born. He said they—he and Quancee—had been waiting for me for a thousand summers."

Glimmers flicker through the panes, moving around the room, as though encircling us with a chain of light. "I believe it. Our stories say the Jemen could foresee the future, just as our shamans do in a bowl of water."

"Speaking of water . . ." Lynx walks to the shelf in the rear, pulls one of the clear reeds down and empties some of its contents into a cup, then he turns to me. "Is your water bag full?"

"Yes. I filled from a trickle of meltwater running down the wall a ways back." I untie it from my belt and hand it to him, watching as he half fills the cup and drinks the liquid down in four long gulps.

My gaze returns to the blinking pane, three red flashes. "Quancee is dying, isn't she?"

"Yes. Did she tell you that?"

"Guess so. I just know it."

"I don't know how long she has to live. Arakie asked me to care for her until the end. I told him I would. Someone must tell her story."

"She has a story?"

"An amazing story. The Beginning Time starts with the birth of Quancee. She guided every calculation . . ." When I frown at the strange word, he says, "Every decision the Jemen made."

I hesitate, before I say, "I want to know more, Lynx, I really do, but we must be going. We don't know how far ahead of us they've traveled. How are you feeling?"

"I'll be better soon. Let me get my extra spear. I keep it out here hidden in a crevice by the door."

Lynx keeps one hand braced against the panes as he weakly steps outside Quancee's chamber and reaches into the darkness to pull a spear from a hidden crack in the rock. He uses it as a walking stick and, stepping around debris, makes his way out to the shore of the ocean.

I follow and stand beside him, searching the luminous black water for movement. I have the vague sensation that I'm floating in a gigantic surreal bubble filled with blue light.

Lynx turns and stares toward the deeper caverns. They recede back into the darkness, angling downward, as though boring a gigantic tunnel through the blackest regions beneath the Ice Giants.

I ask, "Is there any food here that we can carry with us?"

He shakes his head. "When we left we carried everything

we had with us to the seashore. It's my fault. I told Arakie I had to get away from here and back to the Mother Ocean for a few days. He didn't want to go. He said he wanted to die here in this chamber with one hand on Quancee, so she could lead him to the Land of the Dead. I think he knew he only had a few days to live."

I frown at the blue flickers that light the shore. The slight waves bring more ashore and wash a few back.

"We're not going to make it far without food, Lynx."

"Hopefully, they're not that far ahead of us. I'm sorry I slowed us down."

"Wasn't your fault. Could just as easily have been me who slipped and fell." I let out a breath. "The only thing that matters now is catching up with them. A man can live for a moon without food, but I doubt Trogon will give Quiller that long."

In the long silence that follows, I hear a faint melody, like the sacred drumbeats of the Ice Giants, echoing up from the depths. Lynx listens, and the lines at the corners of his eyes tighten.

Even pitched low, for my ears alone, his voice is laced with foreboding: "Let's hurry."

Lynx props his spear and uses it to steady his steps as we walk through the spiky shadows cast by the huge beams dangling above the sea like the toppled remnants of a giant's lodge.

Down the throat of the cavern, orange light flickers. Could be torchlight. Veering around Lynx, I take the lead, putting myself between my sick friend and any threat ahead. As I pass him, I say, "Has to be them."

He nods. "Yes."

28

※

QUILLER

How long have I been walking along the shoreline? I can no longer tell. Down here in this bizarre blue underworld, every sound we make bounces off the water and echoes through the endless caverns, coming back in ghostlike hisses and bumps.

Expelling a breath, I squint into the turquoise gleam. Just like in the last cavern, which was filled with giant cords, all around the circumference of the dark sea, square holes sink back into the rock, tunnels branching off. I can't help but wonder how many Jemen retreated to these dark caverns when the Ice Giants took over the world. Hundreds, at least, and if Trogon is right that these broken beams are the crumbling remains of lodges that were once stacked on top of each other, it may have been thousands.

"Do you think the Jemen lived here before our peoples were created? Or after?"

"After, I suspect." Trogon whispers as though afraid to speak of such things aloud in these toppled ruins, where ancient beings might still walk.

"Then our peoples must have lived here with them. Do Rust People have stories about that?"

When I look over my shoulder at him, I see him clutching

his knife so hard his fist trembles. "We have no stories of living underground in Jemen villages."

"Maybe we didn't live here. Maybe they didn't want us here with them."

His mouth tightens with derision. "That makes no sense."

"Maybe we were outcasts and they left us to fend for ourselves on the cold surface world."

My eyes seem to be having trouble adjusting to the continued darkness. Here and there, licks of flame spring up at the edges of my vision, flicker and vanish. And I'm starting to see small details that were invisible even one hand of time ago, like the tufts of colorless moss growing at the bases of the rocks.

"We could not have been outcasts. They created us. They loved us."

I have to think about that.

"If the Jemen loved us, why didn't they let us live with them? It's far warmer down here than it is on the surface. Surely, if we had ever lived in a place like this, we would have many stories of abiding in darkness with the magical Jemen."

Trogon doesn't comment, but he must be asking the same questions I am.

"To leave us alone with the Ice Giants and surrounded by giant predators, they must have hated us. Makes me wonder why we were such a disappointment to them."

"We were not disappointments," he insists. "Our stories say the Jemen were very proud of us for surviving among the Ice Giants."

Resolutely, I plod around the shoreline, frowning up at the beams that hang over us like the misshapen legs of a magnificent spider. Every cavern contains these ruins, but each new cavern is larger than the last, rising upward into utter darkness, swallowing me until I feel as insignificant as the pinpricks of blue zyme that shine in the sand. Even more astonishing is the fact that I can no longer make out the far shore of the lake. The surface appears to bend in the distance. Has to be . . . I don't know, two days' walk away?

When we enter the next cavern, I am too shocked to continue. "Blessed gods."

My mouth falls open as my gaze traces the shapes of the gigantic half-submerged wheels that fill the lake. Some are broken. Others appear to be whole. Fifty times my height, the wheels tilt against each other at odd angles, as though long ago they fell from the roof and split in half when they crashed into the water.

"We saw things like this," Trogon whispers.

"Where?"

"On one of the islands just off the coast of the far steppe lands in the north. We pulled up our boats and camped there for a few days. The entire island was covered with broken black wheels. Huge mounds of them."

"What are they?"

"I don't know. Some kind of giant rolling crafts that they abandoned? The Dog Soldiers said they could have been the legendary machines that chewed paths deep into the earth. They said at the very end the Jemen were more like serpents, slithering through holes in the ground, than gods." A shiver goes through him and he cocks his head as though listening to a voice.

Night must be falling outside, for the temperature has dropped slightly, enough for mist to begin forming over the black lake. As wraithlike tendrils float across the water and twine through the huge broken wheels, they resemble half-transparent specters gathering in some macabre dance ritual.

"Move. I don't like this place." Trogon shifts his weight from one foot to the other, then prods me in the back with his knife.

When I pass the wheels closest to the shore, I'm so dazed I can't feel my feet walking. I see no rust. The astounding rims of the wheels are black and unnaturally shiny, as though recently polished by the hands of the Jemen. Nothing grows upon them, not even the sparkling blue zyme. In the world outside, our green zyme grows on everything, and it devours iron as though it can't get enough. So these can't be made of cold-hammered meteorites.

I walk until the fog closes in, and I can't see anything except phosphorescent blue swirls curling around my face.

"We have to stop. I can't see my feet."

"No."

"Then light a torch so I can—"

"I'm saving the torches for when we truly need them. Keep moving. She's up there."

"How do you know?"

Trogon's frightened whisper is so low I almost don't hear him: "Don't you hear her? She's been calling my name since we stepped into this cavern."

29

❄

RABBITEAR

I have to keep my wits about me. Despite the fear and awe that fills me, if I start gawking at the rubble of dead gods I will miss Trogon's trap, and surely, there will be one. At some point, he will realize he's being followed. He can't help but realize it. These odd caverns thump and vibrate with each of our footfalls. The larger the cavern, the more our steps reverberate. The only possible advantage is that the echoes make it sound like an entire war party is pounding after him.

Lynx says, "RabbitEar, could we stop for a while? I'm sorry, but I . . . I need to stop."

That's the last thing I want to do, but when I turn and see him staggering along with one hand to his head, I say, "Of course, Lynx."

He tries to ease down to the sand, but weaves on his feet and falls down more than sits. Laying his spear on the sand, he draws up his knees, props his elbows atop, and massages his temples.

"Are you all right?" I crouch beside him.

"Just need to rest. Sorry."

Untying my water bag from my belt, I hand it to him. "Drink. Neither of us has drunk anything since we left Quancee's chamber."

Lynx closes his eyes briefly, then opens them and takes the water bag from my hand.

While he slowly sips water, my gaze drifts across the underworld sea, marveling at the breathtaking relics of the dead. A gigantic tangle of huge cords fills the water here. It reminds me of bison-wool yarn dropped from the sky in a single huge handful, except these cords are so black the eye slides off them, and each strand is as wide as I am tall. The tangle coils and loops all the way to the dark ceiling high above me.

"Lynx, who could spin such a huge cord? Were some of the Jemen giants?"

Lowering the water bag, he shakes his head. "No, but Arakie told me they fashioned gigantic tools to help them build the lodges in these caverns."

"I can't even imagine such tools." When I try, amazement swells my chest until it's hard to breathe. "How deep do these caverns go?"

He lifts a shoulder. "Not even Arakie knew that. He told me this chasm was carved in secret as a final refuge from the war, but only select Jemen were allowed to hide down here."

"Arakie wasn't one of them?"

"No, and he was glad of it. He said he would have rather died a thousand times over than be locked in this darkness until the Ice Giants melted and flowed back into Mother Ocean."

"That was the Jemen's plan?"

"Yes. These caverns were sealed and weren't supposed to be opened until the war with the Giants was over."

"Then why are they open now?"

"All I know is that they hacked apart the cages, and carried their precious animals to a beautiful place to die with them in the open air and sunlight." He takes a breath and slowly exhales the words, "Of course, it isn't in the sunlight now."

As night settles over the world high above us, a bleak fog drifts across the lake and snuggles against our knees. Except for our voices, it's deathly quiet.

It takes me a while to find words. "Sounds like you've seen the final resting place of the Jemen."

Grimacing at the black sea, he continues, "I found it by accident when I fell into a crevasse. I have never felt such sadness in all my life."

"You saw dead Jemen?"

He nods once as though that's all he can muster. "And dead black-footed ferrets and Cymric cats."

"You saw Cymric cats?" My voice is soft with wonder.

High above us two glowing balls of fog, like forlorn comets, slowly drop from the ceiling and travel down through the gargantuan black coils, trailing pale blue filaments for tails.

"I think I would like to see them someday, Lynx. If that's all right."

My friend turns to stare at me. "Are you certain? Dead legends are not easy to gaze upon."

"I'm sure that's true, but once I've seen them with my own eyes, I can let them die and move on."

Taking a deep breath, Lynx shoves to his feet. "Let's go. I've rested enough."

30

***

QUILLER

I wake lying on my side. My hands are tied behind my back and bound to my ankles, which are drawn up behind me. My whole body screams for me to move.

Three paces away, Trogon sits before a tiny campfire with a strange skeleton dragged across his lap. The creature's long tail extends into the water, but the white bones glint in the firelight. Trogon grunts as he uses his knife to pry open the jaws and examine the fangs, twisting the big flat skull first one way, then another.

"I'm awake. You need to untie me. I have to empty my night water."

Trogon doesn't answer.

"I need to get up," I call.

He studiously ignores me.

This is the first time I've seen one of the deep caverns in firelight, and it's breathtaking. The first caves were square, but that changed in the middle of the night. These new caverns are all triangular and, for as far as the firelight reveals, an endless sequence of giant triangles dives down into the earth ahead of us, growing smaller and smaller as though funneling us downward toward some predetermined destination.

"Hello! Can you hear me?"

Trogon flips the skull over in his lap, and the bony tail slaps the water. "I'll be there when I'm finished."

Orange flickers bobble in the slight waves and flutter upon the towering figures painted on the ascending wall of the triangle across the water. I didn't see them last night when all we had was the pale blue gleam to light the cave, but now . . . now I can't take my eyes from them. The spirals stand ten times my height and are made up of linked pentagons and hexagons, all rendered in brilliant crimson, yellow, blue, and emerald green. Magnificent color flows upward toward the apex of the triangle, then twists back down in sinuous patterns that could be serpents twisted together in a curious mating rite.

"If you don't let me empty my night water—"

"Oh, very well."

Resting the skeleton on the sand, he rises and walks over to saw through my bindings with his knife, then he returns to the same place, drops to the sand, and draws the creature onto his lap again so that he can finger the knobby backbone.

My arms and legs feel like dead meat. There's no way I can sit up, not yet. "Is it a fish?" I call. "Doesn't look like a fish. Where did you find it?"

"Just beneath the water over there." He aims with the sharp point of his knife. "It was half-buried in the sand. It's not a fish, though. See these fangs? It's a snake with a huge head and long tail that's barely as thick as my thumb."

"Think his kin still live in the water?"

Trogon gives me a half-lidded look. "When you get feeling back in your legs, you can walk out there and find out. I hope you don't get eaten while you empty your night water."

I use my tingling hands to shove into a sitting position, and pull my legs out straight in front of me. Blessed Jemen, the fiery ache of blood returning to starved muscles is almost unbearable.

I have to grit my teeth before I can stand up and stagger four paces away to empty my night water on the sand.

Trogon tilts his head, watching me, ready to leap up if I make a wrong move. "Now come over here and eat some jerky."

"You're going to feed me?"

"You almost fainted on the trail yesterday. I can't allow that to happen today. Would cost me too much time."

My hands and feet hurt so badly, it's difficult to put one foot in front of the other as I go over and slump down before the fire. The warmth on my face feels deliciously good.

Trogon lifts the skeletal snake by its big flat head and tosses it into the sea with a splash. Then he drags over his pack and draws out a bag of jerky.

My nostrils quiver at the scent of dried meat. I haven't eaten in days. I don't even know how many days it's been, but I was weak-kneed last night when I told him I had to stop and sleep.

Trogon reaches into the bag and draws out a strip of bison jerky. As he hands it to me, he says, "Don't eat fast or you'll throw it all up, and you're not getting another strip today."

"One strip of jerky is barely enough to whet—"

"The Old Woman of the Mountain could be many days away. We have to save what little food we have in case we must walk for another one-half-moon before we find her."

"You're crazy," I say. "There's no one down here. It's just one giant, rubble-filled cave after another."

"Oh," he says with a smile. "She's here somewhere."

Ripping off a hunk of jerky, I slowly chew and swallow. "The rest of the Jemen left hundreds of summers ago, and the caves are open. The Old Woman hasn't been trapped for a long time. She and her lone warrior guardian could have walked out at any time. Why would she still be down here?"

Trogon pulls a strip of jerky from the bag for himself, and

tears off a hunk. Around a mouthful, he says, "Maybe she likes it here."

"No one could like it here."

As though the Ice Giants find that amusing, an unearthly cackle, part chittering, part shriek, rumbles up the triangles, shakes the ground, and fades to stillness in the upper caverns.

"Eat," Trogon orders. "Before I take it away."

I chew another big bite of jerky and force it down my throat, then another. When I'm finished, I wipe my hands on my leather boots. My empty stomach growls and ties itself into painful knots.

"Are you going to throw up?" he asks with a squint.

"No."

"Good." Trogon shoves to his feet and kicks sand over the fire, plunging us into darkness until our eyes, once again, adjust to the pale blue gleam. "Get up. It's time to be off."

"How about some water?" I pointedly glance at the water bag on his belt.

Grudgingly, he unties it and hands it over. I take three swallows before he jerks it back and fastens it to his belt again. "Don't ask to drink again. I'll give you the bag when I think you need it. That or you can lap up seawater. Now, give me your hands again."

While he uses one hand to pull the rope from where it's coiled on his pack, he uses the other to aim the knife at my heart. It rankles, but I extend my bloody wrists. He ties them, then ties the rope around my waist and wraps his hand in the loop.

Gesturing with his chin, he orders, "Take me to her."

"I'm telling you, there's no one down here. We're walking to our deaths for nothing."

Doesn't take long for me to realize, to my horror, that the triangular caverns veer away from the sea and angle down through solid rock, progressively growing narrower as we descend.

When I step into a new cavern, the blue glow fades and the path ahead turns utterly black. The sight chills my bones, for it hasn't been that long since I was lost in darkness like this and felt certain I'd never find my way out. I feel like a mastodon is standing on my chest, squeezing the air from my lungs.

"Stop, little Quill."

His muscular body is silhouetted against the faint gleam from the upper cavern. Trogon unslings his pack and lets it fall to the ground, then he rustles around inside, pulls out his strikes-a-light, and tugs one of the torches from the bundle tied to the pack. Touching the iron device to the shredded bark, he repeatedly clicks it. Each time sparks fly. At last, a spark catches, and he blows upon it until a single tiny flame comes alive, then the torch bursts into flame. When the cavern springs into view, I gasp. The walls are shiny, white as snow, and covered with black squiggling lines. It's rectangular, two hundred hand-lengths wide and twice as long. The triangle peaks at least that far over our heads.

"What is this stone? It's almost transparent," Trogon says in awe. "Chalcedony?"

"I've never seen entire walls of chalcedony."

My senses seem to be skewed, heightened by the scents of damp stone and lichen that's been growing in darkness since the Jemen abandoned these caverns a thousand summers ago. From nearby—I can't tell where—a muffled voice rises. Is it coming from ahead of me, bouncing up from the depths? Or echoing down from above? I'm sure I hear footfalls, someone trotting along the seashore in the upper cavern. My skin crawls as my soul plays out the worst possible outcomes.

I'm staring back toward the upper cavern with my heart thundering, waiting for the Old Woman to appear before my very eyes, when Trogon says, "I don't believe it," and lifts his torch higher.

The darkness retreats, slipping into the cracks in the floor, where it quakes.

"Do you see it?" he asks.

I'm so rattled I just follow him when he breaks into a fast walk, heading deeper into the triangular womb with his torch wobbling, towing me behind him.

The handprints appear first, stamped upon the glistening stone, black with age. Just a few prints in the beginning, blotting out the squiggles, then they become more numerous until the translucent white walls are emblazoned all the way to the apex. Black swaths wash down from high above, as though someone carried huge bowls of blood to the heights and splashed it upon the walls, hoping it would drain down and obliterate the stories of the other Jemen.

"That's a lot of blood. Where did she get so much blood?"

Trogon slowly makes his way across the uneven floor and waves the torch, which draws my attention to the desiccated remains. "Probably from these creatures. Come and look at this."

Trogon edges closer, his torch held at arm's length, and shines it upon the shriveled corpses. They were much larger than Rust People or Sealion People. They would have towered over us. The light plays through gaping jaws and lolling almost-human thighs. None show coloration. They're just bleached out, like carcasses left in the open on glaciers for many summers.

My gaze is again drawn upward to the stipples and streaks of old blood that cover the cavern. "You think these dead creatures were the source of the blood?"

"Yes. Your story killer apparently loved to dip her hands in it and fling it around."

It's not easy determining what happened here. Several o;
the creatures were cleaved down the middle with a gigantic
ax. Others sit upright, as though they came here to die. A few
had their heads lopped off. The cuts are neat, the edges cauter-
ized.

"This was a mercy killing," Trogon says. "These are clean
kills. They were all brought to this cavern and slaughtered like
mammoth calves."

"I don't think so. Some are sitting up, leaning against the
other corpses. And look at their wounds . . . what could cause
that?"

"Forget about their wounds," he says. "What are they?"

Their skulls are monumental, three times the size of our
heads, and their cheekbones resemble beautiful broad shelves
upon their faces. Macabre scales and claws jut from their shoulders, and after struggling to figure out what they are, it comes
to me . . .

"Wings. Blessed gods, they had short taloned wings."

"Yes." Trogon's eyes widen. "You're right. They're giant hu-
manlike beasts with wings. They must have flown through the
blue skies that existed long before the zyme."

I try to envision that and terror fills me. "Did the Jemen
create them, as they did us?"

Trogon smooths a hand over his long beard while he considers the matter. "If they flew through our skies, why didn't our
ancestors leave stories about them? That's not something you
forget."

"Maybe they didn't fly through our skies. Maybe they lived
with the Sky Jemen, and when the Sky Jemen traveled farther
away along the Road of Light, these strange creatures were cast
out, left behind. Maybe that's why the Earthbound Jemen
slaughtered them. The winged beasts flew to earth to survive,
but they weren't supposed to live here."

I grimace at the bodies. I know how things die. Something terrible happened here. Most of these bodies lay where they were dumped, but a few staggered here and collapsed. The creatures must have run or tried to fly away, but they survived for a while after the killing blows, long enough to get back here to die with their kin.

"They were huge," Trogon says in a low frightened voice. "They must have hunted the Earthbound Jemen. I would have killed them, too."

When I take a deep breath, the air is stale and tainted with ancient carnage.

"More!" Trogon suddenly shifts his torch. "See them? Down there." He hurries forward, dragging me by the rope.

When we get there, he shines his torch on a pile of spines and hind legs that were apparently tossed aside after being gnawed clean of flesh. The enormous teeth marks are clearly visible. Some have cat skulls, but human legs. A few massive, pointed skulls, as long as I am tall, also clutter the cache.

Trogon says, "These are not from the winged beasts. See those claws? Giant lizards."

Leaning down, I examine them. "The way the hind leg is attached to the hip tells me these creatures walked on two legs. And they were big. Maybe forty hands tall."

"Giant lizards that walked like humans?"

I finger a tuft of feathers clinging to the foot, and it crumbles and falls like ash upon the floor. "Whatever ate these had huge teeth."

"Probably the winged beasts."

"You mean the Jemen fed them lizards, then slaughtered them and left them to rot? What a waste. One single winged beast would feed an entire village."

"Perhaps there were no villages left to eat them."

When I straighten up, my eyes rivet on the strange sight in

the next cavern. In the fluttering torchlight, the receding columns of standing stones appear beautiful and white, shining with an alabaster radiance.

That muffled voice again . . .

I cock my ear, listening hard for words. It's definitely coming from below us, hidden deep amid the columns.

"Hear her?" Trogon whispers.

31

---- ❄ ----

RABBITEAR

Beyond the cavern of giant wheels, the underworld seems to open like an extraordinary blossom, flaring wider and wider until I'm sure the far shore is two to three days' walk away. My senses are so overwhelmed it's hard to focus on any one thing. We march in single file along the shoreline like ants, dwarfed by the immensity of the cavern, following in the footsteps of Quiller and Trogon.

I turn to Lynx. "I'd have never believed a place like this could exist. What other wonders exist deeper?"

He has his head tilted far back, gazing up at the reflections flashing across a ceiling that rises at least one thousand handlengths above us. It's dreamlike, beautiful, not quite real. And it was built by the Jemen using magical skills that I cannot even remotely grasp.

"I've never explored the deepest levels," he softly replies, but the words resonate.

"Were you afraid to? I wouldn't blame you, especially after you fell into that crevasse and almost died."

"I wasn't afraid. Arakie ordered me not to. He said he had a huge amount to teach me, and this would merely distract me from my lessons. He said I would inevitably explore the ruins of the once-great Jemen civilization, and he pitied me when I did."

"Pity?"

"Yes. I don't know why he said that." As he thoughtfully blinks at the glimmering sea, Lynx adds, "But he was right, of course. I would never have studied. I'd have spent all my time searching these caverns and tunnels."

The tunnels are everywhere, sinking back into the solid rock. On the far shore, tiny squares are visible just above the waterline, hundreds of them. Anything could rise out of those black depths and be on us before we could defend ourselves. It keeps me on edge. My hand aches where I grip my spear too tightly. We've passed a few bones and dried-out bodies, but nothing human. Nonetheless . . .

"That's curious." Lynx gestures. "They look like handholds cut into the wall above the sand."

I twist around to examine the faint line of rounded holes apparently ground into the wall. "Why would the ancient Je-men have needed handholds here? Does the water rise and fall?"

"Water trickles down the walls all the time, but I've never seen the water level rise. On the other hand, I've never been here during the spring or summer when the Ice Giants melt, so maybe it does. It would make sense."

"How old do you think the handholds are?"

"Hard to tell. They could have been cut one thousand sum-mers ago."

I'm trying to imagine what they used the handholds for. "Do you think that when the water rose they pulled themselves along from handhold to handhold in ships of light?"

He just smiles.

Amazement fills me. I can visualize them out there, gleam-ing white upon the black water, just as their ships gleam when they sail through the campfires of the dead.

Dry wood litters the shore ahead, little more than a heap of splinters, but I wonder where it came from. There are no trees down this deep, and the giant beams that dangle above us like pure black spears are not wooden. Perhaps the ancient Jemen dragged in logs to sit upon in their lodges, as we do? We veer around the heap and curve back to walk atop Quiller's trail. She was in the lead here. Trogon's big feet blot out many of her tracks. My sense of panic rears again.

"Lynx, how are you feeling? Can you trot for a while?"

Lynx seems to be watching his feet. Long black hair falls around his face, swaying with his steps, but I can see his tortured expression. "Not for long, but I'll try."

"You look sick. How's your head?"

"Better," he insists. "Hurts, but the pain isn't blinding now. I was just thinking about something."

"About Quiller?"

He shakes his head. "No, about something Arakie told me."

"What?"

"When I was trapped in the crevasse nineteen moons ago, I was freezing to death, hearing voices. In between delirious naps, I heard what I thought was one of the Ice Giants tell a long tale of the terrible war that engulfed the world just after the zyme . . . about death rising out of the oceans near Seacouver and flying around the world gobbling up entire continents. The voice spoke of, well, other things, too, but—"

"What's Seacouver?"

"It was an enormous village that stretched for twenty days' walk along the shore of the ancient ocean before the Ice Giants were born."

I give him an incredulous look. "A village so big it takes twenty days to walk across? That's impossible."

Lynx doesn't argue, just continues, "Anyway, when I told Arakie about it, he said it was his voice I'd heard, and that he had not realized all of these caverns were all connected."

"They are?"

"He said they must be, and that his voice had carried for a great distance beneath the ice." His brows draw together, as though he doubts that.

"Why does that surprise you? I can hear my own breathing echoing. I hate to think what would happen if I were to shout."

Lynx studies the cluster of beams that have toppled across the shore ahead of us. They resemble huge stick-like gaming pieces thrown against the wall. As they waver with the shining waves, the beams seem to be walking toward us. "He never said so, but I always assumed I'd heard him talking with Quancee in her chamber."

Making a valiant effort, Lynx breaks into a slow, methodical trot. I run at his side, saying, "So?"

Lynx lifts a hand and points to the left. "That's northwest, isn't it? I know it's hard to tell down here, and I've never been very good at directions—"

"I can't tell, Lynx. Could be. Why?"

"That's where the crevasse is, down the mountain to the northwest of Arakie's cave. But we're headed due east, aren't we? I mean, I think we are. I've been trying to keep track."

"Then you're better at directions than I am. I'm completely lost down here."

Uncertainty tightens his eyes. "Then I probably am, too. If we're headed northwest, I'm wrong. Forget I said anything."

His dark eyes have narrowed to slits, but that could be his headache.

"Let me see if I understand what's really worrying you. You no longer think Arakie was speaking with Quancee. You think he was talking to someone else in a chamber closer to the crevasse?"

"He must have been."

"The Old Woman of the Mountain?"

"Impossible to say."

When we trot beneath the beams, my heart races. Some lean against the cavern wall five hundred hand-lengths above us, but the rest are propped against each other in a jumble so precarious I fear just the vibrations of our running feet may dislodge them and send them crashing down on top of us.

Lynx puts a hand to his head and slows to walk. "I need to sit down for a few moments."

"Of course, but let's pass through these beams first, then we'll stop."

Taking his arm in a firm grip, I support him while we walk through the fantastic jiggling shadows. It's only when we're ten paces away from the beams that I say, "All right, Lynx. You can sit down now."

He slumps to the sand, breathing hard, and squeezes his eyes closed. "I'm sorry, RabbitEar. I'm slowing you down. Maybe you should leave me behind and run ahead. I'll catch up when I can."

I suddenly feel guilty, because I've been thinking that same thing. More than anything, he needs to sleep for a day straight, but I can't let him, not until I have Quiller in my arms again.

"I've not leaving you behind, Lynx. Why don't you nap for a short time?"

He smiles, nods, but reaches down to pick up a flat pebble, which he turns over in his palm. "No, I just need to rest and think about Arakie."

I prop the butt of my spear on the sand, and watch the sinuous movement of the waves, rhythmically washing the sand at my feet. "About his stories of the Old Woman of the Mountain?"

Lynx skims the pebble across the water. Every place it bounces blue shimmers to life, leaving a stippled trail. "Not exactly. Since the day I first heard it, I've been hearing the voice from the crevasse over and over in my head. I swear to you, it wasn't Arakie's voice I heard, and it wasn't a woman's voice, either."

"But why would he have lied about that?"

Lynx slides a hand beneath his long black hair and massages the base of his skull while he winces. "The only thing I can think of is that he was protecting someone."

Along our back trail, on the far side of giant beams, I glimpse something move. A dart of darkness. Not the wavering shadows. Something solid. Human.

While I keep my eyes on the spot, I continue in a calm voice, as though nothing's wrong. "Who? Surely, if Arakie had a friend, he would have told you about him. Why hide something like that?"

The tall man edges closer, just a faint darkness drifting through the giant beams.

"I have no idea, but in the time that I lived with him, no one came to visit him, and he never left me alone for more than a few heartbeats. So if Arakie had a friend—"

"Please, don't kill me."

The Dog Soldier silently steps through the striped shadows cast by the beams.

"Stop right there!" Swinging my spear up, I aim it at his middle, ready to drive it through his heart.

The tall half-human halts just outside the beams with his arms spread and his hands open, showing me he holds no weapons. His silver cape shimmers pale blue in the reflections.

"Please, I give you my oath, I mean you no harm. I just want to speak with Lynx!"

32

―――――― ❄ ――――――

LYNX

When the Dog Soldier says my name, my aching head pounds. "Sticks, I'm surprised to see you alive. What are you doing here?"

Sticks starts to lower his hands, and RabbitEar shouts, "Keep them up where I can see them!"

His shout ricochets around the cavern, filling it with what sounds like rolling hisses mixed with erratic barks.

Sticks waits until the eerie cacophony dies down before quietly calling back, "I wish to speak with you about the old Je-men. May I come forward?"

RabbitEar takes his eyes off Sticks for a single heartbeat to glance down at me. "We should kill him, Lynx. You can't trust him. His people have been slaughtering ours for a thousand summers."

"No," I say. "Let me speak with him."

"Why? He's of no use to us."

My sense of balance is off. I'm not sure if it's my headache or the wavering cavern gleam, but I must brace my hands on the sand to keep the world steady. "His people are story keepers. They must have stories we do not. I want to hear them. Let him come forward."

RabbitEar glares at me, then waves the Dog Soldier forward.

"Come. But if you make a single wrong move, I'll drive my spear through your chest."

Sticks slowly walks across the sand with his cape swaying around his long legs. When he gets three paces away, RabbitEar walks over to him. "Take off your cape with one hand and drop it to the floor, then remove your pack."

Sticks reaches up beneath his throat with one hand and unties the laces, then slowly pulls the cape from his shoulders and drops it to the sand in a flurry of bluish-silver glimmers. Unslinging his pack, he hands it to RabbitEar.

RabbitEar orders, "Toss it to the floor over there."

"What is your name, warrior?" Sticks asks as he tosses his pack to the floor a pace away.

RabbitEar doesn't answer. He walks forward with his spear gripped in a tight fist. He's watching Sticks when he crouches before the pack, unties the laces with one hand, then dumps the contents across the sand. There are no books inside, just an extra pair of worn boots, a blanket woven from zyme, and several small colorful bags that may be food. RabbitEar roughly shoves them around, as if searching for hidden weapons, before he rises, and says, "You didn't even bring a knife with you?"

"No, but I did collect the bags of food from the dead warriors' packs. At least the bags that had not been pissed on by the lions. Please, there is jerky and grass-seed bread. It's yours."

As RabbitEar rises, he says, "Lift your hands over your head. I'm going to search you."

The Dog Soldier lifts his hands, and RabbitEar pats Sticks down. When he's finished, RabbitEar gives him a curious look. "You really came here with no weapons?"

"I didn't wish you to think I was a threat. I must speak with Lynx. May I sit down?"

RabbitEar seems to be thinking about that. "Yes. Sit, grab your knees, and don't let go."

Sighing, Sticks sits down cross-legged and cups his knees with his hands. In the cavern glow, his dark face and red hair have a curious purple sheen. He continually glances back at RabbitEar where he stands with his spear up, ready to cast.

The Dog Soldier gives me an almost reverential look. "I'm sorry your friend is dead."

"I'll bet you are," RabbitEar taunts. "Was he dead when you got to him or did you strangle him with your own hands?"

"He was dead."

I'm confused by Sticks' awed expression. "What do you want, Sticks?"

"I thought, perhaps, you would tell me stories about him."

Frowning, my eyes trace the low dome of his skull and his heavy brow ridge. *Turkana Boy.* "Why would I?"

"He was, perhaps, the last Jemen alive in our world. Someone must keep his stories and pass them down through the generations."

"I'm not sure he'd want that to be you."

"You mean because the Jemen hated my kind?"

"No, because you have allied yourselves with the Rust People who have tortured and murdered Sealion People—"

"But I have not murdered Sealion People! Not personally." Sticks squares his shoulders and gazes at me with great dignity. "Besides, I am no longer your enemy. I—"

"Really?" RabbitEar says a bit too melodramatically. "When did that happen? Just came to you while you were hunting us down?"

Patiently, Sticks answers, "If I'm hunting you, where are my weapons? Why didn't I bring warriors with me? I certainly could have—"

"Was everyone else killed in the lion attack?" I ask, wondering the same thing RabbitEar is—where are the other Rust warriors? Hiding in the last cavern, waiting for a signal from their sacred Dog Soldier before they attack?

Sticks lightly shakes his head. "Three warriors were dragged down, but the rest of us survived by staying in the ocean until the lions had eaten their bodies. We didn't come out until dawn, when the lions trotted off into the forest and we could see the pride moving along the trail up the mountain. So . . ." he says pointedly. "I could have ordered the last two warriors to hunt you down, or I could have ordered them to accompany me on my journey to find you. I did neither. I released them to go home, and I came after you alone and unarmed."

RabbitEar eyes him severely. "Which means you're either stupid or demented."

"I am neither. It was a gesture of friendship."

An ugly laugh from RabbitEar.

I say, "I think it's more likely that you came after me because you want to get your hands on Volume Delta of the Rewilding Reports."

"I do. Absolutely. But . . ." He fearfully licks his mouth. "I couldn't find it, and I thought, maybe—"

I go rigid as fear explodes in my veins. He was following our tracks. Dear gods, we led him right to Quancee's chamber . . .

"—maybe you would tell me about her."

"Who?"

"The crystal creature in the chamber. She is part of the old Jemen's story, isn't she? Wasn't he her guardian for over one thousand summers?"

RabbitEar takes a new grip on his spear. "Are you saying you think Quancee is the Old Woman of the Mountain and Arakie was her lone guardian?"

Dear gods, RabbitEar told the Dog Soldier her name. How could he do that?

"I . . . I'm not certain of anything, but if Quancee—that's what she is called?—if she is the Old Woman, I think our stories are wrong."

I have to choose my words with great care, because I have no idea what happened when Quancee saw him step into her chamber. Did she speak with him? Sing to him? Allow him to touch her? She's usually overjoyed to see someone. She might have greeted him with affection.

"You didn't hurt her, did you? You didn't panic and strike her or—"

"No, no! I did not. I swear it! I'm fairly sure you are her new guardian. I wouldn't do that, not when I so desperately need to learn from you."

Some of my terror diminishes, but I'm not certain I can believe him. Arakie trusted me to take care of her. If I return and find Quancee smashed to bits . . .

I rub my brow while the tension drains from my muscles. It takes a few deep breaths before I can find the voice to say, "Volume Delta was sitting right in front of you on the shelf in the rear. If you didn't see it, it's because you couldn't read the title on the spine."

The Dog Soldier swallows hard. As he tightens his grip on his knees, his shirt flashes silver.

"You are right." A long pause. "Now, I've just trusted you with a piece of knowledge that is very dangerous. There are only seven of my people left in the world. If the Rust People know, they will shun us, maybe even kill us for deceiving them. We will vanish from the world forever. You don't want that to happen, do you?"

RabbitEar says, "I wish you'd never been re-created."

"How can you say that, when we are the keepers—"

"I've seen you standing at the rear in battles, supposedly

reading from your sacred books to guide the carnage. Hundreds of our people have died because of your deception! So, if Dog Soldiers vanish from the world, the world will be better off."

From deep inside me, I hear my father's agonized weeping on the day he died. No images accompany the sound, and I'm grateful for that, just disembodied weeping that whispers around my head.

"RabbitEar is right. During the battle where my mother and father were killed, I remember seeing the elder Dog Soldier 'reading' from his open book to Trogon. That's when Trogon sent warriors straight at my fleeing mother and father."

Sticks extends his hands in a pleading gesture. "Try to understand! We must survive, too!"

"Put your hands back on your knees."

The Dog Soldier clasps his knees again. His voice is strained: "Please, will you speak with me?"

I hesitate, fearing what he's about to ask, not sure I can ever tell him the truth about anything, but I say, "Ask your questions."

Gratitude and relief soften his features. "What was it like?" he asks with shining eyes. "Living with one of the Jemen?"

"Don't tell him anything, Lynx. You know he'll go back to the Rust People and tell them every word, and they will use it against Sealion People."

Sticks clutches his knees tighter and stares straight at me. "I will not. My only purpose in living is to—"

"First, Arakie was cantankerous," I answer. "A tyrant on the best of days."

And amazing . . .

Memories of Arakie flood through me and grief overwhelms me. Bowing my head, I watch the sand glimmering with blue reflections, and listen to the faint hissing of the waves.

"But he taught you the magical ways of the Jemen, didn't he? You said you learned to read. Did he teach you how to breathe upon the dead and bring them back to life?"

RabbitEar rolls his eyes. "He's staring at you like you are one of the gods, Lynx. Don't be drawn in by this act. He's evil and you know it. And, by the way, what are we going to do with him?"

"I am not evil," Sticks interrupts. "I—"

"He certainly can't travel with us."

"But I can help you!"

"Really? What are you going to do when we find Trogon and Quiller? Will you help us kill Trogon?"

Sticks seems to shrink in upon himself. "No, no, I can't do that. He is a very great holy man. His visions are true! But—"

"See?" RabbitEar says to me. "We need to kill him quick, so we can be on our way. Quiller is in danger every moment, and we're wasting time talking with this half-human. Let's kill him, take his pack of food, and go!"

RabbitEar drops into a warrior's crouch with his spear aimed. He looks like a hunching wolf in his cape, constantly glancing between me and Sticks, waiting for me to give the word so he can end this Dog Soldier's life. My problem is that I know he's right. If we are in a fight for our lives against Trogon, will Sticks simply stand back and let us kill the Rust People's greatest holy man? Or will our new "friend" leap on us from behind and slit our throats?

If no one believes . . . peace . . . impossible.

The memory of Arakie's voice fills me with hope that there is a way to end centuries of hatred between our peoples. There must be a way. For some time now I've suspected the path is through the Dog Soldiers, for they are revered above all others among the Rust People. Unfortunately, I'm not smart enough to grasp how to use that fact to help my people.

With effort, I grip my spear and rise to my feet. "We can't kill him. We may need him."

"What possible—"

"Rust People consider Dog Soldiers to be sacred, almost supernatural beings. They protect them with their lives. That means he's very valuable. We may be able to exchange him for Quiller when the time comes."

RabbitEar's mouth presses into a tight white line. "You're right. I should have thought of that myself."

33

❄️

QUILLER

Hollow thuds, like monsters galloping, shake the ground and pound away down the torchlit passageway of standing stones.

My nerves hum. This long narrow cavern is completely different from anything we've passed through before. The white walls are porous, filled with large holes that catch the amber gleam and hold it like big clamshell lamps. Thousands of them flicker in every direction, even across the ceiling, and numerous tunnels jut off from this chamber.

Trogon holds his torch near one of the standing stones and whispers, "What is this rock? Almost looks woven. See how the pores and channels spiral around the pillar?"

"Could be a sponge that turned to stone," I suggest and finger it with my bound hands. "That's what it looks like."

As he lowers his torch, light streams between the standing stones, blushing color into them. Over the summers, many of the pillars toppled and shattered, hurling chunks across the floor, but two lines of stones still stand and run straight to the end of this chamber, where they drop into the deep alien night beyond.

"Not going to be easy to walk through this mess."

Trogon sniffs the air. "The air tastes strange here. Did you notice? Rakes the back of my throat. None of the other caverns tasted like this."

"No," I reply. "This tastes like the stale aftermath of fallen gods."

Trogon's eyes wink palely in the ghostly gleam as he reaches out, puts a hand on my shoulder, and shoves me hard to the ground at the base of a standing stone. "We're stopping here for a time, little Quill. I must rest, and this is the perfect place. I can tie you to one of the pillars while I sleep."

"I didn't think you ever slept."

"I must be rested when we meet her. There are things I must do that will require great strength, and the past few days have taught me that she is even more powerful that I thought. Now, lean back against the standing stone and extend your legs in front of you."

While I grudgingly obey, Trogon props his torch against a chunk of fallen stone, and watches me through slits of eyes. His fist is clamped around the end of the rope that wraps my waist.

"Good," he says and circles me, looping the rope around the pillar behind me, then around my throat. The next loop tightens around over my chest. He has enough rope to circle the pillar three times before kneeling behind the pillar, jerking the rope tight, and knotting it. Then he rises and walks back to pick up the torch.

"I'm killing the torch now."

As he grinds it out on the floor, the light vanishes, leaving the chamber in utter darkness.

His steps recede, and I hear him lie down seven paces away. Within ten heartbeats, his breathing has dropped to slow exhausted rhythms.

The longer I keep him awake, the better my chances of ambushing him.

I call, "Are you carrying your daughter's bones in the red bag?"

No answer. Just deep breathing.

"It hisses and rattles when you walk."

"Be quiet."

"At first I thought it was just her spirit in the bag, that she was some kind of spirit helper."

"What would you know of spirit helpers?"

I pause for a short while. "I have spirit helpers."

"Not very good ones or you wouldn't have a rope around your neck. Go to sleep."

"My spirit helpers—"

"Are you trying to keep me awake? Perhaps I should come over there and brain you with my club to keep you quiet so I can rest."

The darkness suddenly breathes as wind eddies down from ahead of us and moves through the standing stones, making them sing in faint sweet voices.

I smell the air, trying to identify scents from the world outside, pines or brush, even the distinctive smell of zyme, but that would mean that these caverns twisted around and headed back toward Mother Ocean. I have no idea where we are beneath the Ice Giants, so I suppose that's possible.

Barely audible, Trogon asks, "Why didn't he marry you?"

"Who?"

"Lynx. You said he was supposed to marry you but ended up marrying the woman who was eaten by lions. Did he think you were too ugly to warm his hides?"

"His wife, Siskin, was small and beautiful, and she was very sentimental. Even small things brought tears to her eyes. I'm not like that."

"Stone-hearted woman, eh?"

"No. Practical."

"I see," he says as though it comes as a great revelation. "No wonder he ran into another woman's arms. You would have murdered his soul, and he knew it. Little Quill, the soul murderer. Devourer of men's dreams."

My gaze drifts around the darkness, wondering if that's how Lynx felt. And if that's how RabbitEar feels married to me now.

Trogon laughs softly. "Be glad your husband's dead, so you won't have to watch his dreams die in your hands."

"He's not dead."

As my eyes adjust to the darkness, I notice there's an almost invisible blue gleam here, seeping down from the chamber above us. The white pillars have a soft glow.

"Isn't he?"

"No. I can feel his heartbeat in my soul."

I hear Trogon turn over to face me. His voice is louder. "Echoes of a dead heart. We all feel them. When you've seen as many summers as I have, they are noisy drumrolls that never stop. It's the sad music of our inner lives."

"Drivel."

He makes a husky sound of amusement. "You would have devoured your children's dreams, too, you know. It's just who you are. You and the Old Woman of the Mountain are more alike than you know. Living on the tears and dreams of others."

"We're nothing alike, you old fool. How can you—"

"There are those who devour and those who get devoured. The Old Woman ate men's tears. You eat men's dreams. You are both devourers."

"You ate your mother's soul."

"Actually, I drank it, but you are quite right. I am also a devourer. Now, close your mouth before you're keeping my mother company."

"You don't frighten me, old witch. I see you for what you are. A monster."

"Hmm." It's a barely audible comment.

I wait for him to speak again, but he merely drifts off to sleep and starts snoring.

I can't bear to believe that my family is dead. RabbitEar would have understood. He's a warrior. Jawbone may have understood, even at the age of eleven summers. But my innocent little girls would have stared up into the faces of their killers and just been bewildered . . .

I have to clench my fists to stave off the hatred that fills me.

Soul murderer.

Devourer of men's dreams.

I feel broken inside. Because it sounds like the truth. I just pray I have the chance to murder Trogon's soul and dreams before he kills me.

Very softly, Trogon says, "You're not nearly as brave as your father was."

"My father?"

"Oh." He yawns. "Did you think we killed him outright when we slaughtered your village? No. We captured as many of your council members as we could. Your father lasted the longest. I was impressed. Interestingly, when I asked him about the worst thing that ever happened in his life, all he could talk about was you and his evil brother."

"What does that mean?"

"It means he felt tremendous guilt about the things that had happened to you as a child."

Staring into the darkness, I listen to the blood pulse in my ears while my thoughts wander, sorting memories before I say, "The things that hide in dark crevices in the Forgotten County?"

A long pause.

"Someday, you must pull them out and turn them over in your hands. He'd want you to."

34

RABBITEAR

Standing at the water's edge with the butt of my spear planted in the sand, I lift my torch and send light pulsing over the cavern, trying to see the distant seashore, but it's too far away, and partially obstructed by the giant wheels that fill the water. What strange powers did the ancient Jemen use to carve these wheels? I am very skilled at crafting stone and bone tools, but the immense size of these wheels leaves me looking up with my mouth open. I'm at a complete loss. The edges of the wheels are as smooth as obsidian and just as dark and shiny, but they are not obsidian. Nor are they iron. I don't know what they are or what they could possibly have been used for.

As I lower the torch, shadows flutter upon the water like thousands of orange wings.

The Dog Soldier, kneeling five paces away, doesn't even open his eyes to watch me. When we first entered this stunning chamber, he cried out and dropped to his knees—reciting a magical incantation, I think. It's annoying because the cavern picks up his words as if all the dead Jemen sleeping in the dark whisper back to him.

I find it unnerving.

Pulling my spear from the sand, I head back toward Lynx, holding the torch aloft. The golden gleam plays over the damp wheels, towering walls, and wet sand underfoot, but dies in the distant reaches of this murky underworld.

Lynx lies flat on his back with his spear beside him and the Dog Soldier's pack close by. Black hair streams around his face. Our stash of extra torches is within his reach, just in case. He's been sleeping soundly, his chest rising and falling. I don't want to wake him. He needs sleep badly. But I'm growing more and more anxious to continue on. I keep hearing Quiller's voice, calling my name; she's just ahead of us, almost close enough to touch. I feel the edges of her soul touching mine, feather light, but there, and I know she needs me.

Planting the torch in the sand, I sit down cross-legged near Lynx and draw my spear across my lap to watch the Dog Soldier. The words he speaks are not human words. I've never heard anything like them, and I have the strange feeling that the last time these caverns heard this language it was spoken by the long-dead gods.

How could he know it? Did the Dog Soldiers keep the words as part of their stories? If so, he could be summoning all manner of evil spirits from the air and water, and I wouldn't know it until invisible hands tighten around my throat. I don't like any of this. Despite his value as a hostage, I think it would have been far wiser to have plunged a spear into his heart and left his body to become just another desiccated relic.

The Dog Soldier bends forward, touching his head to the sand, then rises to his feet and stares in awe at the giant wheels.

"Finished?" I call in a soft voice.

Sticks observes me the way an eagle does a fish glinting in the shallows. His silver cape hangs straight down at his sides, but through the gap in the front I see his ugly rusty pendant.

The Dog Soldier gestures to the torch. "You need to give me the torch today and let me lead the way down into the lower caverns."

"So you can snuff it out and run off into the darkness to find your friend Trogon?"

Sticks looks around at the spectacular creations of the Jemen. "Believe me when I tell you that the last thing I want to do is snuff out the torch. I'm very grateful that you and Lynx—" his eyes glow as he gazes at Lynx—"carry extra torches with you." He extends a hand to the stack of torches resting a short distance away, as though he longs to carry them himself.

Tapping my throat, I ask, "Why do you get that weird reverence in your voice when you say Lynx's name?"

The Dog Soldier stares at me as though I'm clearly an imbecile. "He's the only one alive who has been trained in the sacred ways of the ancient Jemen. He is our link to the amazing knowledge of the past."

"Oh," I say with exaggerated politeness. "Well, that explains everything."

Sticks starts to walk toward me, but when I grip my spear in both hands, he stops and wets his lips. "Do you truly not understand how important he is?"

"Don't forget, I grew up with him. I know him inside and out. You don't."

"No, but . . ." Sticks shifts his weight to his other foot. "I suspect I know things you do not."

"Oh, really? Like what?"

Sticks crouches and spreads his hands in a pleading gesture. "I saw the old Jemen when he died. I was looking straight at him."

I glance at Lynx, and am relieved our voices have not woken him. It would hurt him to know the old man was still alive when he left him on the beach. Guilt will plague him for the rest of his life, as it is. In his dreams, he'll relive that moment over and over, changing the way it happened: dragging Arakie with him into the trees, fighting off the lions that pursue him, reviving the old man and seeing him smile up at him.

I know because I live with that kind of guilt.

When I don't comment, Sticks extends his hands further. "Did you hear me?"

"Of course I heard you. You think I'm deaf."

"No, but . . ." He looks puzzled. "You didn't ask about what I saw."

"I don't care what you saw, and if you mention a word of this to Lynx, I'll spear you through the eyeballs just so I don't have to see that ridiculous awe in your eyes."

Sticks slowly draws back his hands and folds them in his lap. "You're a strange man."

"Me? Dog Soldiers are the strangest of all. I wish your people were extinct so my people could stop speculating about who and what you really are."

Sticks blinks. "Sealion People speculate about Dog Soldiers? What do you say?"

Examining him from the corner of my eye, I reply, "We call you half-people."

"Half-people?"

He's clearly offended, so I add, "Half-people with half brains. I mean, look at your skull." I thrust a hand toward him. "Your heads are so much smaller than ours. And the way you stand in the rear during battles, leaping around, waving your sacred books, and gyrating, you're obviously brutish, more animal than human."

Sticks seems taken aback by that, as I knew he would be. Rust People protect and pamper Dog Soldiers, which means he's been treated as one of the most profound holy men in the world since he was a child. To discover that Sealion People think he is little better than a prancing weasel must be disconcerting.

He looks away to frown at Lynx. "I did not know you felt that way about us. No wonder Lynx will not teach me."

"Of course not. I'm sure he thinks it would be a wasted effort."

Confusion strains his dark face. "A wasted effort?"

"I mean, how much can you learn with that tiny brain of yours?"

Lynx heaves a breath and sits up. "You might want to let me speak for myself on that matter." Stringy black hair frames his face.

"You look like mammoth droppings. How do you feel?"

"Better. Thanks for letting me sleep. I needed it."

"I know you did."

Sticks has gone quiet, as though breathlessly hanging on Lynx's next words.

Lynx uses one hand to comb hair out of his eyes and says, "I'll be back."

As he walks away into the darkness, I stare at Sticks with one brow lifted. "Stop looking at him like you worship him. He's just an ordinary man."

"No," the Dog Soldier says with deepest respect. "He's not. He has read the Rewilding Reports with a Jemen teacher. Blessed gods, I would give everything I have for one moon of studying with him."

"Including your life?" I'm listening to Lynx's night water spatter the ground when I aim my spear at Sticks. "I think I could make that bargain work."

Even with his small brain, the Dog Soldier is smart enough to grasp what I'm implying. He looks at my spear, then shifts to watch Lynx walk out to the shore and lift his gaze to the giant wheels, where the torchlight slips around their massive circumferences and dances over the expanse of sea.

"And what makes you think old Arakie was one of the Jemen?"

"I don't *think* he was. I know he was."

I see Lynx nod, a gesture so faint it's barely noticeable. As he walks back and picks his spear up from the sand, the Dog Soldier's wide eyes follow him.

"I've decided that I will teach you, Sticks."

"What?" I say. "Why?"

"Because he saw what happened when Arakie died." Grief tortures his voice. "I need to hear that story. And all of his stories about the ways the Earthbound Jemen died over the centuries."

"What does it matter now, Lynx?"

Lynx and the Dog Soldier are staring at each other as though they are alone and no one else exists in the world. "His stories will help me make the most difficult decision of my life. It's very important that I hear them."

"An exchange, then?" Sticks says in excitement. "We will teach each other?"

"Yes, when this is over and Quiller is safe."

Sticks prostrates himself before Lynx, touching his forehead to the sand again, groveling, saying, "Thank you, thank you! My people will be so grateful."

"How grateful?" I glare at him.

"What do you mean?" He asks as he straightens.

"I mean, you'd better make sure that Lynx lives through this. Do you understand me?"

The Dog Soldier frowns, then as understanding dawns, I see his face slacken. He's suddenly realized that I just told him he'd better be willing to protect Lynx with his life, which includes killing Trogon when the time comes.

Sticks seems to be weighing the price against the benefits, and isn't sure he can do it.

"I asked if you understood me."

"Yes, I . . ." Sticks jerks a nod. "I do, but you don't

understand what a great holy man he is. I swear to you, his visions come true! We all need his wisdom—"

"Stand up. I don't care what Lynx says, I'm going to kill you right now."

"No, no, please!" He throws up his hands in a gesture of surrender. "I will help you protect the Blessed Lynx. I give you my oath."

"No matter what Trogon says?"

The Dog Soldier looks bereft, but he nods. "Yes. Above all else, my people would want Lynx to live."

As I pass Lynx to pull the torch from the sand, I give him a disgusted look and whisper, "Pick up the pack. Wish you'd waited to tell him you'd teach him. That was leverage."

A small smile turns his lips. "I suppose so. Sorry." He picks up the pack and slings it over his shoulder, then holds out his hand for the torch. "Let me lead today. And stay close to me."

"It's better if I stay close to the Dog Soldier. Besides, I'll be able to see the light for a long way."

As he takes the torch from my hand, he murmurs, "That's not what I meant."

35

QUILLER

Beyond the chamber of broken pillars, there's a staircase.

As I ascend each step, narrow and spiraling endlessly upward into the darkness high above me, I have the feeling I'm heading for the surface now. Trogon pants below me. He's been jerking the torch around constantly, flinching at every sound and shadow. He's terrified. I wonder if he hears a voice that I do not? I hear nothing now, except the sputtering torch and the occasional groans of the Ice Giants.

"If the Old Woman of the Mountain is up here," I call down to him, "the Jemen—or the enemies of the Jemen—went to a lot of trouble to hide her tomb."

"She was evil. Both sides hated her."

I search the stairway and the pure white shaft, carved and polished with such extraordinary care. Moisture beads the walls and flows down the shaft like tears. The stairs are increasingly slimy beneath my boots. "I wouldn't want to be buried here. It's too damp. She must be moldering, which would explain the musty scent wafting down from above. Do you really believe she's up there in that next chamber?"

I can see the rounded shape of it, like a fainter shadow at the head of the stairway above me.

"She's there. She must be."

"Do you still hear her voice?"

"No. It stopped when I went to sleep last night."

"If you don't hear her, maybe she isn't up there. Maybe we should go back and search the tunnels in the pillar chamber. This could be a waste of time, and we're running out of torches."

I stop and look down at him four steps below me. He holds the torch in his left hand and his knife in his right hand. There's one more torch tied to the top of his pack. Only one. He knotted the rope that's tethered around my waist to his right wrist. If I leaped off this stair this instant, I'd fall upon him like a hurled rock, probably knock him down the stairs, and maybe break his foul neck. Unfortunately, bound together as we are, we would tumble over each other all the way to the bottom. I'd be just as dead.

When he tilts his head back to look up at me, I see the sweat glistening across his forehead and flowing down his cheeks. His long beard appears to be beaded over with raindrops.

"Do Rust People stories say why the other Earthbound Jemen didn't simply kill the old woman and her lone guardian?"

"Not really. The Dog Soldiers keep a piece of a story called The Last Days that tells of the capture of the Old Woman, but says nothing of her death."

I say, "If our story about the Old Woman feeding on the tears of the other Jemen is true, then they trapped her forever inside a body made of frozen tears as punishment."

"Yes, but your stories are useless idiocy."

Trogon climbs up the next stair and halts, attentively sniffing the air, listening to the muted resonance coming from distant Giants, his gaze darting this way and that.

"Do you feel her presence here?"

"I feel nothing but cold stone." His voice is like the breath of wind in a swamp, fetid, even from three steps below me. "We only have one torch left. We'll search the next chamber. If she isn't there, we'll go back and search the tunnels among the giant pillars. There's a faint gleam in that chamber. Perhaps we won't have to waste the torch."

I turn and look at the stairs above me, silently counting them. Seventeen. Seventeen steps to the top.

We climb in silence.

When I step off the staircase and into the next chamber, I frown at the massive pile of rubble. It looks like an explosion took down most of the roof and buried this small chamber. It's choked with rocks and what appears to be the wreckage of a white stone gate, elaborately painted with squiggling black lines, just like those in the upper caverns. Locked in darkness, there's something terrifying about this place.

"Maybe they did trap her," Trogon whispers.

I jump, for without my realizing it, the old witch has stepped off the last stair and stands beside me. "You think they collapsed the cave on top of her?"

"How else could they do it? She was the greatest, the most powerful, of the Jemen. No half-measures would have worked. If it was punishment, they had to be sure she could never escape."

Trogon abruptly shifts his torch, and through the jumble of debris, far in the back, something winks. Then there's a prolonged glimmer.

Neither of us speaks.

Like specters in a nightmare, we climb toward it over the rocks.

36

RABBITEAR

The huge creatures piled against the wall are macabre.

Reaching down, I pick up a bone and turn it over in my hand to examine it. Birds in the world outside have wing bones much like this.

My gaze lifts to the bleached-out carcasses again. Giant birds with human legs? Or giant humans with bird wings? They are disturbing in a way I cannot even define. As though the bone burned me, I fling it down, step back, and wipe my fingers on my cape, frightened of being tainted by these monstrosities.

"Why would the Jemen create these . . . things?" I ask a little too loudly. My words bounce off the walls and run around the cavern like lost souls searching for a way out.

Sticks clamps his jaw against the emotion obviously constricting his throat. He keeps trying to swallow it down. "Our stories say that at the very end the Jemen created many abominations, praying that they would survive in the new world created by the Ice Giants."

"Are you sure these aren't the Jemen?"

For several heartbeats, he stares at me. "No. No, I'm not. There are very few descriptions of the Jemen. Most are unbelievable. Giants who flew the skies—"

"These grotesque 'things' might meet that description."

Sticks inhales a deep breath and slowly lets it out, before he asks, "What kind of sounds do you think they made when they died? Did they scream, like we do? Whine like lanced wolves?"

"I don't think we'll ever know."

"If they were birds, perhaps they died in silence, listening to their wings flutter."

Lynx stands by the waves, frowning across the water to the opposite side of the triangular cavern where black handprints cover the translucent white wall.

When I cross the sand to stand with him, he murmurs, "The woman who did this . . ." He shakes his head. "She was utterly mad."

"Do you think she killed the huge winged creatures?"

"It's possible."

I try to imagine why the woman—the Old Woman of the Mountain?—would have hated the winged creatures so much that she would have wantonly slaughtered them and left them on the floor like refuse.

"What kind of weapon could she possibly have used to slice them apart like that?"

"Spears of light."

"What?"

Lynx scans the torchlit caverns descending ahead of us, hewn of pure white stone. They seem to beckon humans to enter and be dwarfed by the magnificence of the lost Jemen.

"It's a story that Arakie told me. I didn't really understand a lot of it, except that the enemies of the Jemen used spears of light to knock the Sky Jemen from the heavens and send them tumbling to earth in streaks of fire. Most drifted down as cinders, but a few drove deep holes in the ground and sleep in the dark underworlds to this day."

My gaze traces the bizarre triangular shape of this cavern. "Dark underworlds, like this place?"

Lynx turns to look at me and torchlight flickers in his eyes. "That's what worries me."

The Dog Soldier kneels to run his hands over the old bones in terrible fascination, whispering to himself. Or perhaps to the winged beasts. In the gleam, an occasional gruesome jaw seems to smile.

Without a word, Lynx holds his torch out before him, and leads the way toward the triangular throat that plunges down into the bowels of the mountain.

"Dog Soldier," I call. "Follow your hero."

Sticks rises, blinks at me, then trots to catch up with Lynx. They're talking, but all I hear is the cavern magnifying their whispers so they sound like serpents.

"Walk three paces behind Lynx. No closer."

Sticks whirls around. "But what harm could it do to allow me to speak with him? I—"

"I don't trust you. Three paces behind. Now." I lift my spear and aim it at his chest.

Sticks glumly drops behind, allowing Lynx to get a full three paces ahead of him before he falls in line again.

Slowly, scanning the shadows, I follow the Dog Soldier's fragile silhouette down toward the pale blur of the next pile of bones.

37

❄

QUILLER

Trogon says, "I told you to climb to the top of the rubble pile!"

"I'm trying! It's not easy walking on top of these rocks, especially not with my hands tied. My feet keep slipping out from under me! Hold the torch higher."

He lifts the torch and yellow light flickers down through the rocks. It's like gazing into an oversized rabbit warren. Narrow tunnels slither around and between the stones, almost as though they were burrowed out by an animal.

"There's a shaft about as wide as my shoulders that leads down through the rocks, but I don't think it's wide enough for my hips to—"

"Climb down." His face is a torchlit vision of terror.

"What if I get wedged in there? How am I going to pull myself out with my hands tied?"

"I'll cut your binds, but try not to be stupid," he says as he uses his knife to slice through the bindings on my wrists, then cuts the rope around my waist.

It's the first time I've been free since we were hiking up the steep mountain trail. Trogon shoves me down atop the stones and points with his knife.

"Now, crawl in there. Tell me what you see."

Rubbing my bloody wrists to get some feeling in my hands,

I study the positions of the rocks. "I have to go in headfirst, I think, on my belly like a snake."

"Do it, then."

Lying down, I slide headfirst into the rocky warren. Smells damp and old. The deeper I go, the more certain I am that an icy draft wafts up from below me, twining through the stones, chilling my face. I try to see through the rocks to what lies below. Nothing's there—shadows leaping through debris—but there is a draft. I'm sure of it.

Long before I reach the bottom, I'm aware of a presence. As I maneuver around the rocks through the feeble wash of torchlight, I feel it—a hunger, a buried rage, and terrifying beauty far beyond my comprehension. Black strings of figures appear behind my eyes, like those in the Story Killer Cave, but these trail out into starry darkness that goes on forever. There's a terrifying strength in the strange patterns, as though they hold the secret to understanding the minds of the ancient Jemen who created me.

As I drag myself between rocks, it whispers alien words that filter through my muscles, shivering them. There's no sound to the voice, but I seem to hear it with my flesh. And it creates an urgency in me. I must find her. The need is overwhelming.

Below, I hear the soft scrape of claws in the darkness, and guess she's another four or five hands deep. Then the amber lamps of eyes open, and I stop. Almost hidden in the rockfall, they glow softly.

"What do you see? Did you find her?"

Trogon is too big to fit into this narrow tunnel, but he's keeping close watch on me from above.

I proceed through the cramped spaces, trying to reach the glimmering eyes. As he shifts the torch, I notice the dark gaping holes in the floor, rimmed with ice crystals, which must be the source of the draft.

"There's ice down here," I call up to him.

He grunts. "It's too warm for ice to form in here. Must be somethin' else."

Using my fingertips to pull myself forward, I have to curl my body around a tight curve and slide forward on my side until the tunnel gets wide enough for me to flip onto my belly again and snake forward. But I see clearly now. There's a frozen pool in the bottom of this cave. Torchlight turns the surface faintly yellow.

Maneuvering between two tight slabs, I drop into the next space between the rocks and see a shape in the pool. Something . . . round.

"It is a frozen pool," I call up. "And there's something in it."

"Are you sure?"

"Yes."

Pushing with my toes, I edge toward it until I'm staring down into a frost-covered face.

"Blessed Jemen," I breathe.

"What is it? What did you find?"

"Don't know yet. There's a haze of frost on the surface of the pool."

"Brush it off!"

"I am."

Clearing away the thick rime takes time. As I work, an odd triangular face gradually appears, pale and perfect. Not of this world. She has her eyes wide open, as though she was staring up at someone in terror when she froze solid.

"It's a young woman," I call.

"Can't be. Must be an old woman. Look closer."

"I'm right on top of her, staring at her frozen face! It's a young woman."

She's still speaking to me in strings of black symbols that spin half-remembered dreams inside me, as though the gods twined these images in my very body so that I could not forget. But I have forgotten and that fact fills me with such sadness . . .

I hear Trogon's heavy feet scrambling over the rocks above me. The torchlight bounces around through the rubble.

"Come out. I want to see for myself!"

The ice feels strangely like wax, and I wonder if it is ice, after all. Maybe it's another bizarre creation of the Jemen? I whisper, "Who are you?"

"Who are you speaking to?"

"The woman."

"Is she . . . is she alive? Is she talkin' back?" Fear trembles his voice. Feet scrambling for purchase again.

"No, she's dead. Frozen solid. I was just—"

"I told you to crawl out of there! I must look upon her with my own eyes!"

Her face shines faintly in the dim reflection of the torch. It's so beautiful, so different from my face. I don't want to leave her now that I've found her. I'm certain she is one of the gods, a lost Jemen of immense power.

"Get out right now!" Trogon furiously shoves his torch into the rocks, as though trying to flush me out.

"I'm coming!" I yell. "It's hard to turn around down here."

When I at last manage to wriggle my way around and start to head back, something deeper in the warren moves. Just a shadow, but I'm so startled I gasp.

"What's wrong?" Trogon calls.

My heart thunders as I stare into the glowing yellow eyes of a wolf. These are the feral eyes I glimpsed earlier. He's lying with his narrow snout resting on his forepaws, watching me, as though I'm a curious vole that just invaded his lair. He's unmistakable. The orange gleam shimmers through his thick coat. He's so still and quiet, I almost can't believe he's real.

Arakie's wolf.

Neither of us moves.

An otherworldly sensation creeps through me and I feel as though I'm floating high above my body, hovering near the ceiling. Through the rubble, I see Wolf's eyes. The torchlight has turned them into dancing flames.

I mouth the words, *What are you doing here?*

His chin lifts slightly.

There were no wolf tracks in the caverns above. How did he get here? Probably a silly question. If he spent any time at all with Arakie, this animal trotted down hundreds of tunnels and passageways in search of lemmings. One of the black holes in the floor, the source of the draft, must lead into that maze.

Did Wolf dig the burrow through the rocks so he could lie here and guard her? In utter darkness?

A strange act.

Perhaps someone sits here with him? Someone with a torch? But I see no human footprints.

"If you don't crawl out of there in the next—"

"I'm coming!"

I wriggle through the warren until I reach the top of the rubble pile, then slip out on my belly. "You're never going to be able to get to her. It's too narrow in there."

Shoving me aside, Trogon squints down, trying to see the woman buried beneath the jumble of roof fall. "I can't see anythin' down there except rocks. Are you lyin' to me?"

"No, there's a woman down there in a frozen pool."

"If her face is frozen, how can you be sure it isn't an old woman?" Desperation tinges his voice. "The ripples in the ice could be distortin' the image."

"There are no ripples in the ice. Once I brushed away the frost, it turned crystal clear."

"There are always ripples and ice bubbles in ponds. Given the roof fall, there must also be a lot of dirt clouding the pool."

That's an interesting comment, because he's right. There should be. The pool grows more intriguing by the moment.

"If she was frozen very quickly, there would have been no time for bubbles or ripples to form, and no time for dirt to fall into the pool around her. But the ice does feel strange, like frozen wax."

Trogon's gaze darts over the rubble as though he's considering that possibility. "But it's so warm in here, how could it be?"

"There's an icy draft down there. It probably keeps the pool right at freezing. When she fell in—"

"She didn't fall in." He makes a deep-throated sound of disgust. "She was buried here, then they collapsed the cave on top of her to keep her soul locked in darkness forever."

That makes me sit up straighter. "Like a witch?"

"Of course. She was the most hated of the Jemen." Trogon's breath hisses through his nostrils, sounding loud in this small cave.

"I—I don't think she's the Old Woman of the Mountain."

"She can't be anyone else! Like a bison calf, they drove her and her lone guardian back into this cave, dragged her down, and locked her in a freezing pool forever. Where's her lone guardian?"

I'm staring at the place where the wolf hides beneath the rubble when I answer, "No idea."

Trogon blinks. "That is odd, but you led me right to her, just as my vision said you would."

I shove dirty red hair away from my eyes while I stare at him. His fear taints the air with stale sweat. He must be expecting something, something he has not told me about. Something he saw in his vision. In the dazzle of fluttering torchlight, his bottomless eyes are huge.

"I thought your vision showed you an old wom—"

"I saw old eyes, little Quill, ancient eyes, staring at me

through utter darkness. But I knew it was her, just as I know now this is her tomb."

A soft tingle, like an insect's footsteps, creeps up the back of my neck.

"I must get her out of that pool, and you must help me. She wishes to speak with you, too." Trogon turns and plants the torch between two rocks. "If I can't crawl down there, then we need to move the rocks off her. In the vision, she told me I must lie beside her in her grave."

"Why?"

"Doesn't matter why. I have to do it. Help me with the rocks."

I give him a dubious look. "Some of the rocks are huge. I can't carry them."

"We're not going to carry the biggest rocks, fool. We'll roll them away from her tomb." The torch splutters and almost flickers out. "At least, the stones we can roll away."

"You'd better light that last torch," I warn. "That one is dying fast."

Trogon tugs the last fresh torch from where it's tied to his pack and uses the dying torch to light it. As flames lick through the shredded bark, Trogon tosses the dead torch aside and glances around. "Start pickin' up the smaller rocks and throwin' them down toward the bottom of the rubble pile. I don't think either of us wishes to be in this cave when the last torch dies."

"You're right."

Rising, I grab a rock and heave it, watching as it bounces away down the rubble pile. All the while, I'm remembering the bizarre story he told me about the bird who rolled the stone away from the tomb so that the dead could take wing and flap away to the Road of Light.

Trogon begins lifting and throwing larger rocks.

Amid the loud clattering and banging, Wolf lies completely silent, still as death.

38

✳

RABBITEAR

The chamber is strewn with chunks and splinters of broken white pillars. We walk between the two lines of magnificent standing stones, Lynx in the lead with the torch, then the Dog Soldier, and finally, I bring up the rear.

I step lightly in this realm of the dead, listening intently to the darkness, for I feel ghostly presences moving around me, Earthbound Jemen who perished hundreds of summers ago, but are not gone from this place. On occasion, I glimpse shadows with legs, dodging behind pillars, or leaping away into the light.

We pass what I think was once an altar. Piecing the shattered chunks together in my head, it seems to have been square, painted black and red, a gleaming shape that shines in the torchlight. There's something terrifying about the stark simplicity of the wreckage. Two long rows of pillars leading to an altar. Did they make sacrifices to bizarre gods here? Offerings . . .

Lynx leans over the black squiggles on a chunk of stone, and haltingly says, *"Las . . . ciate . . . ogne . . . sper . . . anze."*

"You read that?" I ask in awe. "What does it mean?"

"Not certain. Something about abandoning hope. It may be a warning, ordering us not to enter."

Ahead of me, the Dog Soldier calls, "We keep a story called The Stoneworkers. It speaks of a time the Jemen dredged white pillars from deep in the sea and flew them across Mother Ocean on the backs of giant birds. The pillars came from a long-gone civilization of temple builders, master stoneworkers who covered the world with vast villages of white sculpted columns like these."

Lynx leans on his spear and lifts his torch higher. "Why didn't the Jemen use their own magic to carve pillars like these? Doesn't make sense that they would pull them from deep beneath the ocean, strap them to the backs of birds, and fly them here."

Sticks moves closer to him. "I suppose not, but the stoneworkers from the lost civilization were their distant ancestors. When they realized the last days were upon them, they didn't want the artifacts and ruins of the glorious stoneworkers to perish with them, so they brought them here to protect them for us—in a future they could not even imagine. Did the old Jemen tell you stories about—"

"Dog Soldier," I say just loud enough for him to hear me. "Step away from Lynx. You're too close."

The dark man turns to frown at me, flaps his arms against his sides in frustration, and halts to allow Lynx to get farther ahead of him. By now, Lynx is so accustomed to me giving the Dog Soldier commands to step back that he doesn't even turn around, just continues down the lane of white pillars with the torch held high.

Sticks says, "Can't I even speak to him from a distance?"

"No."

"But why not? What could—"

"Close your mouth. Are you trying to give away our position to your friend Trogon?"

He grits his teeth, before replying, "No."

"Sure, you weren't. Get in back in line, three paces behind Lynx."

"If I can't speak with Lynx, may I speak with you? Your

people are very primitive, but there may be stories you tell that are worth keeping."

"I told you to get back in line. Do it."

"But what if I tell you the stories my people have kept? They explain so much about what happened—"

"Get in line *now*."

Sticks grudgingly marches forward to the required distance, three paces behind Lynx.

As Lynx passes, the side tunnels briefly come alive with torchlight, revealing chunks of wood and metal, and colorful fragments of glossy materials I do not recognize. Occasionally, I see skulls that are strangely shaped, but clearly human. Brown and shiny, they rest canted on their sides. The empty eye sockets seem to turn to peer at me as the torch passes by. Just skulls. No other bones. Decapitated Jemen? Or the enemies of the Jemen?

Quiller's tracks are crystal clear in the strewn debris at my feet. Trogon was walking off to her left, behind her.

Reluctantly, I call, "Dog Soldier, I've changed my mind. Come walk with me."

Sticks trots back to my side and expectantly stares at me.

"Do you know what happened here in these caverns?"

Excited, he responds, "I think I know some things, but not all of the story. My people kept a story fragment called The Last Days. It speaks of a rebellion—civil war between the Jemen. The traitors stormed the Old Woman's cavern stronghold. There was a horrifying battle. The enemy fell by the thousands, but kept coming. That's why the Earthbound Jemen had to hack the cages apart and make a run for it with their precious animals in their arms."

Glancing back over my shoulder toward the entry far above us, I ask, "If the enemy stormed the caverns from up there, the place we entered, how did the Earthbound Jemen escape? Is there another way out?"

Sticks shrugs. "We don't have that story. I don't know."

I'm thinking about Lynx's tale of finding the final resting place of the Earthbound Jemen and their animals, but I'm not about to discuss it with this strange half-human. "What happened to the enemies of the Jemen? If they won the battle—"

"The Old Woman of the Mountain stayed behind spinning balls of the fire from the air, and casting them at the approaching army." Sticks nervously licks his lips. "But they leaped upon her like ferocious dogs and captured her."

Mesmerized by his telling, I can't take my eyes from his face. "Then what happened?"

He shrugs. "They imprisoned her and one lone guardian in a cave from which she could never again escape."

"Did they kill her?"

"All we know is that she died. We do have one sentence of story that says they carried her dead body away with them to the campfires of the dead. But that's an aberrant story fragment. Probably not true, and that's why Elder Trogon's vision is so important. If we can find her—"

"The enemies of the Jemen flew to the campfires of the dead, just like the Sky Jemen? I've never heard that."

Sticks nods. "Oh, yes, they did. In our story, called The Exile, the enemies of the Jemen chased the Sky Jemen all the way down the Road of Light until they forced them to fly out into the darkness beyond the campfires of the dead."

Behind my eyes, I'm imagining it, seeing the inexorable approach of black permanent oblivion. Sailing on in my ship of light . . .

Slowly, dimly, I begin to understand why the Rust People consider Dog Soldiers sacred. These stories are mesmerizing.

"Do you think our stories preserve different parts of what happened?"

"Until a few days ago, I believed—Dog Soldiers believe—your people are too primitive to have valuable story fragments, but I no longer believe that. Lynx studied with the last Jemen. I'm convinced that he now keeps the most important story fragments of all."

"You actually believe Arakie was over one thousand summers old?"

"I've thought a lot about it in the past few days. There's no doubt in my mind but that he was the Blessed Caretaker from our story, The Doctor, who was condemned to live a thousand summers for his crimes."

As his words resonate through the flickering torchlight, we pass one towering pillar after another, heading toward the end of this long narrow chamber where another square of darkness awaits us. Icy drafts have begun to flow across the floor, chilling my legs. It's been so warm down here that the draft makes me wonder if there's a huge crevasse ahead that's cracked open the surface and plunges this deep. Are we heading for the brink of a freezing abyss?

I fill my lungs, tasting the underworld's ancient cavernous breath.

The nearer we get to the black opening, the colder it gets, and the Ice Giants start making a bleating chorus that resembles a herd of mountain goats warning each other of an approaching pride of giant lions.

Another fifty paces of difficult walking through chunks of rock and crushed stone, then I see Lynx halt. His torch flickers over a white staircase that spirals upward. It's a stunning sight, breathtaking.

"What's that?" I turn to Sticks. "Do you have a story about that?"

He cocks his ear and whispers, "No, but hear the thumps? Sounds like giants walking."

39

---- ❄ ----

LYNX

From just behind my shoulder, RabbitEar whispers, "Someone clearing rocks?"

Moving into the shining white shaft, I stop short and look up. The torchlight reveals winding steps that spiral upward into darkness. The erratic bangs and thuds continue, along with groans.

"Has to be Quiller and Trogon," I whisper back, then search for the Dog Soldier. "Where's Sticks?"

"Just to the left of the entry. You can't see him, but I can." RabbitEar's eyes narrow as he apparently glares at the Dog Soldier. "I told him not to make a sound or I'd kill him." He pauses, before adding, "I should have probably threatened to kill you instead, since he seems to think you're some sort of holy relic."

I step back, forcing RabbitEar to retreat into the chamber of standing stones, and see Sticks watching us with his fists clenched at his sides. Unslinging the pack from my shoulder, I drop it to the floor. Huge chunks of pillars inscribed with more Latin phrases shine around our feet. An old, old language I was only smart enough to partially learn. Now, with Arakie's death, I must ask Quancee to teach me.

RabbitEar, taking no chances, keeps his spear aimed at the Dog Soldier's chest. I don't know what to make of Sticks. He clearly thinks I'm something I'm not, but I can't worry about that now.

I say, "The spiral staircase is very narrow."

RabbitEar's jaw grinds while he examines Sticks. "I know. We'll have to climb in single file."

"But whoever steps off the top stair will be in plain sight of Trogon and a perfect target."

"That's why I get to go first," RabbitEar says in a voice that brooks no disagreement. "I'm much better with a spear than you are."

"Can't argue with that." I tip my chin toward Sticks. "What about him?"

"He can't come with us. We have no way of knowing what he'll do when he sees his sacred elder, the man he considers to be the most powerful holy man in the world. Well . . ." Rabbit-Ear flicks a hand at me. "Except maybe you."

RabbitEar is obviously annoyed by Sticks' awe-filled manner when he speaks with me, and why wouldn't he be? I'm the cowardly boy from Sky Ice Village who got tears in his eyes every time he had to spear a fish for supper. The boy who spent his entire life letting his best friend Quiller fight his battles for him. Even though RabbitEar says he believes I will one day be a great Sealion spirit elder, I am not now, and he knows it.

"If we tie Sticks up and gag him, he could still make enough noise to signal Trogon that we're coming."

RabbitEar uses one hand to smooth his red beard and takes a tighter grip on his spear with the other. For my ears alone, he whispers, "Then why hasn't he done it already? He can hear the thumps as well as we can."

Sticks straightens. "May I answer that question?"

"No," RabbitEar says, and tells me, "We have no choice, Lynx. You have to stay and guard him. If he opens his mouth to yell, kill him quick."

I try to imagine myself doing that and bow my head to stare at the debris on the floor. "Let me go first. I might be able to reason with Trogon."

"That's ridiculous! He's the evilest man alive. As soon as he glimpses your face, he's going to spear you to death."

"Please," Sticks says, "let me speak with Elder Trogon? He'll listen to me."

RabbitEar gives the Dog Soldier a grim disbelieving look. "That's what I'm afraid of. If you stick your head into the chamber and tell Trogon to kill my wife, he'll do it without a thought."

"But I won't do that, because you'll be right behind me on the stairs and you'll kill me. Lynx must go last. He'll be safest there."

"And we have to protect Lynx with our lives, correct?" RabbitEar says in irritation.

Sticks blinks at RabbitEar, as though the answer to that question is obvious, and he doesn't understand why RabbitEar shows such hostility about a simple fact. "Of course."

When I shift the torch to my other hand, the light flashes from the white pillars and casts long moving shadows across the floor. It's unsettling, for they resemble an army of dark ghosts rising up from the ruins. "RabbitEar, I'd rather go first."

He pauses for a long while, studying the Dog Soldier, before he replies, "No, now that I think about it, I'm sure Sticks has to go in first carrying the torch. Then you, Lynx. You'll be right behind him with a knife held to his back. The fear that you are about to kill his sacred Dog Soldier might be enough to make Trogon hesitate. Then you push Sticks ahead of you into the chamber, making room for me to climb up, get a clear aim, and I'll spear Trogon through the heart."

Sticks closes his eyes in pain. "You don't know what you're doing."

RabbitEar pulls his knife from his belt and gives it to me handle first. It's a beautiful weapon, made of mammoth tusk, ground to a sharp point. "Don't hesitate for an instant, Lynx. If you have to kill Sticks to save one of us, just do it."

Trading him my spear for his knife, I use it to gesture at the Dog Soldier. "Sticks, don't force me to do that. Come over here." I extend the torch for him to take.

Sticks walks forward with his arms spread wide and takes the torch from my hand. "I gave you my oath that I would help protect you and I will. But I won't help you kill Trogon. Can you understand that?"

Our gazes are locked when RabbitEar says, "Fine. But if he tries to kill Lynx and you don't throw yourself in front of him, I'm spearing you first."

Sticks looks as though he doesn't quite know how to answer that.

"Get going," RabbitEar orders.

Walking into the white shaft, Sticks uses the torch to survey the staircase spiraling above him before he places his boot on the first step, and slowly starts climbing up.

"One step at a time, Sticks," I whisper. "I'll be right behind you."

"I understand."

It's incredibly wet in here. Beads of water trickle down the walls like rainfall, and drain away into cracks in the floor. When I glance down at RabbitEar, I see him climbing two stairs below me with his jaw clenched and his eyes blazing. He's clutching both spears tightly, ready to kill Trogon the instant we step off the last stair into the chamber above us. I'm sure all he can think of is rescuing his wife from the beast who captured her.

I'm thinking the same thing. Quiller is my best friend and I love her. I'll do anything to make sure she's safe.

40

❄

QUILLER

Trogon is deep in the hole when he puts his shoulder to a huge rock and rolls it out of the way, seemingly so focused on clearing away the path to the frozen woman that he's missed the subtle sounds coming up the throat of the staircase.

I have not.

I thought I heard soft voices earlier, but it could have been the drafts whispering through this chamber. But now I'm certain I hear barely audible boot steps on the stairs. At least two people, maybe three. If they were Rust People they'd simply call out to Trogon. For several moments, I've been trying to figure out who they might be, and my heart is bursting with hope that it's RabbitEar. Mink could be with him and another Sealion man. An elder who was once a warrior, perhaps? If so this has been a very hard journey for him. He'll be exhausted.

The other possibility is that it's Lynx and Arakie. Maybe the old man was not dying, but just ill, and when he felt better, he accompanied Lynx on the journey to find me?

The first possibility seems far more likely.

So, I'm completely surprised when torchlight flutters up the shaft, and an unknown man calls, "Elder Trogon? It's me. Are you all right?"

Trogon is so startled, he drops the rock he's just lifted,

scrambles up out of the hole, and pulls his knife from his belt. Staring breathlessly at the fluttering torchlight, he calls, "Sticks? Is that you?"

"Yes, Elder."

"What are you doing here? I ordered you to stay and guard the old man and—"

Sticks climbs up and steps into the cave with Lynx behind him, holding a knife to Sticks' back. Lynx looks petrified. Sweat-drenched black hair clings to his cheeks, and I can see his knife hand shaking from all the way across the chamber. When our eyes lock, such relief surges through me that I'm lightheaded.

Trogon snatches my arm and drags me close to use as a shield. The point of his knife presses painfully into my throat. "Ah, Lynx!" Trogon shouts. "Drop the knife and step away from Sticks with your hands open or I'll kill your old lover!"

Lynx's gaze darts around the chamber, as though watching invisible figures leaping through the shadows. "Let her go, or I'll kill your sacred Dog Soldier."

Trogon keeps a tight hold on me, but removes the knife from my throat. "If you lower your weapon, I will lower mine. We must speak! There's more at stake here than you know."

Lynx shoves Sticks deeper into the chamber. "The only thing I care about is Quiller. Release her, and we will leave!"

Trogon chuckles. "You won't want to leave as soon as you realize who's buried down there."

Sticks calls, "Blessed Elder, did you find the Old Woman of the Mountain?"

"Yes." Trogon points down into the hole. "She's right here. Buried beneath this pile of rubble. We've cleared most of the rocks that cover her."

A strange expression comes over Lynx's face. The knife he

holds pressed into Sticks' back lowers, and it feels like my heart just fell out of my chest. *What's he doing?*

"Elder Trogon," Lynx calls. "She's dead, isn't she?"

Trogon eyes him suspiciously. "Yes, but—"

"Let me bring her back to life. The old Jemen, Arakie, taught me how."

Stunned, I stare at him. He said the words in such a commanding voice that even I believe him. So does Trogon, I can see it on his face.

"I knew it!" Heedless of the knife at his back, Sticks whirls around to stare wide-eyed at Lynx.

Trogon shouts, "Let's call a truce and talk about this!"

As the Dog Soldier shifts his torch, I see the shadow of someone still in the shaft. Blessed gods, surely Trogon sees it, as well. A small horrible smile turns his lips. His grip on my arm tightens. He's going to kill me if the person in the shaft emerges holding a weapon. I'm of no use to him now, except to heft rocks.

"Lynx, listen to me," I call. "I'm not lying. There really is a strange woman down there."

The shadow in the shaft leaps, as though alarmed at the dreadful sound of my voice.

"Yes," Trogon shouts. "I call a truce! This is more important than any of us realize. She's right here. Can't you hear her voice calling to you?"

The color drains from Lynx's face. "He told me not to try and find her."

"Who? The dying old man? Forget about him. We have found her!" Trogon says.

Lynx slowly, inexorably, pulls his knife away from the Dog Soldier's back, holding it out to the side. "I agree to the truce. But you must toss your knife aside first."

Trogon shakes his head. "Not until your friend still down the shaft comes out."

Lynx turns slightly to call down the shaft, "Come out. And don't make me a liar by violating a truce I just agreed to."

A voice I know as well as my own answers, "You're a fool, Lynx. But I'm coming out."

RabbitEar climbs up the last step with his empty hands lifted above his head. He's wearing a wolf-hide cape with the hood up. The wolf's ears seem to prick when he steps into the chamber and stands just behind Lynx. Lynx is taller, but RabbitEar's shoulders are much wider, packed with muscle.

Where's his spear? He must have a spear.

A sob works up my throat before I can stop it. If he's alive, surely my children must also be alive.

RabbitEar gives me a loving smile, then glances meaningfully at Trogon.

I don't even consciously think about it, for my body knows exactly what he means. I grab Trogon's knife hand and hurl myself toward the floor. The force of the impact makes him let go of the knife. Before he can react, I've grabbed it and plunged it into the big artery in his thigh. Trogon cries out, and lunges for the knife. As we struggle for the weapon, I roll over the torch planted in the rocks. Heat sears my back and I can smell my hair burning before I snuff out the torch.

"Stupid little fool!" Trogon rips the knife away from my hand and shoves me aside like a rag doll. I'm slapping at my burning hair when I hear the hiss.

It's loud in the rock-filled chamber.

"Blessed gods, RabbitEar!" Lynx cries.

Trogon weakly drops his knife. As it clatters through the rocks, I scramble to my feet and see the spear sticking through his left shoulder. With an inhuman cry, he breaks off the spear, then yanks the rest of the broken shaft from his flesh and tosses it away.

"What have you done?" Sticks screams, "We had a truce!"

RabbitEar doesn't waste time answering. He tears the knife from Lynx's hand, and bounds up through the rubble, headed for Trogon with death in his eyes.

41

QUILLER

Before RabbitEar can reach him, Trogon staggers for the hole we've cleared over the burial and slithers down into the tunnel.

RabbitEar rushes to me and takes me in his arms, holding me tightly, kissing my burned hair. "You all right?"

"Yes. Glad to see—"

"I knew I couldn't trust you!" Sticks slams the torch against the floor, beats the flames into oblivion, and plunges the cave into utter blackness.

RabbitEar stops dead, then I hear him almost silently move away. I get on my belly and slither in the opposite direction, heading toward Trogon's pack. We are both warriors. Neither of us wishes to be sitting in the last place Sticks or Trogon saw us. A knife cast in the darkness can still hit its target if it hasn't moved.

My rapid breathing suddenly seems immensely louder. It's absolutely black in here, and the sense of disorientation is extreme. In the rubble below, I hear Trogon grunting as he shoves aside the heaviest rocks around the pool, rocks I could not budge.

Is Wolf still down there, or did he slide away into one of the frost-rimmed tunnels in the floor?

When I try to listen, I distinctly hear Trogon and something else breathing. Must be Wolf. What's he doing? This is not wolfish behavior at all. It's as if he's been waiting centuries for exactly this moment to come to pass and all he has to do now is watch.

Trogon laughs. "Just as I saw . . . in my vision, I'm—I'm in her grave, little Quill. Can you hear her voice now? She's calling to you. Why don't you come . . . come down here and lie with us?"

Lightheaded terror chills my soul, for I long to go down there and do exactly that—lie beside her even if Trogon is there with us. Like a forbidden longing, I can't let something so beautiful, powerful, slip away. Vague images cascade through my mind, glistening places I have never been, forests carved of crystal that sing with the echo of every breath. In them lurks a black fire that I must touch, no matter the cost.

Trogon says, "Come, little Quill. Come and . . . and warm yourself . . . in this pool of hot blood."

My thoughts are racing. I didn't get a very good look at his wound, but I thought the spear was lodged too high to have clipped Trogon's left lung. However, if his blood is already filling the pool, he's bleeding badly. RabbitEar's spear may have cut the big artery above Trogon's heart.

Blessed Jemen, please let it be so.

Gravel screeches. "The pool is melting, little Quill. I can see her face now. Blessed gods, she's magnificent. She has blue eyes. Shining and beautiful."

I frown. It's utterly black, how can he see anything?

"Please?" the Dog Soldier calls. "Let me go to him? I may be able to stanch the flow of blood—"

"Stay where you are," Lynx says.

"But this is not how his vision ends! In his vision, he kills her and she flies away to the Road of Light. You must let me help him, so he can save her!"

"Don't move," Lynx says with deadly intent.

I can't hear RabbitEar. I have no idea where he is.

Where's the torch I rolled over? I feel for it. When I touch it, my fingers close around the shaft and I quietly draw it across my lap, then continue lightly patting the floor until my hand brushes what feels like slick fish skin. The silver cloth of Trogon's pack.

"I can't see you," Trogon whispers. " . . . empty skin filled with blood . . . you still there?"

My hand reaches around inside the pack, shoving aside the book, the lumps of rust, until I find the strikes-a-light.

"You . . . you're all hollowed out, just the shape . . . of a red woman driftin' in darkness. She's coming through . . . coming through the clouds of blood for you." A long pause. "Sticks? Sticks? You there?"

"Yes, Elder! I'm over here."

"Come here, please."

Feet crunch gravel. "He needs me!"

"*Don't.*" Lynx says.

"Why can't I go to him? What does it matter now?"

I've never used a strikes-a-light before, so it takes me a while to feel for the proper position to hold it, then I strike it. A spark flies. Holding it to the head of the torch, I strike it again and again. Finally, the spark catches in the warm bark and a tiny flame flickers to life.

Three paces away, RabbitEar crouches, poised just over the tunnel where Trogon disappeared, looking down with brilliant eyes. The knife is gripped in his tight fist. The instant the torch bursts into full flames, RabbitEar leaps down into the tunnel, hunting his prey, going in for the final kill.

Frantic barking and snarling erupt, and RabbitEar clambers back out of the tunnel. Breathing hard, he turns to me with wide eyes. "Lynx's wolf is down there! He's guarding Trogon."

"My . . . *my wolf*?" Lynx asks as though stunned. "You mean Xeno?"

"Yes, Xeno. He attacked me!" RabbitEar lifts his bloody hand to show Lynx the slashes.

Lynx glances at the Dog Soldier and backs away from him, heading for RabbitEar, calling, "Xeno? Xeno, come here."

Trogon laughs again, but the sound gurgles in his throat. "I can touch her now. She's slick . . . with blood . . . I feel her face. She's blinking."

RabbitEar and Lynx both turn to look at me and I shake my head. "I don't know what's happening. She was frozen solid when I saw her."

"Quiller, bring the torch over," RabbitEar says. "Let's see if we can get a better look."

Rising to my feet, I walk over and hold the torch above the tunnel. Torchlight flickers down through the rocks, casting a maze of shadows.

It's a bizarre sight.

Trogon lies on his side, curled around the woman. As blood rhythmically pumps from his chest and leg wounds, it fills the pool where she rests. Her eyes are wide open, but unmoving. I suspect the blood just melted the top layer of ice and that's why they appear so lifelike. Xeno, the wolf, is stretched out on the opposite side of the woman with his fangs bared, apparently guarding both the dead woman and Trogon.

Trogon groans and his hand feebly reaches down for the red bag on his belt. Bones rattle. "Breathe upon her . . . bring my daughter . . . back to life . . . as you promised."

His gaze is fixed upon the red bag, as though waiting to see the bones spring to life, when his body suddenly tenses up, then relaxes, and his jaw gradually gapes open.

More dream memories rush behind my eyes with such force I have to brace my feet to keep standing. Broken statues lie in an azure field of alien grass surrounded by tangles of bodies. Among them are the twisted metallic fragments of fire-blackened ruins. Shrill wails rise and fall with the wind.

"Is—is he dead?" I stammer. "Let me go down there? Let me make sure."

RabbitEar says, "Wait."

"Give me the knife!" I say and hold out my hand. "I have to go down there."

RabbitEar steps toward me, and wraps one arm around me to hold me tight. "Give it a few more moments, then I'll go down. You don't have to be near him ever again."

I hold onto him with all the strength I have left in my starving body. The steady rhythm of his breathing comforts me and eases the horrific longing rushing in my blood.

When we hear the last breath escape from Trogon's mouth, RabbitEar releases me. Together, we watch it condense in the cold air. For a time, it hovers above the blood pool, before dissipating like fog in sunlight.

"I think he's finally dead," Lynx murmurs.

Sticks bursts into tears. "No, no, it wasn't supposed to end this way. He's supposed to be alive! The Old Woman is supposed to be dead!"

When I glance at Lynx, I find him staring down at Xeno with a strange expression. The wolf has started lapping up the blood and meltwater that covers the woman's body. His muzzle is soaked with it. It's as though he's trying to clean her face so he can look into her eyes to see . . . what?

"I'm going down to make sure Trogon is dead," RabbitEar says. "Can you call your wolf out?"

Lynx kneels on the rocks. "Xeno? Come. Come!"

The wolf ignores him entirely and continues licking the woman's body. As she comes clean, I can tell she's seen around twenty-five to thirty summers . . . or may be much, much older.

How can I tell the age of the most powerful Jemen to have ever lived? Perhaps when she reached a certain age she stopped aging. She has shoulder-length, straight blond hair, like the Rust People, but her face and body are not at all like Rust People—or Sealion People. She's tall and slender in comparison to us. Where we have big heavy skulls, hers is fine-boned and triangular with a pointed chin. She's staring up through wide unblinking blue eyes.

"What do you see?" Sticks calls. "May I come over? Someone must care for Elder Trogon's body."

RabbitEar gives the Dog Soldier a cursory glance. "Stay where you are."

Lynx extends a hand to the wolf. "Xeno? I told you to come. Come now!"

Xeno twists his head to look up at Lynx, and I swear those are defiant human eyes in his head. He growls, and goes back to licking the woman's face.

Lynx gets to his feet. "He's not going to listen to me until he's finished. If he does then."

Annoyed, RabbitEar says, "I thought he was your wolf?"

"I told you, he's not a pet. Let's wait. He'll be finished soon enough. Besides, given the amount of blood in that pool, Trogon obviously bled to death."

"I'm not going to be sure of that until I touch his dead eyeballs," RabbitEar insists.

When the sound of growling erupts, all three of us look down into the tunnel again. The wolf has crawled onto the woman's chest to snarl in her face.

None of us can move.

"Can't . . . be . . ." RabbitEar whispers.

42

❄

LYNX

Sobbing . . .

Faint, rising up from the depths of the hole, I'd swear it's the same woman's voice I heard echoing across the mountain slope outside.

Sticks comes toward us. "Tell me what's happening!"

"He must still be alive. Move out of the way, Lynx." Rabbit-Ear shoves me aside.

"Those aren't Trogon's sobs!"

"Move! I'm going down in that hole, even if I have to kill your wolf."

"Let me go!" Quiller cries. "I want to go down there!"

"No, Quiller, I have to be the one." I grab RabbitEar's sleeve to stop him. "I don't think Xeno will kill me, but he may kill both of you."

RabbitEar exchanges a look with Quiller, then nods. "All right, but make sure the old witch is dead first thing. Understand?"

"Yes, of course."

As I jump down into the hole, the coppery odor of blood gets stronger. I can taste its distinctive tang at the back of my throat. There's an elaborate warren down here. Tunnels run off in every direction beneath the rubble pile, and dark holes gouge the floor. Wolf tracks fill every tunnel and hole I can see in the torchlight. It suddenly occurs to me that all those times Xeno vanished for weeks at a time, he may have been coming here. Why would he do that?

Xeno's bright yellow eyes watch me descend into his lair, but he makes no hostile moves. His long body covers the woman. I can't see anything but her arms and legs in the pool of blood.

When I drop down into the hole beside him, Xeno goes completely still, like a stuffed wolf skin. I ease one hand toward Trogon's throat where he rests on his side curled around the woman.

"Is she waking up?" Quiller asks in a shaking voice.

"I'm checking Trogon, and I don't feel a heartbeat."

"Touch his eyes," RabbitEar orders.

I reach out to touch Trogon's eyeball. He doesn't flinch or blink. "Yes, he's dead. No doubt about it."

Quiller lifts a hand to stifle a sob. The last time I saw her in tears, she had seen six summers. I have no idea what Trogon did to her after he captured her, but . . .

Xeno lets out a low ferocious growl.

"It's all right," I say and cautiously stroke his back. "How did you get down here? Are you all right?"

The wolf exhales a breath that frosts in the cold air, then he rises and moves off the woman to lie on the floor a short distance away, his muzzle dripping.

"You're certain Trogon is dead?" RabbitEar asks.

"Yes, RabbitEar, I'm certain. You killed him."

"Thank the gods," Quiller says.

When I brush aside Trogon's beard and see the woman's face, I am mesmerized. Her blue eyes reflect the torchlight like pools of crystal-clear water. Xeno has licked most of her face clean, but her blond hair is blood-soaked.

Craning my neck, I look up at RabbitEar where he perches

on the rocks above me. "It would help if you could crawl down here with the torch, so I can see better. I need to—"

RabbitEar's sudden intake of breath makes me go rigid.

"Did you see that?" RabbitEar asks.

"What?"

"I thought I saw her blink before you crawled down there, but now I'm sure of it. She's waking up!"

Quiller's fuzzy red halo of hair flickers orange in the torch's gleam. Tears run down her cheeks. "I knew it."

Movement, beside my foot. A sickening blend of curiosity and fear races through my veins. It's her hand, twitching.

When her face contorts and tears drain down her cheeks, I scramble backward, clawing at the rocks to get away from this strange creature that was dead but is coming back to life.

In a feeble voice, she says, "Someone . . . Can you hear me?"

I'm suddenly possessed by the unshakable feeling that I'm little more than a spectral dancer whirling through a shadow-like world at the birth of some horrific apparition.

When she drags herself to a sitting position and drops her face into her hands, I see the shape of her body in the melted wax. A shiver goes through her. "Where am I? Am I . . . alive?"

Xeno stealthily creeps toward her as though he's hunting a deadly lion.

The woman stares at him. "My jailer. After all this time, you're still obeying orders. Such monstrous devotion to duty."

Xeno bares his fangs, and a foreboding sensation fills me. I'm running old Sealion stories through my head, stories of the Old Woman of the Mountain and her lone guardian, wondering if perhaps we got the story wrong. He was not a guardian, but a guard. A jailer assigned to lie here for an eternity of summers, making sure she did not rise from her grave. The keeper of an old and desperate pact.

The woman turns to frown at me. "Who are you?"

I stammer, "I—I am Sick Lynx of the Windborn Clan from Sky Ice Village."

Tilting her head, her gaze methodically goes over my face, then down my arms and legs. "Archaic hominin. Pale skin, but dark hair. You're a Reecur. Denisovan?"

"Yes," I say with a nod. "Denisovan."

She blinks and looks back at Trogon lying on his side in the rubble below. "What year is this?"

"Year?"

"How long has it been since the war?"

I glance up at RabbitEar and Quiller for the answer, but both are gazing down with huge eyes. They appear too terrified to speak. Quiller shakes her head in an almost spastic motion.

"It's been nine hundred twenty-three summers and eight moons since the zyme," I say.

She stares at me as though she has no idea what I mean. "Are you referring to the oxyluciferin 27? The enzyme produced by Bioluminescent Algae Omega? You count from the tipping point of the proliferation of the enzyme in the Pacific Ocean?"

"I—I don't . . . know." I shrug. "We just tell stories of before the zyme and after the zyme."

Her gaze slowly moves away to examine the tunnels running through the warren. "Perfectly logical. It was the moment everything changed. Even in my time, many had started calling it Year Zero."

When she struggles to get on her hands and knees, Xeno stands up and bares his teeth, preparing to launch himself for her throat.

"Xeno," I say, "stop that! Lie down."

The wolf ignores me. As she crawls up through the rocks, Xeno stays right on her heels, barking and snarling.

When she's climbed high enough to see the toes of Rabbit-Ear's boots, she calls, "Help me out of this tunnel."

RabbitEar extends a hand and helps her to climb out of the hole, where she sits upon the rocks and frowns at the other people in the cave.

"Archaic hybrids," she murmurs. "You . . . you're especially interesting. Red hair but dark skin and eyes. Turkana Boy sequence with a touch of neanderthalensis, correct? Or is it rufous albinism?"

I have to twist my neck to see who she's speaking to. Rabbit-Ear and Quiller are still there, but now Sticks has joined the circle. She was clearly speaking to Sticks, but he has gone mute. His chest heaves as though the sight of the bloody woman fills him with revulsion. At some point, Sticks picked up his pack, the pack he gave Trogon at the beach camp, for it now hangs over his left shoulder.

"Please, help me stand up?" she says.

Quiller tries to reach for her, but RabbitEar says, "Stay back, Quiller," pushes his wife aside, and reaches down to take the strange woman's arm, supporting her while she staggers to her feet. Wobbly and dripping, she almost collapses before she manages to lock her knees.

Xeno emerges next, leaps out of the tunnel, and ferociously lunges at Quiller and RabbitEar, driving them away from the woman.

"What's the matter with your wolf?" Quiller shouts as she struggles to return to the woman, but RabbitEar has an iron grip on her arm, keeping her away.

"Let me go!" Quiller yells at RabbitEar.

"That crazy wolf will kill you."

Xeno accents his words by lunging at Quiller snarling every time she times to break free.

Only Sticks remains near the woman, and he looks like a dog hit in the head with a rock. Numb. Stunned. Not understanding what's happening before his very eyes.

Crawling out of the hole, I get to my feet and shout, "Xeno! Go lie down."

The wolf slinks a few paces away, but continues watching the woman with panicked yellow eyes.

She's taller than I am, taller than anyone in this cave, but very slight of frame.

"What is your name?" I ask.

Blinking, as though trying to remember, she stutters, "El— Elektra. Premier."

Quiller and RabbitEar have their heads together three paces away, hissing in frightened voices. I hear RabbitEar whisper, "How could he possibly have known?"

When Elektra shivers, I say, "You must be freezing. Here, take my cape." I pull the bison hide from my shoulders and drape it around her blood-drenched naked body.

"Thank you, Sick Lynx."

"My people just call me Lynx."

When she inhales, tears fill her eyes. "You may call me Madam Premier."

I'm not sure if she weeps because the feel of air moving in her lungs again is painful or she finds it too sorrowful to bear. Her gaze moves over the shape of the cave and the pile of rubble.

"They thought they were so clever, freezing me in a substance that could only be melted by human blood. Poetic f— fools."

Anger briefly flares in her eyes and an earthquake rumbles through the rocks, strong enough to make me stagger, but she's so weak her knees go out from under her and she collapses to the rubble pile. "I need to get out of these caves. I want to breathe clean air and see sunlight again. If you help me, I will reward you handsomely."

I reach down and take her arm. "I'll help you, but it's a long walk to the surface."

She nods and allows me to support her while she gets to her feet again. "Thank you. I'm very cold and weak."

"If we can get back to my cave, I have dry clothing. They're worn hides, but—"

"Bring back his daughter," Sticks cries and points into the tomb at Trogon. "Her bones are in the red bag on his belt. That was the bargain! You would bring his daughter back to life."

Elektra gives him a disdainful look. "So?"

Sticks stares at her as though the words are incomprehensible. "But . . . that's why he came here. That's why he died."

"Irrelevant. I don't care if his daughter is dead."

"Then bring Elder Trogon back! He saved you."

"Don't shout at me!" she rasps, and a tremor runs through the caverns, generating thunderous echoes.

Quiller's eyes go wide as she glances around. "Was that the Ice Giants or—"

"I don't think so," I answer.

Fear is building below my heart. When I turn back to Elektra, I find her blue eyes filled with rage.

She suddenly loses her balance and topples sideways toward Sticks. I hold tight to her arm, but she grunts and sags against me.

Sticks cries out, "I had to do it!" and runs away across the rubble. "She's evil!"

"What are you talking about?" I shout.

When he stops and looks back, panting hard, I see the broken spear shaft in his hand, the shaft Trogon pulled from his wound.

"Lynx, he stabbed her!" Quiller screams.

Like a flower wilting in a winter storm, Elektra slowly collapses in my arms.

43

---- ❄ ----

LYNX

As I ease Elektra's body down upon the rocks, a ghostly calm comes over the cave. There isn't the faintest whisper of air. Nothing moves, no one speaks. Quiller's frosty breaths rise slowly and linger in the cold cave.

"RabbitEar! Quiller! Help me. We have to save her!" Ripping my shirt over my head, I press it into Elektra's wound to stanch the flow of blood. All the while, she gazes at Xeno with utter hatred in her eyes.

"You did this . . . didn't you? So you can . . . move on . . ." Her fingers creep across the floor toward him, as though hoping to kill the wolf with her bare hands.

Xeno lets out one vicious bark and bounds away down the rubble pile, where he leaps onto the top step. His paws thump as he races down the spiraling staircase.

I consider calling him back, but I doubt he'd listen. He looks like he's fleeing the torchlit cave for his life.

"Let her die!" Sticks cries. "Why do you think they locked her in here? She's the reason the Jemen left our world!"

"She's the last of the Jemen, you fool!" I shout. "You are supposed to give her your sacred book!"

RabbitEar leaps across the rocks with his knife in his fist. "I knew I should have killed this filthy Dog Soldier the instant I saw him!"

"No, RabbitEar! Stop!"

Sticks turns and dashes away with his silver cape flaring behind him, disappearing down the winding staircase behind Xeno.

"Why did you stop me?" RabbitEar yells at me. "When he gets back and tells the Rust People that a Sealion warrior killed their greatest holy man, they'll—"

"Please, I need you to help me! And you, too, Quiller!"

Quiller instantly runs forward and kneels beside me, gazing at Elektra with tears streaming down her face. "Tell me what to do?"

"That's a lethal wound in her liver." Gritting his teeth, RabbitEar grudgingly climbs back up the rubble pile and stands looking down over Quiller's shoulder. "She's dying."

"No," Quiller sobs. "She can't die!"

I've never before known this kind of fear. All of my life, I've feared only things I understood, hunger, pain, losing loved ones. The strange creature lying on the rocks before me does not fall into that category. I don't understand anything about her, except that she is legend made flesh, and I must not let her perish from our world.

Forcefully, I press my shirt over her wound, but dark red flows around my fingers. "I can't stop the blood."

"If we carry her outside and find a healer—"

"She'll never make it, Quiller."

RabbitEar glares back at the staircase with his jaw clamped. "When Sticks reaches the Rust villages, they're going to flood up the mountainside and slaughter every Sealion person alive."

Quiller solemnly blinks up at him. "RabbitEar, forget about the Dog Soldier. We are witnesses at the death of the last Earthbound Jemen. We must remember every detail."

When we were children, Quiller was always able to laugh me out of my fears, but this is different. We are both looking down into the eyes of a dying god, and we know it.

RabbitEar says, "Lynx, if you tell me which potions to bring, I'll run back to Quancee's chamber—"

"Quancee?" The woman gasps the name and makes weak swimming motions, as if trying to rise. "It . . . it's still functioning?"

I nod. "Yes, though Arakie said—"

"A . . . Arakie? Dr. John Arakie?" Her blue eyes have gone huge with fear.

"Yes," I answer, not grasping why she is so afraid. "Why?"

"Is he . . . Where is he?"

"Dead. Just a few days ago."

Blood swells at Elektra's lips. She coughs. "Thank the gods. The monster is . . . gone."

I go rigid for a moment. "Why do you call him a monster?"

She frowns up at me as though the question is absurd. "Arakie led . . . rebellion. Billions . . . died."

"Why would he do that?"

"Hated . . . government. After we . . . we rounded up . . . families of scientists, he . . ."

I'm at a loss for words. I knew and loved Arakie. With the exception of my father, he was the best man, the kindest man, I have ever known. The fact that she could call him a monster, the leader of the rebellion, makes me wonder if all our stories are wrong. Maybe the Jemen were not ancient heroes, and that possibility terrifies me. It means everything Sealion People believe about the enemies of the Jemen is wrong. If Arakie led them, they may have been the true heroes . . .

Rising, I walk away from her.

She lifts a hand and imperiously gestures to Quiller. "Come here . . . young woman."

A few moments ago, Quiller was frantic to get close to Elektra, but now she refuses to budge. "What is it?"

"That boy . . ."

"What boy?"

"Broken . . . boy . . ." Silence falls while Elektra struggles to gather the strength to say, "If you care . . . kill him . . . save him from what's . . . ahead."

RabbitEar gives Quiller a strange look. "Is she talking about Jawbone? Our son?"

Elektra holds Quiller's gaze for as long as she can, then, drowsy with death, her head lolls to the side and the struggle goes out of her face.

"How could she know about our son?" RabbitEar asks.

"Maybe for the same reason he knew her name."

"He knew her name?" A strange sensation works its way through me. "Your adopted son? The Rust People child you found after the lions destroyed his village?"

"Yes, why?"

"How is that possible?"

Quiller shakes her head. "I don't know, but it's the last thing he said to me before I left the cave to walk away with Trogon. Jawbone told me that Elektra had been talking to him through the air. I didn't know what he was talking about."

I walk over and place my fingers against the artery in the Jemen's throat. "There's no heartbeat."

"I don't understand any of this," RabbitEar says. "What just happened? How could she come to life again only to die moments later? What possible purpose—"

"He told me the dead had to take wing," Quiller says, and curiosity fills her eyes. "Take wing and flap away to the Road of Light. Trogon said it was the only story that would save the world."

RabbitEar grimaces. "The nonsense of a madman."

Nervously licking my lips, I shake my head. "I'm not sure she is dead. She's one of the Jemen. How can we tell if she's truly dead or just hibernating like a great frost bear waiting for spring thaw?"

"Move away from her, Lynx," RabbitEar half-shouts. "Let's get out of here. I don't want to wait around to see if you're right."

RabbitEar wraps an arm around his wife's shoulders and pulls her toward the staircase.

As a final act, I plant the torch in the rocks and smooth bloody blond hair away from her face. I don't close her eyes, but leave them open so she can watch the last glimmers of flame until they perish in the darkness. It's not sunlight, but at least it's light after centuries of darkness. As I back away from Elektra's still body, torchlight flutters over the white walls as though consuming them in an unholy conflagration.

RabbitEar and Quiller halt at the top of the stairs, and he calls, "Come on, Lynx! That torch is going to die any moment."

44

LYNX

I walk in the rear as we pass the entrance to Quancee's cave, and I can hear her singing to me in a sad lilting voice, calling me to her.

"Soon," I promise. "I have one final task before I return to you."

Ahead of me, RabbitEar and Quiller walk side by side. Quiller keeps skipping stones across the surface of the paleo-ocean just to see the brilliant blue patches of phosphorescence blaze.

Quiller turns and calls, "What is this place, Lynx?"

"The ocean before the zyme." I can hear the longing in Arakie's voice when he first explained this to me. "The blue is bioluminescent algae. Same family as the zyme, but zyme spreads a thousand times faster. This paleo-ocean twists around through hundreds of caves and caverns."

She grimaces, as though she did not understand many of the words I used, but she just nods and turns back around to whisper to RabbitEar. I can see it in her tight eyes when she looks at me. I'm not the same person she knew just a few moons ago. I've become alien, a creature that no longer fits into the Sealion People—a people without a written language or books, or anything more than simple math that can be counted on the fingers.

Skirting the edge of the slight waves, I watch their boots press into the sand, fill with water, and become shining blue footprints. RabbitEar continually turns around to look at them in fascination.

The vast web of heavy black beams dangling like gigantic spider legs above us shimmers. The beams thrusting up from the water are the brightest, almost turquoise.

When we reach the ledge, I watch RabbitEar hand his spear to Quiller. He climbs up first, then he extends a hand to her. She takes it, and he pulls her up into the mouth of the tunnel that leads through the last cave and then into the air and light. I can already tell it's sunset outside, for the gleam that fills the tunnel is deep amber. After a few days in the cavernous underworld, I crave the surface world with a desperation I'd have never thought possible.

"Your turn, Lynx." RabbitEar extends a hand down to me. Silhouetted against the faint sunset gleam, his red hair and beard appear orange.

"Thanks." I grab his hand and allow him to pull me up the rock face into the tunnel.

As he turns, he wraps an arm around Quiller's shoulders, and they walk together through the tunnel. It's a comforting sight. Their love for each other seems to warm the cold air. I hurt her once, not so long ago. He will not do that to her, and I'm grateful for that.

When RabbitEar gets to the other end of the tunnel, I hear him rasp, "Blessed gods, what's he doing just sitting there? Doesn't he know we want him dead?"

"Wait!" I trot to catch up with them and duck out into the inscription cave.

Sitting cross-legged in the square entry with a book open in his lap, the Dog Soldier seems mesmerized by the stunning vista. It's snowing outside, a thin, dispirited snow falling lightly across the distant tundra dotted with smoking volcanoes. His cape flows around him like a pool of liquid silver.

RabbitEar and Quiller give me questioning looks.

Quiller says, "Does he want to die? Surely he heard us coming."

"I'm sure he did," I answer.

"Then why didn't he run? I can hit him from here. That's a short spear cast," RabbitEar says as he lifts his spear.

"Wait, please."

"Bad idea, Lynx." RabbitEar scowls at me.

"Let me just speak with him for a few moments."

Without waiting for a response, I trot ahead toward the Dog Soldier. He doesn't turn, just stares off into the distances as though he knows I won't kill him.

Stopping two paces behind him, I call, "What are you doing here, Sticks? I thought you'd be long gone by now, headed back to your people."

A shake of his head.

He still has not turned to look at me. I veer wide, go to the opposite side of the entry, and lean my shoulder against the stone to stare down at him. I see the title of the book now, *The Wisdom of the Desert. Thomas Merton.*

The Dog Soldier has tears in his dark eyes. "I saw him," Sticks says in a soft reverent voice. "Just like the old Jemen on the beach."

He's been crying for a while. His eyes are puffy and red. "What did you see?"

"Remember the story? The Jemen had to learn to change into animals to survive the cold after the Ice Giants were born."

"I remember."

"On the beach . . ." he starts in a low voice that builds in strength. "I was treading water in the ocean when the pride of lions trotted over and lay down near your friend and started whining and growling. I thought it was some sort of lion death ritual. They seemed to be mourning him. Then I saw something happening to the old Jemen. Hands seemed to turn into paws. I thought I was imagining things. I didn't understand until the pride trotted away and I slogged out of the water and saw him."

"Saw what?"

"A huge lion lay on its side, the biggest lion I have ever seen. It lay in exactly the place where he had lain. That's when I knew for sure that he truly was one of the Jemen." He looks up at me. "And I knew you were his last student and I had to find you."

My throat constricts with grief. Bowing my head, I blindly stare at the ground. There are wolf tracks pressed into the windblown snow. As Father Sun descends toward the western horizon, the slanting light fills them with shadows. Four toes. Xeno's tracks.

"Do you see?" Sticks whispers, as though afraid to speak too loudly of such magical things.

The realization sinks in slowly, as though my mind doesn't quite believe what my eyes are showing me.

Sticks extends one finger and points out the transformation, one track, two tracks, then the wolf tracks become boot prints that move away down the snowy slope. The beaded pattern is clear. The same beaded boot pattern I saw on the mountain before I found RabbitEar. After standing guard for so many long, long winters, winters where he saw his people vanish among the campfires of the dead, and the world go cold and dark, I wonder if he wears the boots of the dead in remembrance of precious things now gone forever?

"*I saw him change,*" Sticks insists. "Just like the old Jemen on the beach."

I search the stunning vista, looking for any sign of

movement. Bison graze down by the pine grove, their coats shining with freshly fallen snow. No other movement.

"Where do you think he is?" Sticks asks. "Where did he go after her death?"

Behind me in the cave, I hear RabbitEar and Quiller talking, probably wondering what's taking me so long to decide about the Dog Soldier.

Sticks turns to them and glares at RabbitEar. "That one. He shall be known as the Betrayer."

I look back at RabbitEar, who's fingering his spear, and I think about the centuries of murder and hatred between the Rust and Sealion Peoples. I can hear Arakie's voice telling me to believe that peace is possible.

Turning back, I peer down at the Dog Soldier.

In the same patient teaching voice that Arakie used with me, I say, "No, he shall be known as the Deliverer, for he delivered a great evil into your hands so that you might destroy it and save our world. You shall be known as Sticks the Virtuous."

The Dog Soldier blinks and looks away. After several thoughtful moments, he asks, "And Quiller? What will she be called?"

"She will be known as the Guide, for she guided Trogon the Prophet to the Old Woman of the Mountain's tomb."

Sticks' eyes blur. As though he's telling the story in his head, he softly says, "And you . . . You will be called the Dog Soldier's Blessed Teacher?"

He watches me with hopeful eyes.

I take a deep breath and hold it in my lungs for a time while I study the boot prints and think about Xeno, about his devotion to Arakie, and his lonely howls that serenaded so many of my nights here in these caverns.

My footfalls echo softly as I step out of the cave into the drifting snowflakes, searching for his trail. A line of shadow runs across the snowdrifts, perfectly straight, angling down toward the distant sea. I wonder what he hopes to find there. Perhaps he's gone in search of Arakie's body on the beach. Will he stand guard over it, as he has always done?

"I must bury a friend," I say, "beneath a mound of stones on the mountain. It was the way of his people and what he wanted. Will you come with me?"

Old memories are coming upon me fast. I feel weary, bitterly weary, knowing I've lost Arakie and Xeno, and I'm alone and simply not up to the tasks ahead.

"Yes, I will." He clutches his book to his heart and slowly stands up.

The scents of wet earth and glacial meltwater are suddenly strong on the air.

"There are a few things I must do first."

With glowing eyes, he asks, "Are you going to Quancee? To say goodbye, before we—"

"I'm going to gather up a few things, my extra cape, my pack, and to explain why I'm leaving again. It will break her heart. She's always so happy to see people." With a sigh, I add, "And I must explain to my friends why they cannot not harm you."

"Shall I wait for you here, Blessed Teacher?"

The title will take some getting used to. I don't like the sound of it, but I say, "Yes. I'll return shortly."

Sticks kneels before Xeno's tracks and uses one finger to reverently trace the shape of the beaded boot prints, while I walk back to where Quiller and RabbitEar wait for me.

45

As I get closer, RabbitEar stabs a finger at me. "Don't you dare ask me to let him live! Do you have any notion what's going to happen when he returns to his village—"

"Why did you break my truce?"

He closes his mouth and blinks, before saying, "I don't take orders from you, Lynx. Trogon had to die."

Quiller nods. "Yes, he did. He was evil."

"Just like the Dog Soldier." RabbitEar glares at me. "He has to die, too."

I bow my head, and softly say, "He is my student now and I owe him my protection." In a pleasant voice, I ask, "You will grant me that right, won't you?"

RabbitEar glowers. "Not happily."

The love letters and mathematical formulas scribbled across the walls seem to float in the air, things of paint and blood and hope, almost invisible in the soft darkness. I feel their power filtering through me, stirring longings in my bones for things I fear I will never find.

"Lynx, come with us. We're going home." Quiller tightens her arm around RabbitEar's waist. When RabbitEar looks at her, his eyes shine with love. "Sealion People are so few in number now, we need every—"

"I have other obligations, but I will be there before the Moon of Tundra Flowers."

She looks sad. "But our people need your guidance more than Sticks does. And your brother Mink would want you to come home with us."

"I want to come home. Believe me, I do. But I can't. Not for a time. And I have a great favor to ask of you."

RabbitEar and Quiller both stare at me. He says, "What is it?"

"Please ask our people to wait for me. I must be the one to tell them the story of what happened here."

"You mean we can't say a word about—"

"Yes, that's what I mean."

Quiller frowns. "Why can't we tell them?"

She stares into my eyes, trying to see the boy she knew not so long ago, but when her brows draw together I know she can't find him. For that matter, I can't either. My innocence vanished after Arakie's lesson on the concept of zero in the ancient world. After that, it was one revelation after another until Sick Lynx of the Sealion People was little more than a memory.

My thoughts are disconnected, overwhelmed by the events of the past few days. I'm not sure I have the ability to clearly explain my reasons, but I say, "Because the Dog Soldiers are right. Stories heal. I need time to weave the story well enough that it will last a thousand summers."

Quiller looks at RabbitEar and sees him nod before she softly says, "All right, Lynx. We will all be waiting for you."

46

LYNX

As Sticks and I tramp down the forested mammoth trail toward the bay, my pack rattles on my back. The zyme has just started to glow, turning the raw misty evening faintly green.

The litter that Sticks drags behind him bangs and clatters over the frozen tracks in the trail, and he keeps making pained sounds, as though towing the litter is a great indignity for a Dog Soldier. When we stopped in the mountains to gather poles to make the litter, he looked appalled. His people do not do hard labor among the Rust People. All of their needs are taken care by others. I suspect my lessons are going to be hard for him in more ways than he has perhaps imagined—just as Arakie's lessons were for me.

Crystalline, pale green icicles spike down from the branches above and around us, twinkling in the last rays of Father Sun's light; here and there through the trees, I catch glimpses of the towering Ice Giants. In the next few moments, as the zyme glow intensifies, they will shade deep green. But for now they are surreally blue, their jagged peaks rising into the sky like broken-toothed monsters from the Beginning Time. Their moans are low, agonized. I feel them observing me with cold infinite patience.

The scent of pines is strong here.

I look back at Sticks. His dark face runs with sweat. Does he feel the Giants watching him? He may, but for me it's more than that. I have the terrible awareness of being known by the Giants, as though they have watched me since before I was born, watched and been sublimely disappointed. At the edges of my hearing, I detect whispers and barely audible laughter, the discourse just too faint to make out.

"We're almost there," I call. "The trail levels out in another ten paces or so."

"Thank the Blessed Jemen."

Using a hand to shove aside a low-hanging bough, I walk out of the trees and onto the mammoth trail that circles the shore of the bay, and my steps falter.

Arakie lies alone on the sand just where I left him beside the old beach fire. The bright color suddenly vanishes from the world, leaving it colorless and bitterly cold. Our lodge still stands, though the bison hides that cover the mammoth-rib frame have been torn loose and flap in the wind. I have known for nineteen moons that this day was coming, but now it seems harder than ever to imagine burying this great man—a man I barely knew.

I draw my lion-hide cape more tightly around me, suddenly chilled to the bone.

The Dog Soldier gasps when he sees Arakie. "I swear to you! He was not a man when he died, he—"

"I know," I softly say. "It's all right."

I plod forward like a prisoner walking to his own execution. The closer I get to Arakie, the more the deep sand drags at my boots, as though the world itself is trying to hold me back.

Chewed bones and torn silver clothing scatter the beach from the camp all the way out to the crashing waves. I count two skulls. The other warrior's head may have been carried off into the forest by a lion to be eaten later.

When I drop my pack to the ground near the old fire pit, my strength dies. Arakie's eyes are closed. He looks peaceful. He should be torn apart, nothing but his gnawed bones left. Instead, his body is untouched and he's half-covered with sand. All around him, lion and wolf tracks mark the ground. Did the predators try to cover him up, to bury him?

"Forgive me for leaving you behind," I whisper and crouch down to brush aside his thin white hair over his wrinkled face. His skin is icy cold. "I should have been here. Doesn't matter that you ordered me to leave you behind. You needed me, and I knew it."

What were his last thoughts? Was he watching a thousand summers pass across the canvas of his soul? Or was he worrying about me? I pray he was watching his long-dead wife and children running across a warm meadow to meet him, to guide him to his Land of the Dead.

Sticks tows the litter up along the other side of Arakie's body and kneels down. Bowing his head, his lips move with quiet words, an ancient Dog Soldier prayer to the Jemen.

When he looks up, he searches the beach, noting the bones, then points to the blue ball with the red slash and white dots sewn onto Arakie's worn hide shirt. Across the ball, the letters N and S are clear, but I'm not sure what the two upside down Vs mean. Are they upper-case Greek lambdas? I always meant to ask . . .

"What is the blue ball on his shirt? Is it an ancient Jemen symbol?"

"I asked that question once. Arakie got a sad look on his face, as though if he answered he'd be violating some old pact of sacrifice and remembrance."

"If it's secret knowledge, you do not have to reveal—"

"No, it's not secret. It was his clan symbol. He called it 'the meatball.' He said it didn't matter that they had been gone for a thousand summers, they were still his people. He was a deeply loyal man. He believed in what the meatball stood for, what his clan stood for."

"Jemen clans." Sticks seems baffled by the concept. "We have no stories about their clans. This is the first time I have heard one named. I wonder what other clans they had?"

"Perhaps we will discover their names together when we read the Rewilding Reports."

Awe shines in his eyes. "I hope so."

Through a long exhalation, I say, "Help me get him on the litter?"

"Of course. Where will we take him?"

"Up into the forest on the mountainside. There are plenty of stones there."

"Yes, Blessed Teacher."

Gently, we lift Arakie's frozen body onto the litter, then I take the poles and tow my friend across the sand and into the forest shadows flickering with zyme light. Sometime in the past, the largest pine blew over and its roots left a deep hollow in the earth.

"This is a good place."

When I bend down and take Arakie's shoulders, Sticks leaps to grasp his feet, and we lower him into the rocky hollow. He looks thin and frail down there, barely more than skin shrunken over bones.

"Now what do we do?"

"We cover him with rocks," I answer.

Pines whisper and seem to lean down to watch as we gather stones. It takes another full hand of time to completely blanket him with rocks. By then darkness has consumed the forest, and the tip of each pine needle shines green in the zyme light.

Stiffly, I get to my feet and dust the dirt from my pants. The monstrous booms of the Ice Giants tumble down from the high mountains and pound the air around us.

"Will you pray over him?"

"No." I lightly shake my head. "He didn't ask me to, and I'm not sure he would appreciate it. His spiritual beliefs were deep, I believe, but he never spoke to me about them. He was a very private man."

Sticks accepts this, but appears disturbed by my lack of funerary tradition. "Do you think he would mind if I pray?"

"He would not mind."

Sticks closes his eyes, but speaks no words aloud.

I'm grateful for that, for grief has constricted my throat, the grief of lessons unlearned, of books not opened, of ancient Jemen stories not heard—the loss of my friend's voice in my life.

While Sticks prays, shadows dance among the pile of stones. I can't see him now, not even a patch of his cape. I think Arakie would be happy about that. He now rests beneath a mound of stones on the mountainside, just as he wanted.

Kneeling down, I scoop up a handful of dry pine needles and twigs to use as fire starter when we get back to camp and tuck them in my cape pocket.

By the time Sticks opens his eyes, the shrill, sweet notes of windswept pines fill the darkness.

I clutch my cape closed at the throat and start back down the trail for the beach camp. Sticks walks beside me, his steps almost silent in the duff.

"Let's go and build a fire," I say. "We can warm ourselves while we piece together the story of the past few days."

"Yes, Blessed Teacher."

For a moment, clouds pass before the pale green disk of Sister Moon and the forest goes dark, illuminated only by the dim zyme glow. As they pass, I pick up my pace, break out of the trees, and inexorably head for our old beach camp.

"What will we do tomorrow, Blessed Teacher?"

"Tomorrow morning, you will return to your village and tell the Rust People that their great prophet Trogon is dead, and he died to save the world from monstrous evil."

"I . . . I will tell the story? Not you?"

"As of tonight, you are the story keeper, the keeper of the greatest story of all time, for both our peoples. Once we have it pieced together, you will tell it over and over around winter fires in different villages."

Solemnly, he answers, "Yes, Blessed Teacher."

"But you must tell it faithfully, leaving nothing out, adding nothing. Do you understand?"

"I am a Dog Soldier." He appears deeply offended. "Once story fragments have been kept, it is a ritual violation to change one word of the story and punishable by death."

When I say, "As it should be," my heart is pounding my ribs like a lump of iron in my chest. The story must be powerful enough to still the hearts of people a thousand summers from now.

The driftwood pile I gathered many days ago is still around the old fire pit, but it's been scattered by animals and Wind Mother. I begin picking up and stacking the wood.

"Will you go with me to the Rust People village?"

"No, I must return to speak with Quancee to prepare her for your arrival. I will expect you by the end of the moon."

Sticks' head dips in a nod. "Yes, Blessed Teacher."

Propping the pieces of driftwood against one another to create a tent in the old fire pit, I say, "Then you will accompany me to Sky Ice Village, and together we will tell the same story to Sealion People."

Sticks looks very reluctant to openly expose himself to Sealion People, rightfully fearing he will be killed on sight for the crimes of his people. I can see it in his taut expression. "Will the Deliverer be there?"

"Yes. And the Guide. And a small number of others. But no one will harm you. You are under my protection."

"I hope they respect that," he says hesitantly, probably recalling the truce I established with Trogon that was instantly broken by RabbitEar.

I've thought a lot about that, about why he did it, not that it matters now. What's done is done. But it was an important lesson for me. I am not yet a man that my own people will listen to . . . and I must be.

Reaching into my cape pocket, I pull out a handful of dry pine needles and twigs and carefully place them in the middle of the driftwood tent, then I drag my pack over and untie the laces to pull out my two fire sticks. Laying the punky stick, covered with holes, on the ground, I place the sharpened point of the hardwood stick in a hole and begin spinning it between my palms. When the punky wood in the hole turns red, I dump it into the fire pit on top of the old pine needles and wait until a tiny flame licks up before adding more twigs from my pocket.

An emerald veil of mist glistens around us as we both extend our freezing hands to the flames.

After a few moments, I rise and go to the dilapidated lodge. Shoving aside the flapping bison hides, I crawl inside and reach for one of the books Arakie brought to read in the firelight while he died, *The Masks of God*. In the back of the book are several blank pages. Clutching it to my heart, I crawl out of the lodge and walk back to the fire.

Swallowing the lump in my throat, I pull a blackened twig from the fire and turn to a blank page. Sticks watches me. As I begin in a low halting voice, I use the twig to write the words that must never be forgotten:

"The beginning of the Book of Sticks the Virtuous, the Blessed Dog Soldier who witnessed what came to pass in those days . . ." I look over at Sticks. "Continue the story. Slowly, so that I may get the words right."

He stares at me in silence, then with deathly seriousness, says, "Forasmuch as many have taken in hand . . ." He waits for my writing to catch up. " . . . to set forth those things which are most surely believed among us about the Jemen . . . these are the events delivered unto us who were from the beginning eyewitnesses and sacred keepers of the story . . ."

Long into the cold windy night, I huddle closer to the fire with my twig against the page, carefully recording my own soft words: "And they went out quickly . . . and fled from the tomb, for they were afraid."

When I lift the twig from the page and blink down at the words, Sticks humbly asks, "Is it finished, Blessed Teacher?"

"I think we need one more sentence, but I'm very tired, and my thoughts won't coalesce."

Sticks draws himself up with great dignity, and asks, "May I speak the last sentence?"

"Of course."

Wetting his lips, he reverently says, "And Sticks the Virtuous went forth into the world as it was in those days and testified of these miraculous things and wrote of them, for they are most assuredly true."

I pause to consider the sentence, how it will be understood not next moon, but centuries from now. "Yes, good. I like it."

Placing my twig in the fire to blacken the tip again, I carefully write the words down in clear black letters so that no one may forget.

47

***

LYNX

As I hike up the snowy slope toward Arakie's cave, I can see the Road of Light that paints a white swath across the glittering night sky. Has he reached the campfires of the dead? He should have by now. I've been worried about how his Jemen ancestors greeted him. Did they welcome him like a returning hero and honor him for leading the rebellion against the other Jemen . . . or did they turn him away from the camps of the dead and force him to walk the lonely forest trails as an exile among them?

There is so much I do not understand; it's bewildering.

Ducking beneath the icicles that cover most of the cave, I enter the faint blue gleam and continue on, passing by the inscriptions. My gaze lingers on the bloody handprints, but not for long. Quancee's mind has already reached out for mine in a feather-light touch, her happiness at my return deeper than words.

"I'll be there soon."

I slowly negotiate the dark tunnel, then drop over the ledge and walk straight back, stepping around the debris that clogs the path to her chamber. Arakie was never alone here. I know that now. She was with him always, even when he wandered far from these caverns, but they had a special relationship born of centuries of relying on the other for everything.

I halt before entering her chamber to stand alone in the darkness with the cave chill biting into my face. Through the blue flickers I see Quancee flashing three red, three green, then three red signals: the plaintive strain of desperation that she's been flashing across centuries. *Help me.*

There is only weariness and grief in my heart, for I know I will never be able to help her. Not even Arakie could heal her wounds.

Stepping into the crystalline chamber, I stroke the shining panes that I imagine to be her face. "I buried him. It was hard, Quancee."

Sinking down to the floor, I rest my back against her, and a warm fluid sensation fills me as she surrounds me with what I can only describe as love.

"I can't believe he's gone."

Her panes shimmer as though with tears of grief.

Leaning my head back against her shining face, I gaze upward and softly say, "Quancee, please tell me about the enemies of the Jemen? Who were they? Why did Arakie lead a rebellion—"

"Let me answer those questions."

Surprised by the strangely accented voice, I scramble to my feet and stare at the man standing with one hand braced against a toppled roof beam. His body is darkly silhouetted against the blue glow of the algae in the paleo-ocean, but I can see that he wears one of Arakie's old capes, worn thin, dozens of holes poorly patched.

The sensation of love I felt from Quancee has vanished, and I feel her trembling. *She's afraid of him.*

I stammer, "Can—can you?"

His hand slowly falls to his side and he walks one step closer to me, until I can see his brown hair and preternaturally blue eyes. He has the same small oval skull and pointed chin that

Arakie had. "Quancee knows many things, but I am now the only one who knows the whole story."

Fear coils in my belly like a living thing. I long to back away from him. Instead, I plant my feet. "Please start with why there was a rebellion. The government rounded up the families of the scientists. Arakie's family?"

His mouth tightens a little. For a long time, he stares at me. "And mine." He pauses and takes a deep breath. "First, I am Vice Admiral Steven Jorgensen of the National Aeronautics . . ."